Heroes

For Mara.

With thanks
to Marc Côté, Jan Geddes, Anne McDermid,
Tom Noyes, Miles Wilson, Michael Winter, and the
Ontario Arts Council.

H E R O E S

a novel

Ray Robertson

THE DUNDURN GROUP

A SIMON & PIERRE BOOK
TORONTO › OXFORD

Editor: Marc Côté
Design: Scott Reid
Printer: Transcontinental Printing Inc.

Canadian Cataloguing in Publication Data

Robertosn, Ray, 1966-
Heroes

ISBN 0-88924-292-5
I. Title.
PS8585.O3219H47 2000   C813'.54   C00-930044-9
PR9199.2.R62H47 2000

1   2   3   4   5   04   03   02   01   00

Canadä

THE CANADA COUNCIL | LE CONSEIL DES ARTS
FOR THE ARTS | DU CANADA
SINCE 1957 | DEPUIS 1957

We acknowledge the support of the **Canada Council for the Arts**, the **Ontario Arts Council** and the **Book Publishing Industry Development Program** (BPIDP) for our publishing program.

Care has been taken to trace the ownership of copyright material used in this book. The author and the publisher welcome any information enabling them to rectify any references or credit in subsequent editions.

J. Kirk Howard, President

Printed and bound in Canada.
✿
Printed on recycled paper.

Dundurn Press
8 Market Street
Suite 200
Toronto, Ontario
M5E 1M6

Dundurn Press
73 Lime Walk
Headington, Oxford,
England
OX3 7AD

Dundurn Press
2250 Military Road
Tonawanda NY
U.S.A. 14150

All the proud fathers are ashamed to go home.
Their women cluck like starved pullets,
Dying for love.

Therefore,
Their sons grow suicidally beautiful
At the beginning of October,
And gallop terribly against each other's bodies.

James Wright
"Autumn Begins in Martin's Ferry, Ohio"

If you can't beat 'em in the alley, you can't beat 'em on the ice

Conn Smythe

Let's talk. All right, I'll talk. I'll talk and you'll listen. You've done enough talking for a lifetime, anyway, and I guess I could use the practice. I've had one drink and I'm going to have another, but even if I have just one more after that I'm not going to get drunk. Dark wood panelling covering these walls; plenty of pistachios and smoked almonds *gratis* all along the length of this oak bar; every bent elbow in here covered in serious shades of sober grey tweed: this just isn't that kind of place.

But even if it was that kind of place I don't want to get drunk. What I want is to get a little bit tipsy and feel the wiggle of my toes in my socks in my shoes and breathe a deep after-work breath and on the way home pick up a Vegetarian Deluxe Pizza from Papa Ciao's and eat my dinner in front of the game on television tonight. I'm a vegetarian now, you know. And no, all those lectures you used to lay on the old man and Mum and me every night at supper on the systematic mass slaughter of our fellow animal friends haven't finally managed to sink in after all these years. For me, it's just a health thing. I mean, talk to any scientist worth his test tubes and he'll tell you that too much animal flesh in your diet is like eating pure poison. So wipe that grin off your face, little sister, for me it's all about doing what just makes sense.

Anyway, the hockey game starts at 7:30 and I've got to stop off and pick up that pizza, but I've got some time. Maybe now's not when we ought to finally sit down and say all the things that should have gotten said already, but it looks like it's the best I can do. Tough luck for you, I guess, but I'm the only brother you're ever going to get. Too little or too late, we're stuck with each other, Patty. Me and you. Stuck.

So let's talk. And let me call me Bayle and you I'll call Patty. Because, to be honest, I'm just not ready for that naked "I" all by itself just yet. But then I was never even half as brave as you. I'm not even sure if I ever want to be.

But the game doesn't start for another couple of hours and it's nice and dark and quiet in here and at least we're finally really going to talk, so who knows? Maybe there's time yet for you to teach your big brother Peter a thing or two about being brave.

PART ONE

1

"So I cold-cocked the Gook sonofabitch right in the face. And that, young man, is the name of that tune."

Bayle shot the remains of his one-and-a-quarter-ounce bag of unsalted peanuts and considered his options. Telling himself that demanding thirteen baby bottles of Canadian Club whiskey and shouting ancient Greek maxims at whoever attempted to interfere wasn't going to be one of them, he forced his attention back to the copy of Sextus Empiricus's *Outlines of Pyrrhonism* opened up on the tray in front of him. Only the feigned studying act seemed capable of slowing down his American aisle-side seatmate's steady flow of assorted tales of Yankee glory.

He was, he let Bayle know almost immediately upon boarding during the stopover in Cincinnati, an ex-air force man of twenty-three years, had served three and a half of those years proudly defending the Free World in Korea, had voted for Reagan twice and would have a third time if they would have let him, and guessed that if English was good enough for Jesus Christ it sure as hell should be good enough for the United States of America. The man also let Bayle know that he was fairly confident of an ETA in Tulsa, Oklahoma, of 1:35 p.m.

Bayle admitted that he wasn't sure what his own ETA was and tried to concentrate on the Empiricus with the explanation that he had to study for a big exam when he returned to Toronto. The man volunteered that Bayle looked a little old to still be in school. Bayle answered back a little defensively that he wasn't just in school, he was in graduate school, a Ph.D candidate in philosophy with a speciality in Greek Hellenism, specifically the works of the third-century sceptic Sextus Empiricus. The man looked at Bayle like he'd just confessed to never having eaten a Big Mac or wanted to go to Disneyland.

Therefore, he who suspends judgement about everything which is subject to opinion reaps a harvest of the most complete happiness.

Brain, as usual of late, encountering difficulty sticking to the page, Flying is a lot like whiskey, Bayle thought. Stop right there; metaphors, no. No thank you, no. Always taking you places you don't want to be.

The window next to him viewless since he'd pulled down the plastic cover immediately upon locating his seat, the other passengers surrounding him the same for their assorted food-and-drink-shovelling-and-slurping, paperback-turning, *U.S.A. Today*ing, and laptop-punching, Bayle scanned the plane for possible diversion.

An elderly nun one seat ahead of him on the other side of the aisle absently fingered a small silver cross hanging from around her neck as she read from a worn, black Bible spread out on her lap. She lifted her head from the book from time to time to smile a soft smile at no one at all and everyone. For the official record, as far as Bayle was concerned, Christians were just Platonists with a bleeding cover boy, the very metaphysically mucky antithesis of the clean logical lines of hard sceptical indifference that world-wary Empiricus had laid down two centuries after the celebrated J.C.'s lifetime. Still, he couldn't help but envy the nun her slightly glazed state of happy labour.

Bayle closed his eyes and leaned back in his seat, not the first time in what felt like a very long time that a bad case of purpose-envy turned his thoughts toward immediate membership in that not-so-exclusive Canadian Club so often frequented by all those similarly anxious for two thick fingers of quick liquid meaning. Which is to say Bayle wanted a drink. Or two, or three. Or eight.

In the eighteen months since he'd passed his foreign language exams and written his period and subject tests all Bayle had to do was defend his dissertation and he was done, would have his doctorate. Bayle, however, on the brink of official sceptical citizenship, felt like nothing so much as a swaggering secret virgin frightened out of his false macho bluster by a seasoned hooker's impatient command to either make it happen or to put it back in his pants. Whatever else in the past year and a half he couldn't put his name to, this, without a doubt: the dreaded shrunken truth-table; to wit, fear, for some reason, of the philosophical finish line.

At the same time, power-drinking and resultant alcohol-assisted hi-jinks of varying degrees of self-depravation more nights a week than not at renowned Queen Street West dive Knott's Place, a practice that was doing absolutely nothing for his liver, his stalled interest in his work, or his relationship with his girlfriend of almost three years, Jane. Particularly vexing was Bayle's recent inclination for leaving late-night Empiricus and strong spirits-soaked messages on the answering machine of the early-to-bed and early-to-rise Jane, the former never failing to hang up when the latter managed to make it to the phone, Bayle — regardless of what Jane's call display might say to the contrary — never failing to deny afterward all knowledge of the calls.

None of which should have necessitated that he travel a thousand miles away from home to write an article on minor-league hockey in the American mid-west for *Toronto Living*, a monthly magazine catering to the interests of young Canadian professionals. Except that in Bayle's case, it did.

He opened his eyes to the warm smile of the nun, her pleasantly age-scarred face staying with him even after she'd moved herself stoop-shouldered down the aisle to the washroom at the back of the plane. Although Bayle and his sister, Patty, had been raised as good Canadian agnostics — "God is love," Bayle's father had impatiently answered his pubescent son's between-periods theological awakening, eager to give his attention back to the Maple Leaf-Red Wing playoff game playing on the livingroom television — Patty had undergone what their mother referred to as her Catholic Thing.

By Grade 11 Bayle's sister had successfully convinced their recently widowed mother that the cost of allowing her to complete her high-school years at a private, downtown Toronto Catholic school — and not at the nearby suburban Etobicoke public high school — was well worth it, both because of the superior education she would be receiving and because she likely wouldn't have to spend the majority of her free time fighting off the sometimes crude advances of her male classmates. Even by her first year of high school, the hockey-playing, beer-guzzling Etobicoke boys never knew quite what to make of tall, brilliant, and undeniably beautiful Patty.

Of course, to Bayle — and Bayle alone — Patty had immediately revealed her true motive: the wonderfully sinful thrill of reading the Catholic Church's entire *index librorum prohibititorum* right under the nun's noses.

"But we're not Catholic," Bayle had protested.

They were lying where they did whenever Patty really needed to talk, backs to the carpet on the floor of her bedroom, undergraduate university man Bayle making the trip back to Etobicoke because Patty had called him up the night before with "some really incredible news, Peter, I mean, really, really, incredible news." Their heads were almost touching although neither was able to see the face of the other, only the plain white ceiling up above. A record of Gregorian chants, another recent enthusiasm, moaned from Patty's Simpson-Sears stereo.

"Just think," Patty said, ignoring her brother's objection, "this time next year I'll be in the lavatory at Lorreto's smoking the day's first cigarette and cracking open *Our Lady of the Flowers.* Genet was on the list for years, you know."

"Lavatory" was one of a handful of linguistic leftovers remaining from what their mother still called Patty's British Thing. This after, successively, the Kennedy Conspiracy Thing, the Punk Thing, and the Ecology Thing. A faded Union Jack and *The Complete Works of Rudyard Kipling* lay cardboard-boxed and buried in the garage under their mother's broken sewing machine and Bayle's old hockey equipment, never spoken of between any of them.

"Look, Patty," Bayle said, "I really don't want to be the one to spoil your party, but, uhm ...."

And he didn't. Not really. But he did. Almost always, Bayle did.

From the womb, it seemed, Bayle knew that two and two were four and couldn't ever forget it, as fine a disposition as any level-headed logician or any pisser on any number of other people's parades of passion as could be asked for. But who really wants to be the one going around with a calculator reminding ten-year-old kids playing ball hockey in the frozen street all day that the odds of their growing up to be just like their hockey-playing heroes are just about as good as their being struck by lightning twice in the same afternoon? I mean, who? Who really wants to be that guy?

"But what?" Patty said. "But what, Peter?"

"I mean," Bayle said, "I'm not an authority or anything, but the way I understand it there's this one little thing you've got to have to be considered a Catholic."

"What little thing?"

"Well, God."

He couldn't see them, but Bayle could hear his sister scratching away at the backs of her hands. Every one of Patty's new enthusiasms was born of a sudden burst of maniacal energy culminating in chafed red hands and wrists. Cortisone and — for brief periods, when it got bad enough — yellow dish gloves to discourage contact with the infected skin area helped, but only the inevitable loss of interest in whatever up to that point had absorbed her so entirely signalled the beginning of the healing process for his sister's rubbed-raw skin.

And like a lone teetotaller in a sweaty room full of raging drunks, like a voyeur standing around with his hands in his pockets at an orgy in full swing, when Patty was like this, at her scratching fervent worst, frankly she made Bayle just a little bit nervous. Might even have scared him a little. All right, she scared him. Scared the hell out of him. Bayle came to inherit a guilty relief at the sight of his melancholy sister's perfect white hands.

Patty didn't say anything. After a while, she got up to flip over the record, the monk's chanting eventually giving way to the snap, pop, and dull thud that announced that the needle had gone as far as it could go, that the music was over. Worse than the sound of the scratching, Bayle hated to hear his sister silent.

Patty flipped over the record. A hundred perfect voices of unshakeable devotion poured out of the cheap speakers.

"Sometimes," she said, "I don't think you listen to me, Peter."

"Quick little piece, isn't she?" the grey-haired man beside Bayle said. Bayle's frantic attempt to get the passing stewardess's attention and, at the same time, not appear as absolutely intoxication-desperate as he suddenly was, resulted only in the sort of wide-eyed and full-toothed smile that is usually accompanied by a caption underneath asking Have Seen This Man? and advising the use of extreme caution. "Don't worry, though," the man continued. "She'll be back this way sooner or later."

Just then the nun returned from the bathroom looking just as beatific as before. Bayle wished she was a flying nun and that she would take a three-thousand-foot fucking leap out of his sight. No sister of mine. You're not my sister.

"See?" the man said. "Here she comes now. Sooner than later, too. The little honeys can run all day but they can't hide forever."

Metaphysician heal thyself, Bayle thought. Look the little honey straight in the eye and tell her what you want. Need.

The stewardess stopped the cart in the aisle and rested her hands on slightly bent knees to better hear Bayle's question. Bayle looked up from his seat at the mascara and smile looking down at him and pointed out his heart's desire.

The woman told him how much his drink cost and Bayle paid her. The grey-haired man had another paper cup of complimentary coffee, took three packets of sugars and two containers of cream, two packages of free chocolate chip cookies, and six napkins. The woman asked Bayle if he himself might like some cookies for later. Bayle shook his head, no, said he didn't think so, no, so the woman gave him two more packages of peanuts and three additional napkins instead. Each in his own fashion, Bayle and his seatmate set to work on their loaded-up trays.

Bayle pushed the silver button on his armrest and eased back in his seat, sipping at his drink. Before long, the older man's alternating long coffee slurps and quick, rabbit-mouthed cookie nibbles sent him reluctantly forward in his chair and back to Empiricus.

Leaning over the book, fresh sip of whiskey taken in and glass on its way trayward again, a single drop of Canadian Club escaped his mouth, rolled onto the topmost part of his bottom lip, held for a fraction of a second on the lower, and then splashed onto page four, a large liquid point of punctuation falling directly onto the middle section of Book 1, Chapter i:

> We make no firm assertions that any of what we are about to say is exactly like we say it is, but we simply declare our position on each topic as it now appears to us, like a reporter.

Bayle watched the wet dot slowly soak its way through the page, the whiskey's brown gradually turning into the page's white.

A wet dot slowly soaking its way through the page, Bayle thought; the whiskey's brown gradually turning into the page's white. Period. Not a metaphor or symbol to be seen for as far as the eye can see. None.

2

BAYLE'S VIEW on the bus ride to the
arena varied little. Storehouses, heavy machinery
operations, dairy processing plants; two or three of
each of these as the miles and the airport fell behind.
But mostly fields. Alone at the back of the bus, in
every direction he looked, mid-western American
fields. Wheat usually, he supposed. But now, mid-
October, just fields. No matter which way he looked,
he couldn't see where any of them ended.

Then, rising out of the miles of empty farmland that surrounded it, the arena, grey and massive, an enormous concrete vegetable, suddenly all that was his consciousness. Nearer: HOCKEY TONIGHT! Closer still, on an unlit marquée suspended over the entrance to the rink:

Warriors vs. Wichita 7:30 p.m.
Tickets $8 Adults $6 Seniors/Youths
Listen to WUUS, The Voice of America's Heartland!
Featuring the I.M. Wright Show Every Weekday From 2
Until 5 PM

Drinkless for over an hour now, the usual signs of sudden alcohol-cessation coming on strong (dry mouth, drowsiness, sharp hunger), neophyte reporter Bayle nonetheless decided he should at least try to take some notes — although of what, he wasn't sure. He pulled a pen and small notepad out of the breast pocket of his suit jacket. The pen sported the slogan Safety is a Way of Life at Ontario Hydro, one of literally hundreds Bayle's father had accumulated over his thirty-plus years on the job, all of them identically stamped.

Writing instrument and paper at the ready, each held loosely in either hand, Bayle continued to watch the flat brown fields persist through the bus window. After a few impotent minutes he put both back in his pocket.

Because he was the only passenger, the driver by-passed the bus stop where the highway met the concrete border of the adjacent parking lot and dropped Bayle off directly in front of the main arena entrance. Bayle thanked the man and stepped down from the bus, positive that even if worse came to worst he himself could never be a bus driver. Eight hours a day of nearly non-stop motion, and at the end of it, back to exactly where you started. Blue collar existentialism. A pot-bellied Sisyphus who doesn't make change.

From his wallet Bayle removed a slip of paper that contained in his own handwriting the gate number the public relations director of the Warriors had told him over the phone to look for. "Legible notes will make or break a good journalist," Jane, his girlfriend and employer for the next week and a half, had told him.

"I bend," Bayle had replied. "Sceptics bend."

After a Jane-convened lunch a week before, after Bayle had suggested a rare quiet rendezvous at his place for later that night (for Bayle, a much needed just-say-no evening), Jane had promptly countered with another idea: nine days of Bayle alone in an American prairie state writing an article on the minor-league hockey boom in the mid-western and lower United States for the magazine she worked for.

Bayle wasn't a journalist, hated to travel, and, if still impossible to walk by a newspaper box without peeking through the smudged plastic pane to see how the Maple Leafs managed to do the night before, didn't really demonstrate that much interest in hockey anymore, the death of his nearly fanatical Toronto Maple Leafs-loving father six years before the final step in Bayle's gradually diminishing interest in the game. So of course Jane was pulling his leg about the trip. And just how leg-pulling unlike her, too.

They were in her office in the Manulife Centre, the ant-scramble below that was midday Toronto Jane's well-earned associate-editor's view. Bayle slumped against the wall next to the curtainless window and waited for the punchline to Jane's joke, wondering how to kill the remainder of the afternoon until she got off work at six. It was, of late, a not uncommon dilemma.

"I think you should go away for awhile, Peter. Away from Toronto. Away from us." Jane leaned back in her black leather swivel armchair, thumb to chin and forefinger to temple, as sure a sign to Bayle as any that, for whatever reason, she was serious about the trip.

Whether negotiating the fee for a new graphic-design artist for *Toronto Living* or making a sexual advance toward Bayle, Jane was, when it came time to do business, all business. A few times she had even managed to combine the two activities, having Bayle go down on her while she haggled over the speaker phone with freelancers about their pay, the college radio station's afternoon reggae program softly playing in the background, the non-musical Jane's favourite furnishing of work-place nookie rhythmic cover. But that was strictly once upon a time. Bayle was hard pressed to remember their last shared act of even missionary kindness; actually, hard pressed to even remember the last time he'd been hard.

"You want to send me away?" Bayle was having a difficult time processing this. He felt like a problem pre-teen being farmed out to summer camp. Running a puzzled hand through his hair, he absently touched the fresh bandage on his forehead, this the end result of last night's closing-time scuffle between himself and another Knott's Place patron over who would have the last play on the jukebox. In the morning Bayle had felt more foolish than hungover or injured. He never even listened to the jukebox. "Have things really been so bad?" he asked.

"I've been patient, Peter, you can't say I haven't been that. But to be perfectly honest, this whole self-destructive bit is wearing a little bit thin. Actually, real thin. The drinking, the fighting, and now the little phone messages on my machine. It seems like every time I turn around you've regressed a couple years younger. I'm afraid that one day I'm going to find you ten years old and wanting me to drive you to hockey practice."

Bayle put his finger in the air to make a point. Realizing he didn't have one, he let it fall back down. He did manage a thin, "What 'little phone messages?'" but the remark didn't seem to register. Bayle didn't pursue the point.

"As to why you seem so intent upon pissing away your chances of getting a good teaching job by not defending your dissertation and getting on with your life, I don't know. I really don't. Everytime I try to discuss it all you can say is that you guess you've been having a hard time concentrating on your work lately and that you guess you don't know why. Frankly, I'm starting to believe you."

"So naturally you think the answer is for me to spend some time with a hockey team," Bayle said. He was hoping that the obvious sarcasm in his voice would undercut her machine-gun logic. The artillery kept coming.

"I don't know what the answer is, Peter, but I'm getting the feeling that you aren't getting any closer to finding out what it is, either. I think you need to reflect real hard on you and your career and whatever it is that's got you so stuck in neutral. It's really only a three or four day assignment at most, but let's double that, let's make it nine days. You haven't been out of the city in years. Maybe the time and distance will help. It couldn't hurt. Besides, none of my regular feature writers wants this story. I also know that your scholarship money is gone and that you owe your landlord two months and counting in back rent. Not to mention the five hundred I loaned you last month. Not that I can't wait to get the money back until you get back on your feet again with your first teaching job. But you're fully aware, I think, of my feelings about cash transactions of that sort between those intimately involved — the sooner it's off the books, the better the relationship. The job pays $1500."

In spite of the fact that Bayle *was* dead broke, into his girlfriend, mother, and landlord for just over two thousand dollars, he wanted to demolish Jane's argument, to count off just a few of the many things he could be more profitably doing with his time than hanging around a minor-league hockey team, to point out to her the utter absurdity of her even suggesting the idea.

Instead:

"You know all I've ever done for the magazine is a little proofreading and a few of those Around Toronto pieces," he said. "And those things don't even have a by-line. Who says you'd want to publish what I'd come up with?"

Notwithstanding his predictably Ivory Tower disdain of Jane's chosen profession, what he regularly referred to as "germalism," Bayle had, over the past unoccupied year or so, periodically found employment at Jane's magazine. The jobs he was given were easy — proofreading, line-editing, the occasional two-hundred-word tongue-in-check account of the

annual auto show or this year's dwindling Santa Claus Parade
— the pay as decent as the work was utterly anonymous. Ideal
employment for the out-of-work and sceptically uncommitted.

"You're a Canadian male between the ages of 7 and 84 so
you obviously know the game," she said. "And in spite of too
many years of intellectual masturbation at the university
you're still intelligent enough to do a decent enough job, I'm
sure. The rest of it is just basic reporting etiquette."

Bayle looked down from the window at the everywhere
car and pedestrian confusion. "Is this your business-like way
of giving me an ultimatum about our relationship? Offer me
an out-of-province assignment I can't afford to turn down?"

Jane's instinctually analytical way of conducting her life
had attracted Bayle before they'd even met, an ad in the back
pages of NOW magazine advertising for "an extremely
rational, career-first professional woman looking for good sex
and occasional non-sexual fellowship with an equally rational,
career-first professional man" if not exactly setting Bayle's
heart pitter-pattering, at least making a direct hit to his
Empiricus-inspired ideal of disturbance-free companionship.
Five dizzying weeks during the first year of his doctorate were
as close as Bayle had ever come to letting the man-woman
thing take over and tell his head what to do.

Susan, a new student to the program like himself, could
quote Descartes in the original, would make Bayle laugh and
laugh with tales of her hopelessly small-town home town of
Oxford, Mississippi, and had the sexiest damn southern
honeyed voice Bayle had ever heard, in real life and in the
movies both. And in the single-minded devotion she showed
for Montaigne, her philosophical pet and intended speciality,
she reminded Bayle a lot of Patty at her own frenzied focused
best. But when Bayle found himself once too often out-and-
out love-stoned in the stacks of Robarts Library, lost in a daze
of springtime magnolia visions of the hundreds of freckles on
Susan's bare chest and shoulders and how the ivory whiteness
of her skin was only all the more beautiful for them — this,
instead of bearing down on the latest journal article dedicated

to Empiricus in *Scepticism Quarterly* — thankfully he had had the foresight to do what he knew he had to do and nipped things in the bud. Sure it had hurt at first, but it was the right thing to do. Whenever he'd meet Susan's eyes of inexplicable hurt in the hallways of the philosophy department afterward, he'd lower his own eyes and remind himself how he'd done the right thing.

And if Bayle had grown to occasionally wonder of late what it would be like to share his life with a woman not quite so Jane-like, someone who didn't insist that neither party under any circumstance employ the word "love" (as hopefully ambiguous and potentially troublesome an expression as has ever been known to humankind, she'd pointed out) or ever spend more than two consecutive nights together (familiarity unfortunately but undeniably breeding contempt, she'd noted), it was, Bayle concluded more than once, only because the grass is always greener. He told himself that, all things considered, the grass on his side of the fence tasted just fine and to can the romantic-love-as-panacea-to-all-that-ails-you crap. Jane fulfilled his needs and he her's; it was really as simple as that. Chew your cud and don't rock the pasture, Bayle.

"Don't get emotional about this, Peter," Jane said. "At least I'm making a suggestion. That's more than you've done for over a year now."

How bad had things gotten? He honestly found it difficult to tell. Intellectually speaking, he knew that the way up and the way down were always one and same, the whole thing depending, of course, on whether one was up or down. Which of course was simply Heraclitus's way of saying that it was quite possible Bayle might have been so fucked up now for so long that it might have begun to feel like normal. Which really wasn't much help. The pre-Socratics rarely were.

"I'm giving you a chance, Peter," she said. "Take the job."

Bayle didn't answer. The pragmatist in him said to carefully weigh the pros and cons of the trip. The pragmatist in him, however, was little heeded these days, not since an occasional late night at the Graduate Student Union over a few shared pitchers had given way to routinely consuming large quantities of whiskey and exchanging blows over such timeless philosophical questions as whether "Feel Like Makin' Love" or "Satisfaction (I Can't Get No)" was the more fitting last-call jukebox selection at Knott's Place.

"All right," Bayle said. "I'll go." The traffic lights down on Bay Street flashed green and all the little toy cars were suddenly on their way again.

Who knows? he thought. The time alone and the distance away really couldn't hurt. Also: necessity is the mother of invention. It might have been Sextus Empiricus or it might have been Ann Landers, Bayle at that moment really didn't give a shit which, only hoped that a grain of truth existed in the cliche that said that there's a grain of truth in every cliche. Nine days to become who I used to be: entire worlds have been created in less time.

Besides, Bayle thought, it might be fun to watch some hockey again. Seemed like a lifetime since the last time he'd seen a good game up close.

Finding gate number A-1, Bayle waited in line behind a thin woman in tight blue jeans and too much makeup with what looked to be her son, a teenager in steel arm supports. The boy wore a baseball cap, wrist bands, and windbreaker all emblazoned with the logo of the local team, the Warriors. The woman looked Bayle up and down.

"Office should be open any minute now," she said.

Bayle nodded. "Great, thanks." He looked at his watch. Two o'clock. On time.

The three quick drinks on the plane had been acknowledged by now for what they were: a mistake, but only a minor one, with no lasting repercussions except a little dry mouth. Bayle hated to fly and the drinks had seen him through. He checked his watch again. Not even two. Early, in fact. He pulled off his suit jacket and threw it over his shoulder, suddenly aware he'd packed all wrong for the trip.

The radio had said it was 28 when he got up at a quarter to seven for his flight from Toronto, but it had to be at least eighty degrees now. Eighty degrees and humid as hell on October 19th. *Toto, we're not in Canada anymore.*

Suspended by his braces, the boy swung around and faced Bayle. "Are you a ppppplayer?"

Bayle looked at the boy, then quickly to the woman for help.

"He wants to know if you're one of the Warriors." She eyed him up and down again, smiled. "You're big enough to be a player."

Louder this time, "Are you with the tttteam?"

Immediately, not wanting to hear the boy speak again, "No," Bayle said, "I'm not. I'm not a player. Sorry."

"Oh," the boy said, attention falling between his white high-top running shoes to a quarter-sized spot of mud on the cement walkway. He didn't shift his body, still faced Bayle, eyes steady stuck on the clump of wet brown. The CLOSED sign in the ticket window flipped over to OPEN and the woman quickly approached the counter.

"What've you got left behind the visitor's bench?" she asked.

"Row six all right?"

"Yeah, that's good. Two adults." She took a twenty-dollar bill from her pocket and pushed it under the glass window toward the young girl behind the counter. "Hey, Paul," she called to the boy. "Right behind the Wichita bench. Row six."

The boy slowly raised his head, eyes darting left and right in search of some place to call home. Eyes meeting Bayle's, "Ggggget them," he wailed. "Ggggget ... Wwwwwichita!"

The woman received her change, took the tickets, and she and her charge slowly moved away.

Knowing he shouldn't but doing so anyway, Bayle stared at the boy until from behind the counter he felt the eyes of the girl on him.

"Can I help you?" she said.

"Yeah, I ...." But he'd forgotten the question he was supposed to ask. All he could really do was stare.

3

"And where, Mr. Bayle, have they got you staying if you don't mind me asking?"

Dark brown suit; black dress shoes; no jewellery; hair cut
short but not too short; medium height and build; no
distinctive physical features, body mannerisms, or verbal
idiosyncrasies: Samson, the Warriors' director of public
relations, appeared to Bayle's eyes and ears so ordinary he
almost wasn't there, the perfect corporate citizen. His hands
were folded neatly, as in prayer, on top of his desk, empty but
for a small computer, fax, and phone.

"A place called The Range, I think," Bayle said. "I
actually haven't checked in yet. It's a bed and breakfast over
on ... I forget the name of the street. My editor, Ms. Warriner,
she made the reservation."

"Main. The Range is on Main Street, right downtown.
That should help you adjust a little bit to small-town life."

"I figure I'll be pretty busy working."

"I'm sure you will," Samson said, "I'm sure you will. And
speaking of work, I've got a phone call to make and you
should have a look around the arena before the boys hit the
ice for their skate." Bayle took this as his cue and rose from his
chair on the other side of Samson's desk. Samson remained
seated, turning pages in a manila folder labelled, Bayle could
see, with his own name and that of the magazine he was
working for.

"As far as things on my end go, Mr. Bayle, everything
seems to be in order for your stay with us. Here you are."

Samson handed him a media pass with Peter Bayle-
Journalist, *Toronto Living*, All Access, typed on it. It felt
strange to Bayle to see his own name attached to that of a
clearly defined profession. A life-long student, he had never
really thought of himself as anything before.

"Thanks for everything," Bayle said, holding up the pass.

"Just let me know if there's anything you need in the way
of information about any of the players or the team. Because
that's my job: information." Samson pulled a business card
from the top drawer of his desk. "The powers-that-be will tell
you different," he said, handing over the card, "but I'm the
one who makes things happen around here."

Right or left? Bayle stood alone outside Samson's office, Karen Carpenter from somewhere above softly bewailing rainy days and Mondays. There's a possible vocation, he thought. Bayle pictured himself as a muzak disc jockey programming Neil Diamond and orchestrated Beatles hits, pleasantly absent all day long in a thorazine and chamomile tea stupor. Form following substance, he reflected that the whole operation was probably entirely computerized.

Coffee. Not Little Italy cappuccino, no, but from the glass-covered and office-partitioned hallway to his right a waft of heart-pumping java bristled Bayle's nose. Yesterday at this time he was sitting at Bar Italia drinking his second cup of Toronto's best cup of coffee and trying to decide whether panini or stracciatella would go better with Wednesday's hangover. Yesterday at this time he was back in the city, back in Toronto, back home.

Bayle loved Toronto like only someone who wasn't born there can. To anyone who didn't know better, he *was* from Toronto; to everyone else, begrudgingly Etobicoke born and bred. Etobicoke: a yearly swelling sea of pre-fabricated houses and citizens flooding to life after World War II with the influx of fertile war veterans and thousands of equally breeding-proficient Eastern European immigrants added to the Canadian mosaic mix, each camp believing unquestionably that you are born to be born, to work, to have children, to watch said children grow, to retire, to watch grandchildren grow, and to die. And, if blessed, your children and theirs after them the same.

But from his first nearly delirious subway trip downtown at age six with his father to see the Leafs at Maple Leaf Gardens ("One more stop and this is it, Peter, The Gardens, and pretty soon all of Canada's going to be watching *us* on T.V. tonight, son, because tonight *we're* going to be on 'Hockey Night in Canada'") to a moody teenager's nosing through Harbord Street secondhand bookstores on dreary February afternoons (the wonderfully melancholy mustiness of two-dollar paperback classics and mint tea and oatmeal muffins filling up the shop) to, eventually, an actual dweller of the Big Smoke himself, every morning waking up knowing that the shooting anew of the movie of his life (with three million anonymous extras and plenty of hundred-year-old architecture as backdrop) was the privilege of anyone lucky enough to inhabit a real city, Toronto claimed Bayle as one of its own and Bayle it as his.

But Wednesday, Bayle reminded himself, was yesterday, and yesterday was the day before today, today being the first day of the nine-day countdown toward Bayle-as-he-used-to-be.

Right, then, he thought: See the suits first, save the players for later. Either way, he'd have to talk to them all anyway. Jane had insisted on lots of quotes.

Steaming styrofoam cup of coffee from the secretary's office in hand, Bayle tapped lightly on the door marked James Duceeder, General Manager. "Yeah, come on in," the voice inside barked. A loud radio dominated the office. "Samson said who you were. Be with you in a minute."

Which reminds me of something I heard on the way in to work this morning, folks. What do you call one thousand civil servants on the bottom of the Arkansas River? Progress, folks, progress. We'll be right back after these important messages from our sponsors. And remember, folks, if it's not Wright, it's not right.

"Ahee hee hee. You ever listen to this guy?" Duceeder said, standing in the middle of his office, pointing with his thumb to the radio on top of his filing cabinet. "He just kills me, really."

"No, I haven't. I'm actually not —"

"That's right, Samson did say you were from Canada, didn't he." Duceeder clicked off the radio and sat down on the front of his desk. "Well, you will if you hang around these parts long enough. Proud to say that every one of our games is on the same station Mr. Wright is on, WUUS, AM 590, the Voice of America's Heartland. Have a seat."

Duceeder looked like he sounded; maybe more.

"I don't know how much Mr. Samson told you about the article that I'm writing, Mr. Duceeder, but what I'd like to —"

"Jimmy D."

"Excuse me?"

"Jimmy D. My friends call me Jimmy D."

"Okay. Well, Jimmy D., I thought that I'd just drop by today and introduce myself and say that I hope that over the next week or so we can talk a little bit about you and the job you do with the Warriors. No big deal, just about the team, the league, and how a minor-league outfit like the Warriors operates down here." Bayle surprised himself, sounding almost as he imagined a journalist should.

"Yeah, Samson put something on my desk about your coming, but I don't see how I can help you very much. I'm just an old hockey guy from way back. Coach Daley says to me he's short an experienced defenceman and I make a trade for an experienced defenceman. I'm just a wheeler and dealer, I'm just a hockey guy. Not much I can really tell you beyond that."

Great, Bayle thought. My first interview and the G.M. pleads the fifth. He brought to mind Jane's solution for dealing with what she called a journalist's worst enemy, "the silent ones." Simple, she had said. Just get them talking about everyone's favourite subject.

"Were you born in the Midwest, Jimmy D., or —"

"As a matter of fact, I'm originally a Canuck like yourself. Different neck of the woods though, a fair bit farther west, Medicine Hat, in Alberta. Came down here in seventy-five? Seventy-six? Mid-seventies, anyway. Long enough to call it home even if I do miss the hunting they've got up there this time of year. But I guess you could say I'm pretty much Uncle Sam red, white, and blue all the way through now. Met my wife Carol down here."

Duceeder picked up the large gold-framed picture that dominated his desk and handed it to Bayle. "That's the little lady right there with our son, Bill. The starting guard on his high school basketball team and a straight-A student two years running. He'll be fourteen in a couple weeks." Bayle smiled at the photograph then smiled some more wondering when it would be technically okay to politely set it back down.

"Jimmy D.!" A middle-aged man's bespectacled and virtually hairless head grinned itself around the door frame of Duceeder's office.

"Hey, you guys get in here for a minute, will you?" Duceeder shouted. He turned to Bayle. "Now here are a couple fellas who could really help you out with your story. Peter Bayle, I'd like you to meet Ted Able and Bob Munson, the radio play-by-play guys for the Warriors' games. Ted, Bob, this is —"

Able, the one whose bald head Bayle had first seen, grabbed Bayle's hand and pumped it vigorously. "No need, Jimmy, we just ran into Samson. How you doing? Ted Able."

"So the glossies are suddenly interested in minor-league hockey now, are they? What's the angle?" Munson, about the same age as Able but without glasses and with hair, stood with his hands on his hips, looking Bayle straight in the eye as he spoke. The sleeves of his suit jacket were pushed up almost to the elbow. Bayle suspected toupee right away.

"Geez, Bob," Able said, "ease up, will you? This guy's big time. This isn't Davidson from the *Eagle*."

At this, Duceeder's face flooded red, a previously nearly imperceptible vein on his forehead instantly throbbing blue. "Damn it, I told you before not to mention that prick's name in this office and I'll be damned if —"

"Easy now, Jimmy D., easy. I was just trying to point that it's not likely that Petey here is biased in the same way as our old friend —"

"Don't!"

"— our old friend at the *Eagle* is." Able gave Bayle a friendly, conspiratorial look. "You've got to understand right from the get-go, Petey, that the beat writer for the Warriors is what we in the hockey media refer to as a left-winger."

"Left-winger, shit," Munson sputtered. "Cock-sucking belly-aching liberal scum-licking —"

"You said a mouthful there, Bob," Duceeder said. "You said a mouthful there."

"Easy now, you two," Able said, "we've got company here, remember?" Able turned his attention back to Bayle. "Anyway, we'd be happy to chat with you anytime you like. You might even want to come up to the booth sometime and see how a couple of pros do it, right, Bobby?"

"We're late."

Able looked at his watch. "Geez, you're right. Well, we'll see you gentlemen at the opener tonight."

"You boys take care," Duceeder said.

Munson already out the door, Able called ahead to his partner, "Just a sec, Bob." Able turned around in the doorway. "Hey, Jimmy D.," he said.

"Yeah?"

"Guess what you call one thousand civil servants on the bottom of the Arkansas River?"

"Aheh heh heh. That guy just kills me. Really."

4

"FUCK SAMSON. Samson is irrelevant to me. I don't hear his bells and whistles, you understand? I've got a sick power play and Wichita tonight and you want to know if you can talk to me for a couple of minutes. Forty-three percent of all hockey games are won on the special teams and we can't score on our backup goalie in practice with a two-man advantage. And you want to know if you can maybe just have a few words with me. You want to talk to me, you talk to me about Wichita's penalty-killing unit. You happen to know anything about the four-corner rotating box they're using this year? You got any idea if they're still committed to dumping and chasing or are they giving that quick little Russian they picked up over the summer the green light to make a play if he's got it? You know if Unger is still taking all their deep face-offs? I didn't think you so. We're playing a team tonight that's about ten times better than the one we beat four straight in last year's playoffs and who would like nothing better than to come into the Bunton Center and kick our ass all over the place on opening night in front of our own fans. And you would like to have a few words. You want bells and whistles, you go talk to Mr. Samson. And while you're there, you can tell Mr. Samson that Coach Daley is too busy trying to get his hockey team to the league championship to have any time left over for team autograph sessions, Warrior car-washes, or Meet the Fans Day. You tell Mr. Samson that Coach Daley doesn't hear bells and whistles, you understand? And for Christsake, shut that door behind you."

Thus spake Coach Daley.

Bayle closed the door behind him, mentally crossing sports reporter off his list of potential occupations.

5

WANDERING THE bowels of the arena, Bayle wondered who or what next. Except for Jane explaining to him some journalistic do's and don't's and equipping him with a few folders full of articles on the hockey boom in the U.S., he was essentially on his own. And the article was going to be the easy part.

If genuinely confounded as to the reason why, Bayle nonetheless knew that something in his life was seriously amiss, it being simply too large a leap in lifestyle from committed young thinker to getting-older-all-the-time idler — thinking, more than one booze-bruised night, whether he himself should be committed — to explain away his change in character as something like the mere sowing of a few late-twenty-something oats. Until recently, work, and particularly his study of Empiricus, had never been anything less than Bayle's chief reason for getting up each day; holidays, for example, never a period of reduced-load hollow ritualizing and increased socializing, but always a time of increased production, an opportunity to do more of all he ever really wanted to do.

But now Bayle was up to double-digits when it came to the number of times he'd given his advisor, Smith, a definite date when he would finally defend his thesis as best as he apathetically could and get on with getting on with his career and spreading the wise word of Empiricus and all that the old Greek sceptically did not stand for. Bayle more than once wondered why he just couldn't be sensible about the whole thing like he knew his old man would have.

For thirty-two years Walter Bayle put in his forty hours a week at Ontario Hydro because it paid the bills. End of story. What he lived for, though, were his Maple Leafs, Bayle's father's love of Toronto's home-town team making its way into nearly every life lesson the old man sent Bayle's way.

"See, a family is lot like a hockey team, Peter," he'd tell thirteen-year-old Bayle sent home from school early with a black eye and a note for his parents. "Everyone in the family has to look out for the other guy and make sure they're doing okay. So when those older boys at school were giving Patty a hard time and calling her names because she wouldn't talk to them, then it's your job to make sure that your teammate — your sister — is all right. You understand?"

Bayle scratched his head. "So you mean you're not mad at me?"

"Mad at you, hell," his father said, tearing the teacher's note in two, "I'm proud of you, son. What do you say we round up your mum and Patty and see what's the flavour of the month down at Baskin-Robbins?"

Maybe because just as soon as he could crawl onto his father's knee to watch the Leafs on T.V. Bayle was a devoted hockey fan too, he never shared Patty's irritation at their father's exclamation to their mother at the conclusion of every Friday night's meatloaf supper, "Well, it's Miller Time, Ann, and 'Hockey Night in Canada' is twenty-four hours away and counting and I think the Leafs are going to get lucky this weekend." That Miller beer wasn't sold in Canada for the majority of the years Bayle and his sister were subject to their father's week-ending mantra only infuriated Patty further. Bayle tried in vain to convince her that maybe she didn't understand their father because she wasn't a Maple Leaf fan herself. Patty replied in rare, brother-bashing form that although Bayle was in university now and her older brother, he still had the very real capacity to be a real idiot sometimes.

"He works hard," Bayle said. "Just because he's not a twelfth-century mystic doesn't mean that what he does isn't important."

"Do you ever hear what I say? Do you? I told you, *I* could care less what he did just as long as *he* cared about it. There are peasant women in Guatemala who work with their hands for months — for months — to make one piece of —"

"There you go again."

"There I go again what?"

"Guatemalan peasants. Christ, Patty, why does everything have to be so romantic with you?"

"Maybe you're not romantic enough."

"Yeah, well, maybe if you were a little less romantic you wouldn't have to spend half your life wearing yellow —" Bayle stopped himself, but not soon enough. He somersaulted from hate to pity to self-loathing, all in the same regretful moment.

41

Although they were in Patty's bedroom she was the one to storm out. One of the two flung yellow rubber gloves reached its intended target, but Bayle wished it was only the start of several months of intense physical torture. On his back on the carpet he pulled the glove off his face, but didn't rub away its sting. Bayle had made his sister cry.

"No, sir, no problem at all, be glad to do it. It be okay if I sort of continues on my way here, though? I got sixteen restrooms to clean up before game-time tonight, and that ain't even figuring in restocking the toilet paper and towels and such."

Janitors hadn't made it onto the list of potential interviewees Jane had put together for him, but, coffee gone and bladder full and walking in on a working but willing subject, Bayle felt thankful for the opportunity for something to do. Situation normal, he thought: lost in space and stumbling around looking for the nearest men's room.

"How long have you been a custodian here, Mr....?" Names. Always get the name first. Jane had told him that.

"LeRoi Jefferson if you're writin' it down, Roy if you're just saying it. At the Bunton Center, you mean?" Bayle nodded. "Been head janitor here since '89. Course, before the hockey team came along I was just part-time, helping out whenever there'd be a truck show or rodeo, a music show now and then for the kids, a gun and knife show — lotsa gun and knife shows. And after working that assembly line at G.M. for all them years before they closed up shop in '87, I don't mind telling you it wasn't easy making ends meet on part-time wages with six little ones at home. This here hockey team the best thing that ever happened to this old boy. Excuse me now, I got to get at that toilet where you're standing." Bayle quickly moved out of the doorway of one of the washroom's stalls.

"Thank you," Jefferson said. He pushed his cart right up to the stall and slowly got down on his knees inside. Kneeling directly in front of the toilet bowl, he reached behind himself, eye level with the contents of his cart, and carefully selected a wire brush and container of cleaning fluid. He began squirting and scrubbing away.

"Do you follow hockey much, Roy?" Bayle asked, looking at the man's back as he spoke.

"Well, to tell you the truth, and I hope this don't spoil the writin' you doing none, but I got to admit that I ain't much of which you'd call a real big fan of the game, myself. They got what they call an Employees' Night here once a season and I been a couple times, brought the family down, you know. But if you want the honest to God truth, I have the hardest time just following that little puck around. Thing no bigger than a hamburger and you're supposed to keep track of it while all these big fellas be whippin' by, fallin' over each other?" Bayle laughed. Jefferson looked over his shoulder, grinned.

"Couldn't meet a nicer bunch of fellas than them hockey players, though," Jefferson said. "No, sir. You know what they done every Christmas for the past three years? Give me a bottle of C.C. You know what C.C. is?"

"Canadian Club?" Bayle said, happy to know the answer to something for sure, even if something he knew he shouldn't have known about so well.

"That's right, Canadian Club, sippin' whiskey, from Canada. And expensive, too. Sure. That's good whiskey, that C.C." Jefferson stood up from the toilet and surveyed his work. "Okay, we're about done in here. Let's move on down the hall."

Bayle trailing right behind, Jefferson pushed the cart ahead of himself down the empty arena corridor. Slightly chilled, even in his jeans, suit jacket, and long-sleeve shirt underneath, it had been years — since he was a still-playing teenbopper — that Bayle had been in a hockey arena so early before a game. He couldn't see it from where he was standing, but the muffled motor noise of the zamboni machine getting the ice ready for the Warriors' practice echoed throughout the Bunton Center's cement halls. He found the sound unexpectedly soothing.

Until:

"I told you that I'd tell you when they were sharp enough. You just keep sliding that blade, Lefty. When I've seen enough sparks, I'll be sure to let you know." Around the corner of the corridor an athletic-looking black woman about Bayle's age covered almost entirely in a tight-fitting silver shining space-traveller costume closely watched a pair of white figure skates being sharpened by an elderly white man standing over a skate-sharpening machine, a cigarette dangling from the corner of his mouth. "And I'll tell you right now, Lefty, I don't want to hear about how many other pairs of skates for the players that you've got to do by tonight. People come to see me do my thing just as much as they do theirs." Under her left arm the woman carried what was obviously the headpiece of her uniform, a bucket-shaped silver helmet with painted-on scowl and punched-in air holes for nose and mouth. Leaning against the arena wall was an accompanying rifle-length plastic weapon of some sort.

Following Jefferson inside their destination, another men's washroom identical to the one they'd just left, "Is she with the team?" Bayle asked.

"Yes, sir, she works here. That's Gloria. She's the Warrior."

6

"C'MON, feel it."

"McDonald, what the fuck?"

"He wants me to feel his wrist."

"Just feel it. Feel the difference."

"Dippy, I don't want —"

"Dippy, tell me why you want McDonald to feel your wrist. Wait, don't answer that, I don't want to know."

"Is it time yet?"

"Dippy says he's 5 percent bigger than last year from working out all summer."

"C'mon, Mac, you're the only one who knows how big it was last year, feel it."

"Dippy, I'm naked, I don't want to feel your goddamn wrist."

"Sounds like it didn't bother you too much last year."

"We were arm wrestling, Robinson. And we were both drunk."

"That's how it always starts. A little arm wrestling, a few beers, and before you know it —"

"Hey, fuck you and the horse you rode in on, Robinson."

"What time is it? Is the zamboni off yet?"

"Just once, eh? Just tell me if you think it's bigger, that's all I'm asking."

"Calisse, feel that big sonofabitch's wrist, will you? You two start to give me headache."

"You want him to shut up, you feel him, Trembley."

"He is your countryman, not mine, Monsieur Robinson. I say if Monsieur Dipper's wrist is to be felt, it should be by one of his own, no?"

"Trembley, can't you lay off the politics at least until the regular season starts?"

"Liberation, my friend, it knows no season. Didn't they teach you that at that community college you almost graduate from?"

"You make this stuff up as you go, Trembley, or has the Separatist movement issued a phrase book this year for all you Frogs travelling outside Quebec?"

"Oh, there is a book, Monsieur Robinson, and your name, believe me, it is in it."

"Machine's off!"
"Shit."
"Really?"
"Shit."
"Seriously?"
"Let's go!"
"Pull my sweater down, will you?"
"Hand me that tape."
"Busted lace! Lefty?"
"He's already out there."
"Damn. Who's got a lace?"
"Good skate, guys."
"Keep it loose out there, guys, stay loose."
"Tabnernac, what kind of fucking tape they buy us dis year? Made in fucking Disneyland, I bet."
"Let's have a good one, boys, nice and easy out there."
"Let's go, let's go."
"Quick skate and Wichita tonight, gang."
"Everybody let's go, let's have a good one out there."
"Good skate, boys."

"Trembley, how come we're always the last two out of the room?"

"Monsieur Robinson, I do not know."

"Trembley?"

"Oui?"

"You ready to get this thing going tonight?"

"I believe I am, yes."

"Trembley?"

"Oui?"

"Who's that guy in the suit jacket?"

7

A LITTLE before four Bayle called it a day. Having talked to more strangers in one afternoon than in five years of graduate school combined, he ached for an empty room and an endless echo of "No comment." One of the chief attractions of the philosophical profession was that most of your colleagues were long dead. If you happened to find yourself bored or annoyed with a third-century Greek it was always nice to know you could just close the book on him. Living people were almost never as accommodating.

A bag in each hand, with a lowered right shoulder Bayle pushed open the heavy front door of the arena, the rink's manufactured chill melding with a warm, almost moist wind coming off of the enveloping flatland. He started across the car-speckled parking lot toward the empty aluminum bus-stop bench. Halfway across the blacktop a blue pick-up pulled up alongside.

"You going into town?"

"I think I am," Bayle said. "Main's in town, isn't it?"

"It's in town. Get in. I'm going your way."

The owner of the truck kept one hand on the wheel, the other on a silver flask, and his eye on the road. He dressed like an old-time reporter in a black-and-white Gary Cooper movie: worn felt hat, rumpled grey suit, battered Oxfords. The truck was without air-conditioning and both windows were rolled all the way down to admit a warm breeze. The man's collar was wet, his tie loosened, the top button of his white shirt undone. He noticed Bayle eye him sideways every time he took a drink.

"If you don't like the way the driver conducts his business I can let you off at the next bus stop."

"I didn't say anything," Bayle protested, turning slightly in his seat, looking at the man fully for the first time. He was probably in his late-fifties but seemed at least ten years older. Booze, Bayle thought.

"No," he said, "that's true. You didn't." He raised the flask to lip level, paused, then tucked the silver container between his legs. "Davidson," he said, free hand offered over, eyes never leaving the highway.

"Peter Bayle."

Davidson slowly shook his head a few times up and down, as if the solution to a problem he'd been hard pressed to answer had suddenly been supplied to him. He retrieved the flask and held it toward Bayle across the front seat.

"A little early for me," Bayle said, smiling good-naturedly. The too many cups of coffee he'd had at the arena had almost compensated for the drinks he'd consumed on the plane.

Having to be back at the rink in less than four hours, he didn't
want to tip the balance again.

"I thought it might be," Davidson said. He snapped back
the flask and resumed with his silent sipping and steering.

Apart from confirming his identity as the Duceeder-
enraging sportswriter from the local newspaper, Bayle's
intermittent attempts at luring Davidson into a discussion
about his job covering the Warriors were met with throaty
grunts and, when Bayle mentioned Duceeder, a sustained
groan. By the time they hit the outskirts of town Bayle had
conceded Davidson as a journalistic subject. Bayle turned his
attention to the town now outside his window.

The truck idled at a red light. Davidson rested his free
hand on top of the steering wheel, the flask stuck in the glove
compartment since they'd entered the town proper. They
appeared to be in the middle of the business section of town —
banks, insurance buildings, and other grey two-and-three-storey
structures of unidentified but presumably similarly solemn
purpose dominating the small-town U.S.A. scene. Except that it
was a business day, Thursday, at five to four in the afternoon,
and there wasn't one person on the street. Bayle gave Davidson
his address and asked if today was a local holiday.

"If it is, nobody told me," Davidson replied.

"Then where is everybody?"

"Malls," Davidson said. "Like flies on shit, the outlet
malls out on I-35. Welcome to middle America, son."

Just as it announced itself, Main appeared to be the
town's main street. Every fast food franchise Bayle had ever
heard of and many that he hadn't dotted the thick
commercial smear, a couple of flag-whipping car dealerships
and several boarded-up store fronts providing slight respite
from the gleaming landscape. Bayle even managed to spot a
few human beings inside some of the restaurants. Davidson
lifted his left pinky off the steering wheel and pointed at a
passing gas station.

"Twenty years ago they started giving you a discount if
you pumped your own gas. Self-service they called it. You

pumped, you paid less. Now you don't have a choice and they charge the full price anyway. You know why?"

Bayle was following the rising numbers on the building fronts, anxious not to miss his hotel. "Not really, no," he said.

"Because the average idiot in this country can't remember anything farther back than his last crap, that's why. Because now he can't even *imagine* not pumping it."

The truck finally pulled up outside of where Bayle was staying, The Range, a two-storey, brown-shingled house of late-nineteenth century design with looping ropes in the shapes of lassos affixed as bucolic adornment to its front. Painted wooden horses grazed on the front lawn, a single frozen cowboy with a drooping moustache and an enormous ten-gallon hat swinging eternally a wooden lasso of his own over his head. Underneath the wood-burnt sign planted in the middle of the yard that announced the name of the lodging, a smaller shingle suspended by two silver chains declared:

Welcome To The Range, Pardners!
VISA, MASTERCARD, AMERICAN EXPRESS
and LOCAL CHECKS ACCEPTED

Beside this, another sign, this one identical to those that dotted the tiny lawn fronts of what seemed to be every other building on the street, announced THIS BUSINESS/HOME IS PROTECTED BY CDH PROTECTION SERVICES 24 HOURS A DAY 365 DAYS A YEAR. Protected from what? Bayle wondered. Cows?

"Well, here you are," Davidson said. "Home on the range." It was the first time he'd smiled since Bayle entered the truck.

Bayle got his bags out of the truck bed and stopped beside the driver's side window. "I appreciate the ride," he said. "But believe me, it's not home."

"That's what they all say," Davidson replied. He shifted into drive and drove, leaving Bayle standing alone in the middle of the street.

8

BAYLE SIGNED in, paid for his entire stay in advance with the company credit card Jane had given him, and went right to his room. Mrs. Franklin, the proprietor, had been hospitable if reserved. A trim middle-aged woman with close-cropped hair and upscale cowgirl looks (smart jeans, silk vest, clearly expensive reptile-skin-of-some-sort cowboy boots), she noisily worked on a hard candy between her back molars and pointed out that he should let her or her nephew, Ron, who worked the evening shift at the front desk know immediately if there was anything they could do to make his stay at The Range in any way more pleasant. She made it sound like a threat.

Bayle thanked her and headed up to his third-floor room, identified not by number but mid-western epithet. Bayle was staying in the Great Plains Room.

She stopped him before he got halfway up the stairs. "I forgot to give you your complimentary copy of the *Eagle*," she said, disappearing behind the counter. Bayle came back down. A copy of the American Constitution, a "Wright is Right-WUUS 590" bumper sticker, and a framed movie still of a youthful Ronald Reagan horseback with guns ablazing were appended to the wall over the desk. Mrs. Franklin caught Bayle's eyes lingering over the photo. Joined him.

"I suppose some people do prefer to remember Mr. Reagan in his Presidential clothes — suit, tie, and all the rest of it. And he certainly did cut a striking figure, don't misunderstand me. But for me, even when he was serving the American people in the White House for all those years, he was still Ronnie of the West, always ready to do the right thing no matter how many of the bad guys had him surrounded. My nephew I mentioned earlier, Ron, my sister's boy, he's named after Mr. Reagan." A sigh. "If only some of that can-do attitude were as easy to give." She turned away from the picture.

"Anyway, here's your paper," she said. "As of tomorrow morning you have to pay for your own. There's a box out front by the door. If you need change ask at the desk."

Bayle took the paper, thanked her again, and went off in search of the Great Plains.

Laying on the bed, Bayle put the newspaper down on his knees, rubbed his eyes, and read the headline again (*WARRIORS TO LEAVE TOWN? Million Dollars in City-Ordered Renovations to Bunton Center Could Drive Team Out of Town Say Owners, Bunton Groceries*). So that's why Davidson is *persona non grata* around here, Bayle thought, reading on: it was his articles in the paper a few months back that put the city inspector onto the problems with the arena.

The story went on to say that over one hundred full- and part-time local jobs would be lost city-wide if Bunton Groceries were to relocate the team.

Bayle thought about the janitor he'd talked to that afternoon, Jefferson, and his six children, then the boy he'd seen in front of the arena earlier in the day, wondering what would happen to all of the Warriors apparel the kid had been wearing if the team decided to move. Row after row of unwanted Warrior t-shirts, sweatshirts, and baseball caps hung in second-hand-shop abandon before Bayle's eyes, a sort of Platonic Form of uselessness weighing upon his mind. He shook the thought from his head and decided it was time to unpack.

Except for the busily humming air-conditioning unit and light fixtures and electrical outlets, the room was meant to resemble a turn-of-the-century pioneer's quarters. Bayle laid away his clothes in the mirrored oak dresser, put his dissertation, folders of hockey articles, and laptop computer on top of the heavy mahogany nightstand, and, the white porcelain chamber pot pushed underneath the bed, placed his air purifier on the level below and switched it to ON.

Bayle owned three air purifiers, none of which he ever bothered to insert a filter into. One of the machines he kept at his place, one he left at Jane's apartment for when he stayed the occasional night, and the third, what he called his "traveller," a smaller unit, he left permanently in his suitcase for his rare trips away from home.

Filterless, each supplied more than simple white noise to drown out nighttime urban honks and howling, however, the machine's deafening quietude manufacturing a near-perfect auditory translation of the sort of peace of the intellect and emotions that Bayle from the beginning had sought out in studying philosophy. But even desire-denying Empiricus, he had to confess — as close as Bayle had ever gotten to finding in the written word eradication of emotional, moral, and metaphysical confusion — even Empiricus could not duplicate the depth of stillness of Being produced by the little machine's uniform humming, the encompassing mist of droning certitude it provided never failing him for its soul-soothing effect.

Bayle laid back down on the bed and let the murmur of the machine spill over him. Flat on his back, a hand-embroidered feather pillow placed gently over his face, the steady whir that now filled the room received dirty him like a filled-to-the-brim hot bath. Although he easily could have nodded off — the long flight of this morning, the drinks on the plane, the non-stop chatter of today, the day's unexpected heat and humidity — he resisted his closing eyelids so as to experience wholly one of his most favourite of feelings, impervious awakedness, Bayle's own secular take on the Christian's ideal state: *in*, but not *of* this world.

From underneath the pillow Bayle peeked at his watch. Nearly four-thirty; three hours until face-off. Enough time to plug in his computer and input some of the notes he'd taken at the rink, maybe even have a look at a few of the files. Still deliberating, his eyes fell upon the discarded newspaper lying at his side on the bed, the story of the Warriors' potentially devastating move staring up at him, the Warrior-outfitted teenager from that afternoon once again coming to mind. Bayle closed his eyes.

On his back, on his side, on his stomach, on his other side, on his back again, Bayle could not get settled, the spell of the air purifier unable to plough him under. Later, sitting up on the edge of the bed, none the refreshed for his attempted hour of rest, That's odd, he thought. That's not like me.

9

"WELL, GOOD evening, Mr. Bayle. Sit yourself down over here beside me. You can help fill out the buffer-zone between James here and Mr. Davidson when he arrives."

Fifteen tiers of seats above the ice surface, the Bunton
Center press box wasn't much more than a twenty-foot-long
open-air linoleum counter at the south end of the rink.
Several three-legged stools tucked neatly underneath, the
counter itself was bare but for some ancient coffee-ring stains
and Samson's folded hands. Bayle would have preferred to be
by himself buried somewhere high in the nosebleeds, but this
was where Jane would have wanted him to be. He took the
offered seat between Samson and Duceeder. Since that
afternoon Duceeder had reasserted the part in his thinning
hair and changed his coffee-stained tie.

Hand-holding couples; overflowing families; even a few
timid-looking solo supporters: all checked over their ticket
stubs again and again, all walked up and down the cement
steps of the arena trying to find their way. Although it had
been years since Bayle had last been inside a hockey rink —
with his father, to a Maple Leafs' playoff game five months
before the elder Bayle's death, the hard-to-get post-season
tickets a celebration of sorts of Bayle's father's seemingly
successful post-op recovery from the cancer — the arena was
just as he remembered an arena being a half hour before a
game: lights low, the ice in shadow but still brilliant white,
the air late-fall, early-morning fresh.

With Patty beside him in the backseat of the family Buick,
and already suited up in his hockey equipment at home in
preparation for that weekend's Pee Wee game — but running-
shoe footed, Bauer skates stored in the trunk — Bayle would
every Saturday afternoon listen to his father at the wheel of
the car go through pre-game strategy:

"These guys on Dolson Mowing, these guys have got
speed and know how to use it, Peter, these guys like to skate.
So don't get caught standing around out there, okay? Don't let
your man get away from you. You're just as big as they are, so
use your size, make your man pay for his space out there, keep
him honest. Remember how we saw Sittler take care of Clarke
last Saturday night? Do it just like that, Peter, just like number
27, just like the captain. Get all over him, son. *Make him pay.*"

Once actually inside the rink Bayle's father would drift off to smoke and talk with the other puffing fathers in the cloudy arena lobby while his mother would buy Bayle and his sister hot chocolate and their choice of one treat each from the canteen before joining the other coffee-drinking hockey mums at the shiny shellacked picnic tables. Bayle and Patty would leave the grownups behind and sip their hot chocolate and eat their candy bars and watch the hockey game being played before Bayle's own from the freezing wooden rink-side bleachers.

Even when the boys from his own team would begin to arrive at the arena Bayle would sit with his sister in the stands. Not because his parents said he had to, but just because he liked to. Bayle's teammates were Bayle's teammates, but mostly they bored him. Even if six years his junior, Patty never bored Bayle.

"I don't know why they call us Pee Wees, Patty. It's just what they call us, I guess. I never really thought about it."

"Peter, if you hold your cocoa like this the steam warms up your nose and then it heats up the rest of you. I wonder why it's like that. Why do you think it's like that, Peter?"

"Patty, save some of your Snickers for later. Look at me: I've only taken two bites out of mine and you're already almost done."

Patty stopped attending Bayle's hockey games when she discovered that cricket was the national game of Great Britain. Bayle tried his reasonable best to convince her that as much as she might want to be — and even though Canada *was* a part of the Commonwealth — she'd always be Patty Bayle from and of Etobicoke, Ontario, Canada. But Patty had decided to become a British subject.

Bayle quit playing hockey not long after. He was going into Grade 9, just starting high school, and there were other, more interesting things he wanted to do with his spare time. Like going out for football. And dances, and girls.

After Patty had quit coming to his games, and just before he hung up his skates for good, Bayle had been struck by the fact that no matter how hot you got when you were down on the ice playing — even when you were sitting on the bench between shifts — how incredibly cold it was to just sit in the stands by yourself and watch a game, no matter how interesting the match-up. He'd never realized just how cold it was to sit up there and simply watch.

Bayle knew he should ask Samson and Duceeder about the story in the *Eagle*, should probably try to work the team's threatened move into his own projected article somehow, but before he could formulate a properly journalistic question Davidson was making his way toward the press box.

Mindfully slow, like a man walking a tightrope without looking down, Davidson advanced up the aisle, a can of Coke in one hand, a portable computer and small printer hanging from the other. As in the truck earlier that day, he looked only in the direction he was going.

"Mr. Davidson, good evening," Samson said. Bayle nodded. Duceeder didn't lift his gaze from the zamboni circling the ice.

"Samson," Davidson said. He removed his old suit jacket and carefully folded it and placed it on the counter. He pulled a stool from underneath, sat down, loosened his tie, plugged the computer into a jack underneath the counter, lowered his head, and immediately began punching hard at the keys of the laptop. Even from one seat over Bayle could smell the liquor.

"Mr. Davidson," Samson said, "this is the young man I was telling you about downstairs."

Without looking up from his small computer screen, "I've had the pleasure," Davidson said.

"Oh, wonderful. As I'm sure I remarked to you earlier, Mr. Bayle here is a fellow journalist. Only this is not one of your typical ink-stained wretches. From what I understand, before too long we'll have to call him Doctor."

"That a fact?" Davidson replied.

Actually, more of a running theory, Bayle on the inside

answered. On the outside, however, he smiled like a perfect idiot. Yes yes yes, a veritable doctor, yes. Capable of healing the metaphysically ill in three sagacious visits. Your tuition cheerfully refunded if no relief afforded to your aching *weltanchung* within the first two months of treatment. If all else fails, take two Platonic dialogues and call me in the morning. Bayle wondered if zamboni drivers suffered from vertigo. Probably a union job anyway, he decided, probably have to know somebody. Bayle didn't know anybody.

Davidson kept working away at his laptop. Duceeder watched the zamboni make its final laps around the rink. Samson, hands still folded in front of him, smilingly beheld the filling-up seats all around him.

WE WILL WE WILL ROCKYOU
WE WILL WE WILL ROCKYOU

A blast of tinny rock and roll that Bayle knew indicated that the players' appearance on the ice was imminent jumped out of the arena loud speakers.

"Christ, Samson," Davidson said, "the warm-up hasn't even started yet. Are you selling ear-plugs at the concession stands now?" Davidson didn't look well; in fact, fingers peeled tight around the edge of the counter, face only a shade or so darker than the white handkerchief sticking out of his front pant pocket, he looked like a prime candidate for either a heart attack or a sustained bout of vomiting. Or both. Bayle wondered if it was the shock of the loud music or simply his day-long tippling catching up with him. Or both.

"Not a decibel louder than it was last year, Mr. Davidson. You're just getting a little bit long in the tooth, I fear. Besides, it doesn't seem to bother our young friend here very much. Mr. Bayle? Does the public address system seem to be operating at an acceptable volume to you?"

"I guess," Bayle said.

"There you are," Samson, smiling, said in Davidson's direction.

"Well, if Mr. Bayle *guesses* it's just right, than I *guess* it must be," Davidson said. He shot Bayle a look of thorough disgust only compounded by his physically pained expression. "Are the stats ready yet?"

"Cynthia will have them for you in five minutes," Samson answered.

Hands flat on top of the counter for support, Davidson pushed himself up and put his jacket back on. "I'm going to the can. Tell her to put the new statistics beside my notebook. And ask her to bring me another guidebook. I forgot mine at home." Davidson walked away from the press box as carefully as he had arrived.

Waiting until Davidson had moved out of earshot down the stairs and into the arena lobby, "I honestly don't know how you can talk to that bastard, Samson," Duceeder said. "Should've done like I said last winter and banned his ass from all media-access spots for being intoxicated on arena property. We do have the right, you know. It is in the arena by-laws. Make him fill out his damn game reports from the first-floor john. See how serious he is about writing articles on the condition of the Bunton Center then."

Surprising himself, not knowing he was going to say it until he did, "But it's not his fault," Bayle said.

Samson and Duceeder turned around in their seats.

"I mean, if the Bunton Center's unsafe, he was just doing his job writing about it, right?"

Duceeder scowled, Samson actually smiled, if a little sadly; both men looked back down at the ice.

Well, *it's true*, Bayle thought. Right?

10

"YOU MUST be the hockey guy my aunt was talking about. Welcome to Shitsville, U.S.A."

Envisioning an early night preceded by a diligent attempt to make sense of some of what he'd managed to jot down during the game, an admittedly sluggish but hard-hitting four to one Warriors' victory — including two bloody fights, both draws, between the Warriors' Dipper and the league's other premier enforcer, Wichita's Bladon — Bayle asked the teenager staffing the front desk of The Range if there were any coffee or pop machines in the building. His first live hockey game in years had put Bayle in the mood for a cup of hot chocolate.

"Pop? You mean, like, soda? Yeah, down the hall to your left, right past the lounge." Before Bayle could move away, however: "Hey, wait a minute, almost forgot, this came for you. No charge." Bayle looked at the sheet of shiny paper and exhaled hard through his nostrils. It was a fax from Smith, his thesis advisor. A thousand miles away, he thought, and he still manages to be in your face. Bayle folded the page in two and stuck it in the inside pocket of his suit jacket. Later.

"So who won?"

"What?" Bayle said, looking up.

"The game. Who won?"

"We did. I mean the Warriors. Four-one."

"Go team."

"You follow hockey?" Bayle asked.

"Nah. I'm more of a — what would you call it? — individualist in my sporting tastes." A crooked grin to go along with his black leather jacket and Metallica t-shirt coloured the remark slightly enigmatic. Bayle, however, refused to ruminate; Bayle wanted a cup of hot chocolate.

"You hitting the sack? It's not even eleven. Not going to take in all the sights and sounds the big city has to offer?"

"I think I saw just about all I needed to see today," Bayle said.

"Yeah, you got that right."

"So what's with all the heavy safety precautions then, all the security signs on everybody's lawn?"

"Drugs, so they say," Ron answered.

"Drugs?"

"So they say."

"You mean like drug trading, gang violence, that sort of thing?"

"The only logical career choice for any energetic young American entrepreneur from the wrong side of the tracks with no silver spoon stuck in his mouth and who doesn't want to work at Burger King for minimum wage his entire life. So they say."

Bayle waited for further clarification. None apparently forthcoming, he said goodnight and headed down the hallway looking for the coffee machine. The boy called out after him:

"Right on. You too. Have a good one. And if you need anything, just, like, you know, let me know. Anything. You know?"

The coffee machine offered regular and cappuccino, two special blends, Swiss mocha, a non-alcoholic Irish coffee, something called "Premium Blend," Earl Grey, Orange Pekoe, and English Breakfast teas, but no hot chocolate. Maybe it's a Canadian thing, Bayle thought.

Hot-chocolateless, he opened the door to his room. He put his coffee on the nightstand and lengthwise on the bed flipped through his notepad. Quickly learning here nothing he hadn't already seen and known three hours before first hand, he picked up one of the informational files Jane had instructed the *Toronto Living* research department to put together for him. Three quarters of an hour later Bayle put the folder back on the nightstand.

Although admittedly slightly depressing to learn that the number of Canadian professional hockey franchises was steadily diminishing each year and that every day new teams seemed to be popping up in unlikely American cities like Memphis, Nashville, and Atlanta — all due to a woefully weak Canadian dollar and the huge tax breaks many booming American cities were willing to hand out to sports franchises — Bayle knew that none of what he read should be allowed to affect him all that much. Empiricus dictum number one: Freedom from disturbance means suspension of judgement. If, like clean water, raw timber, and maple syrup, Canada's game was becoming just one more Canadian export steadily seeping south, well, then, Empiricus dictum number one. When all else fails, Empiricus dictum number one.

Bayle went into the washroom and plucked out and put in their disinfected white plastic place his contact lenses. On his way back to bed he pulled to one side the window curtain and paused to let affect the full effect of a rear parking lot-lit pastiche of beam swirls and pulsing light spots, an overflowing tub of electric honey being glub glub generously dumped all over the nighttime black world, the entire wonderfully incomprehensible sighted sensation a woefully near-sighted man's sole compensation for never being able to lie down for even a quick nap without having to first remove from his eyes two pieces of water-permeable thin plastic. (Guilt-free, full-blown irrationality: a crystal-clear sceptic's sweet-treat of refreshing confusion for the brain.) Of course, Patty had always been the exact opposite.

When eleventh-grader Bayle got his first pair of glasses and told his sister not with awe but just because it was true how weird it was to now see things he hadn't even known were there before and how much clearer everything else looked, Patty had immediately insisted that she wanted glasses just like Peter, that she wanted to see all the things that she hadn't been seeing up to then too. Bayle's parents tried their best to explain to their eleven-year-old daughter just how lucky she was that she didn't need to wear glasses, that her eyes were beautiful just like they were, and wasn't she glad that she didn't have to wear anything that might keep everyone from seeing just how beautiful they really were?

But Patty wasn't buying. Sulked and sulked for weeks. Sat on the floor a foot and a half away from the television screen watching cartoons hoping for failing eyesight. Bayle would silently pass by the livingroom on the way from his bedroom to the bathroom and push his new glasses up the bridge of his nose and hope that somehow his little sister got what she wanted. But it wasn't to be. Patty had been cursed with perfect vision.

11

MID-SUMMER '95, the summer
after Bayle's first year of aspiring doctorhood, and a
rare Sunday dinner at the Bayle home with Peter back
from the city, just before Patty refused to leave her
room altogether and before Bayle's mother decided
her daughter's recent case of the blahs was something
more than just another one of her temperamental
daughter's many moods and got her a nine a.m.
appointment with Dr. McKay, their family doctor,
Patty never managed to keep.

Bayle hung his suit jacket up behind the kitchen door and kissed his mother on the cheek and asked where Patty was.

Overseeing several bubbling pots on the stovetop and without turning around, "Where else?" his mother said.

"It's just Patty, mum," Bayle said. "She'll snap out of it. She always does."

Since his father's death three years before, it had fallen upon Bayle to absorb the majority of his mother's exasperation over the emotional Ferris wheel of Patty's highs and lows. The beeping red light on his answering machine usually meant a Patty update from Etobicoke from his mother. Lately, his machine had been awful busy.

"Maybe you can get her out of her funk, Peter," his mother said, poking her fork into a pot of rolling, boiling potatoes. "I don't know what's left for me to say to that girl. Eighteen years old and with three different universities offering her full scholarships and your sister has to be coaxed into eating her meals and to wash her hair once in awhile. I tell you, I'm glad your father's not around to witness this. A man like like him who had to work for everything he ever got in his life would have just killed for the opportunities you and your sister have had handed to you. And don't fool yourself. There are plenty of other kids out there just as smart as Patty who would take her spot at those schools in a minute. Those universities aren't going to wait on her answer forever, you know."

Bayle nodded.

Granted, Patty could be a handful, but their mother was no picnic either. According to her, all that Patty really needed to do to keep herself on track was to settle down with a hardworking union man like her and Bayle's dear old dad, get a house of her own in Etobicoke to call her own and fix up and look after, and start pumping out three or four future Ontario Hydro workers. That would keep her busy. That would keep her head out of the clouds.

"I guess I'll go see how Patty's doing," Bayle said. He waited for a response. His mother kept lifting and replacing steaming pot tops.

"That macaroni and cheese sure smells good," Bayle offered.

Turning around from the stove, oven-mitted hand on her hip, "It's brocolli quiche," his mother said.

"Well, it sure smells good anyway."

"Tell your sister that," his mother said.

Bayle said he'd relay the message.

By themselves briefly before dinner and right through every second of it, Patty chin-in-hand indifferent to her brother, her mother, the food on her plate, and every scrap of conversation encouragingly volleyed her way — all to a degree Bayle had never witnessed before. Since the recent collapse of her nearly two-year-long Catholic kick (a new record for continued fixation), Patty had been aloof the few times Bayle had spoken to her and not too good at returning his occasional calls, but that was, he'd thought, just a part of her usual post-engrossed state.

But three months after she'd donated her rainbow-of-a-closet full of variously coloured rosaries and the complete works of Thomas Merton to the Salvation Army and resolutely gone to bed at four in the afternoon on the day of her Grade 13 graduation from Lorreto's, no new things of earth-shaking importance spilled from Patty's lips that Bayle and everyone else within earshot just *had* to know about, none of the usual nervous signs of giddily revving up for the inevitable next Big Thing evidently revving.

And with hands, Bayle couldn't help but notice, as flawlessly white as her face remained stonily blank. Blank and thin. Just as beautiful as before — maybe even more so for the deep, soul-searching saucers of eyes that now dominated her face and seemed to look not so much at him as through him — but thin. Bayle was watching his sister disappear. He shovelled down his vanilla ice cream with canned peaches in heavy syrup on top for dessert in record time.

Patty could tell he was ready to bolt. She sat up straight in her chair and pushed around with newly found energy the food on her untouched plate, even managing to put down a few mmmm-mmmm-good swallows as she hurled every ounce of her energy and attention Bayle's way like a possessed used-car salesman pumped up on one too many cups of coffee and with an end-of-the-year monster bonus on the line if he can move just one more of these new beauties off the lot by the end of the afternoon.

"I know U of T has the biggest faculty and the most famous alumni and they're offering a full tuition waiver and the most scholarship money and of course I'd be close to you downtown and that would be great but Kingston is so old and beautiful and Queen's has the second highest number of Ontario high-school scholars in their freshman class and then there's UBC and it *would* be kind of neat to just pack up and move out somewhere you've never been before and start a brand new life you know what I mean? What do you think I should do, Peter? They're all sort of breathing down my neck. The next move is mine. I really do have to make a decision soon."

Bayle's mother grinned over her own ice cream like a delighted new lobotomy recipient, thrilled at her too-thin and too-quiet daughter's suddenly miraculous return to the living. Between this and Patty's sudden chatty liveliness that bordered on the out and out hysterical Bayle could only wipe his mouth with a paper napkin and go for his coat. Can't stay, no, thanks, really, really have got to go. Mountains of laundry await. Mountains.

Patty bobbed up from her chair.

"Just give me a second to clean up a bit and grab some library books that should have been returned downtown ages ago and I'll go back with you," she said. "There are some books that you can only get at Robarts that I've been meaning to check out for awhile now." She stuck a limp green bean in her mouth and skipped off down the hall before Bayle could open his, or his happily astonished mother close hers.

Bayle's mother ambushed him at the back door.

"Be patient with her, Peter," she said. "This is the first

time your sister's shown any interest in going anywhere or doing anything besides sleeping all day in I don't know how long. But don't baby her, though. She's a smart girl. She won't stand for that. But be encouraging. If she wants to talk, let her talk. If she doesn't, that's fine, too. But don't treat her like one of those sick kids they send off to Florida for their last wish, either. Don't give her a reason to feel sorry for herself. If you ask me, that's half the problem right there."

"Half of whose problem?" Patty said, appearing in the kitchen doorway. Standing there in faded blue jeans and her favourite Property of U of T Athletics sweatshirt Peter had bought for her for her sixteenth birthday, a stack of library books plastic-bagged and tucked neatly underneath one arm, her long blond hair tied into a no-nonsense ponytail with a piece of blue cloth, she almost looked like Patty of old ready to rush right off with *important things to do,* ready to chase down the intricacies of this season's once-and-for-all obsession.

"Nobody's," Bayle said, pushing open the kitchen door. "Let's get going. We want to get downtown before Robarts closes."

But the library did close without them, although not the Brunswick House. How Patty managed to talk him into taking her there Bayle wasn't sure, even less so after the untold glasses of soapy draft beer they'd downed before closing time. The "Brunny," as it was affectionately known to the students at the university, was a nearly hundred-year-old U of T legend, an enormous German beerhall-styled bar with the historical plaque out front to prove it and the widely understood mission of providing the cheap alcohol and crowded seating conditions condusive to rampant flirting and a wide variety of undergraduate stupidities. Throw in an aging beer-hall diva given to drinking too much gin and groping the football players and whose piano sing-a-longs were not even hooted at affectionately anymore, just flat out ignored, and you had just the sort of place Patty would ordinarily have loathed.

But it was, Patty enthusiastically informed Bayle on the subway ride downtown, on the list of the "Must See and Do" places the U of T Student Association had mailed to her in their recruiting package over the summer, and she pretty-pleased Bayle into just one beer before they hit the library. Although Bayle said he doubted if whether or not she liked the Brunswick House would be a determining factor in where she spent the next four years of her academic life, he'd always been fairly hopeless in the face of his sister's rare but powerful pretty-pleases so they got off at the Spadina stop instead of St. George and had their hands stamped and beer spilt on them by a rowdy table of Cheezy-throwing Commerce students before they had a chance to exchange a word.

And when Patty ordered four more glasses of draft when Bayle was in the washroom, saying, when he returned to the table with a disapproving frown, "Have I told you I've had a less-than-wonderful summer? Sometimes a girl just has to let down her hair and relax, you know" (pulling away the piece of blue cloth that held her ponytail in place, bushels of greasy, blond hair falling and falling down as she did so, a mischievous smile peeking through the mass of unkempt hair covering her eyes), they were off and running. Where to, exactly, Bayle had no idea; and, what was worse, a strong suspicion his sister didn't either. Both of them running, though, this without question.

He tried to be patient. When Patty didn't immediately follow up her mini-confession with anything else about her summer-long gloom, Bayle kept ordering more beer while watching along with her with a kind of repulsed fascination the furious attempts everywhere they looked of four hundred increasingly fuzzy faces giving it everything they had toward making sure they didn't end up going home without an intoxicated stranger in tow or, at the very least, a hangover worth bragging about over breakfast. As the beer Bayle and his sister consumed and the hours they sat there began to add up, the room itself seemed to buzz louder and louder, to transform itself into a swarming drone of pure riotous sound.

They drank on, Bayle drinking and waiting, Patty drinking
and saying nothing.

When they were finally spit out of the Brunswick House
at two a.m. onto bar-emptying, suddenly-swarming Bloor
Street, the cool night air produced entirely different effects in
brother and sister. More than a little drowsy from all the
alcohol, Bayle bought two veggie dogs for Patty and himself
from a busy vendor strategically camped outside the
Brunswick House doors to scoop up the hungry post-drinking
crowd (Patty still swearing off all meat but for occasionally a
little fish on Friday — Ecology Thing leftover fusing with
recent Catholic Thing remnant). Bayle walked over to Patty
talking to a group of frat boys milling around in front of the
bar and handed her her veggie dog. He'd prepared it for her
just the way she liked it: plain but for a deep double swipe of
mustard squirted right down the middle.

Patty said thanks without even looking at him and carried
right on with her spirited conversation, letting the weiner and
bun hang limply by her side as if Bayle had handed her an
old shoe he'd just found on the street. A cab crept its after-
hours crawl in front of the bar and the frat boys quickly hailed
it and piled in, waving and calling out Patty's name as they
jammed in, promising to see her there.

Before Bayle could even ask:

"Guess where we're off to, bro?" Patty said, putting her
arm in his, other hand still holding on to the now almost
vertical, dribbling veggie dog.

His already-eaten own having only made him even
sleepier, Bayle didn't want to go anywhere. Especially with
three drunken brothers of Phi Beta Whatever with obvious
lecherous designs on his kid sister. "Let's go home, Patty,"
Bayle said. "If we hustle you can still make the subway back to
Etobicoke. Let me carry your bag. I'll return your books for
you tomorrow. You can check out those other books you
wanted some other time."

"Oh, Peter, it's a speakeasy and I've never been. Nothing
special to a big college man like you, I'm sure, but think of

your poor innocent sister locked away in suburbia and so
painfully naive in the ways of the world. Pretty please?"

"Sorry," Bayle said, Patty's sugary plea surprisingly easily
resisted through simple exhaustion. "Only one pretty please per
every twenty-four hour period and you've already used up
today's quota in getting us to waste our evening here. C'mon,
pick up your bag and let's go," he said, starting in the direction
of the subway stop. "I might get to bed before three o'clock yet."

Patty dropped her arm from his. Hurled the mustard-
emitting veggie dog off into the night and scattered the plastic
bag full of library books into the street with a perfectly placed
soccer kick mastered during her British Thing.

"I haven't been out of that *fucking* house in three *fucking*
months and I'm going to an after-hours bar with you or
without you," she said. She shot up her hand for an
approaching cab that immediately stopped.

"Are you coming or not?" she said, already in the back
seat, hand on the inside door handle and ready to slam it
shut, Bayle could tell, if he answered No.

By the idling taxi's headlights Bayle picked up each of the
booted library books one at a time, handing them over in a
neat pile to his sister when he finally got in beside her.

When they reached the Dundas Street address the frat
boys had given her, Patty forgot the books in the backseat of
the cab, Bayle luckily spotting and retrieving them when he
got out to pay, reminding her as they headed for the Chinese
restaurant that a negligent library record can haunt you your
entire life. Patty said she'd try to keep that in mind.

After the special tea was ordered and produced — lukewarm
beer in a small tin pot, two tiny white Chinese teacups to
complete the Spartan service — and the fraternity boys
summarily dismissed — "I'm sorry," Patty had said, looking
directly at the tallest and best-looking one, all three of them
spotting and happily tramping over to her and Bayle's table,
"you've obviously mistaken me for someone who would waste

her time talking to someone like you" — Bayle and his sister settled into pretty much a mirror of their Brunswick House routine, Bayle waiting for the dam to burst, Patty content, it seemed, to simply watch the river flow.

Much tepid beer under the bridge later, indeterminable hour somewhere between very late and very early, like Bayle's, Patty's teacup seemed a permanent part of her hand by now, even if for the last long while rarely to lips lifted. A cowboy-booted and sideburned Queen Street hipster sitting with a tall black-haired beauty excepted, the customer constitution of the restaurant had changed several times over since Bayle and Patty sat down hours earlier, leaving brother and sister Bayle the sole teacup-tipping constants.

"God, drinking is stupid," Patty said, pushing away her cup.

Bayle sat up in his seat, chair scraping. He forced his eyes painfully wide, Patty's words stirring him from what, before tonight/this morning, he would have thought virtually impossible, open-eyed sleep.

"I guess it makes sense, though, doesn't it?" she said. "Anything that makes you feel even the tiniest bit not bad for ten minutes now has just got to make you feel like absolute shit for ten times longer than that later."

Bayle really didn't have any thoughts on the subject. Bayle was still trying to wake up. He blinked both eyes violently and repeatedly in an attempt to lubricate his eyeball-sticking, dried-up contact lenses.

"Maybe we should eat," Patty said. "That's supposed to help, right?"

"I was thinking vegetable fried rice and hot-and-sour soup about an hour ago," Bayle said, "but figured the food would put us to sleep."

"You mean put *you* to sleep." Slight smile.

Bayle smiled back. "All right, so you got all the tenacity genes in the family," he said.

Patty picked up her tea cup of warm beer again and sipped at it absently. "Yeah. Yeah, that's me all right," she said. "Tenacious Patty. Yeah, that's me."

Then, louder — and as she went along, gaining enthusiasm for her subject, louder and louder still — "Yeah, Tenacious Patty," she said. "That's it. I think I'll start up my own line of woman's wear. The Tenacious Patty Line. For the Truly Active Woman Intent on Getting Ahead in the World and Staying There. You know: severe, two-piece business suits of stylish armour with shoulders *out to here* just like a hockey player's with not an inch of mortal flesh showing and all styles available in the identical shade of grown-up grey. Five-inch black high heels that say, Yes, I've got legs up to my neck you'd just love to slobber all over, but I'm also the toughest negotiator you've ever had the misfortune of encountering, each pair furnished, it goes without saying, with a shining silver razor blade carefully concealed inside the left shoe for those extra-tough bargaining sessions. And brand new this season! Don't call it a purse! Don't call it your bag! It's the all-purpose Tenacious Patty Satchel! To the ignorant eye, it's true, just another flimsy lady's accessory, but to the happily initiated, everything you need and then some to keep healthy, wealthy, and wise out there in the cold, cold world of commerce. Snub-nosed Barreta. Easy-to-access switchblade. Even a vial of hydrochloric acid for tossing in the faces of one and all who — no matter how hard you try; no matter how hard you try and try and try — just don't seem to get your point."

Most of the restaurant was looking their way now. Patty looked up at her brother. Patty looked through her brother. Crazy — no other word for it — crooked smile and hot salt tears. Like being caught in the middle of a violent thunderstorm, Bayle thought, on the sunniest day of the year.

The situation clearly called for Bayle at his absolute worst, Bayle the emotional commiserator. He placed a tentative hand on his sister's trembling shoulder. Patted her there a few times softly. Smiled a hang-in-here smile. Awkwardly drew his hand away. Felt in his gut just as petrified as she looked. "Patty ...."

"Oh, let's just get out of here," she said.

Bayle didn't know what to say so he got up and settled the

bill at the cash. When he came back from paying, their table
was empty. An instant of panic. But then the guy in the
cowboy boots and sideburns smiled and pointed outside at
Patty sitting on the cement step of the restaurant embracing
herself against the cool of dawn. Bayle smiled a relieved
smile back at the man and said thanks as he walked past his
table, forgetting Patty's library books stacked on the floor
beneath her chair.

Bayle and his sister ate their breakfast specials in silence, the
dust-caked white curtains hanging beside their window table
useful at least in preventing too much of the ripening
morning sun from spilling through. After the egg yolks had
been mopped up and the coffee cups refilled twice over there
really wasn't much left to do. All around them the restaurant
hummed alive, the early Monday morning breakfast crowd
with their freshly cracked newspapers and just-scrubbed faces
infectious for their beautifully foolish excitement over the
start of just another day, the start to just another week.

Bayle felt his stomach turn a joyful tumble at the thought
of putting Patty on the subway and getting himself home to
bed so that before too long he could get right back up and
head off to the library and return to work on the final paper
for his summer-school class. The seminar itself had been a
disappointment, a fourteen-week snooze of a survey through
"The Rationalists," the paper topic he'd been assigned almost
equally as boring. But the thought of showering and shaving
with purpose and carefully packing up his bag with a clear
mission in mind and hours and hours of uninterrupted quiet
time ahead of him to accomplish it pushed back the
weariness of the hour, the effect of the rare hangover, even
Patty's long silences and troubling outbursts.

But really not so troubling. Because Patty was going to be
all right, Bayle thought, picking up his coffee cup, draining it
to its dregs. Hell, she *was* all right. Nearly nineteen years old
and still living at home would put anybody on the road to

becoming unglued. But soon enough she'd be out of there, starting university herself, and when that happened ....

"Didn't we pass an art store on the way over here?" Patty said. She pulled open the curtain to one side and strained her neck left then right then right then left to find what she was searching for. She looked like somebody who was afraid they were being followed.

"An art store?" Bayle said. "You mean like a gallery?"

"No, that would be called a gallery, wouldn't it? I mean an art store, a store that sells canvases, paints, brushes — all the things that a person who wants to paint needs to have to — There! There it is!"

Her face almost pressed to the window, she kept rapping the end of her index finger against the glass. Bayle shielded his eyes as best he could from the sun and squinted to see what she was seeing.

"Where? I don't —"

"Over there, right over there," she said, voice rising, knocking harder on the window pane. "Right next to the post office."

Bayle finally saw what she was looking at, a small, nondescript, cement-brick shop about two blocks down Spadina. "Okay, okay," he said. "Now I see it." He let the curtain drop and sat back in the red-vinyl booth and rubbed his eyes. "But what do you want with an art store?"

Picking up her coffee cup, blowing on it although it was already cool, "I'm thinking about doing some painting," Patty said. "Actually, I've been thinking that maybe I'll take a year off to see if I really like it and if I'm any good. Who knows? Maybe I'll apply to art school next year. They say that O.C.A. has one of the best programs in the country."

"This is the first time I've heard of any of this," Bayle said.

"Well, now you have."

Bayle shook his head. "Patty, you can't just decide to become a painter. I mean ... you just can't." Patty looked away, looked back out the window. "Besides," Bayle said, "I don't even know if that place is an art store."

"Oh, it's an art store, all right," Patty said, bouncing up from her seat. She held out her hand.

Bayle placed his hand hesitantly in hers; suddenly tuned in to what she wanted and tried to pull it away.

"Oh, no," he said, "no way."

"C'mon, Peter, it'll only take two minutes."

"No way, N-O, no."

"Just two minutes, that's all I'm asking. We've been up all this time anyway, what are two minutes more?"

"Two minutes more are two minutes more than we should be awake and not at home asleep."

Patty hadn't let go of his hand. She grabbed on to his forearm and wrist and slowly pulled him to his feet.

Face to face inches apart on the floor of the busy restaurant, waitresses gliding by like ghosts in white support shoes sentenced to carry bacon-and-egg-laden plates throughout breakfasts of eternity, Bayle suddenly saw his eight-year-old sister laughing with her hand over her mouth and asking him for the last bite of his Snickers bar, all that was left of her own chocolate treat a crumpled brown wrapping paper lying discarded under the stands at the hockey arena.

"Please, Peter?"

"No more pretty-pleases?" he asked.

"I thought you said I'd already used all my pretty-pleases up for today."

"New rule," Bayle said. "From now on, just as many pretty-pleases as Patty Bayle wants."

12

BAYLE CHANGED his mind about stepping out; took the boy at the front desk Ron's advice and decided to try a place nearby called Larry's that didn't have much to recommend itself other than you didn't need to own a car to get there.

The walk from The Range to the bar was short, no more than ten minutes, but Bayle's t-shirt was soaked through by the humid night by the time he got there. He opened the bar door and stepped inside, the air-conditioned cool of the room momentarily stunning him, though not unpleasantly.

A fuzzy big-screen television, fifteen-cent chicken wings, and waitresses who smiled so hard you feared they might hurt themselves provided the unexpected environment for an altogether dimmed room full of middle-aged, middle-class, sour-faced white males. Larry's aroused slight interest only in that it was, in the context of Bayle's barroom experience, something of an anomaly: in sum, a thoroughly debauched sports bar. Nearly midnight now, the all-sports cable station soundlessly replayed a monster truck pull taped earlier that evening from somewhere in Idaho. No one paid much attention to the screen, but Bayle sensed that its absence would have been quickly noted. The tables of men kept the two waitresses working the room running, the sort of drinking going on throughout clearly not of the merely recreational sort. Bayle could feel the room's angry heat.

Fuck it, he thought, eyes on him as he moved from the door to the bar. I need a drink.

The room musicless and the sound on the television muted, a steady babbling and occasional sharp shout nonetheless made it necessary for Bayle to lean forward with forearms on the bar when ordering his drink. The bored looking bartender seemed to be the only one in the place who didn't have something to say.

"C.C., straight up," Bayle said.

Tongue stuck deep in his cheek, the bartender shook his head.

"Canadian Club, no ice," Bayle, louder, repeated.

"I heard you the first time. Never heard of it, and we don't got it."

"Give him some of the bird," a voice farther down the bar said. "Put it on my tab." Bayle turned to see Davidson taking a sip from his glass sitting by himself at the other end of the bar.

Bayle took the Wild Turkey the bartender sat down in front of him and, not knowing what else to do, awkwardly raised it in Davidson's direction. Ignoring the gesture but looking at Bayle now, "Sure wasn't 'Hockey Night in Canada' out there tonight, was it?"

"A little slow," Bayle replied, "but not bad." The bourbon tasted good; different from regular whiskey, almost sweet in its sting, but good. He took another, deeper sip.

"A *little* slow? Christ, I could've laced up and not looked out of place."

A slight smile cracked Bayle's face. He took another drink and surveyed the room. Three baseball-capped and full-bearded men sitting at the table closest to the bar high-fived one another with a palm-reddening intensity and noisily called out for another round. Back home Bayle would have pegged them for civil servants in the Ontario Ministry of This or That out for a couple of rowdy beers and the game. Here they could be planning a lodge meeting or a bank job, he really couldn't tell.

Bayle always felt this way when he was in the States. Even as a kid when he and his dad would travel just across the border to Buffalo to see a game at the Auditorium, as soon as the border guard waved them through and his birth certificate was back in his wallet, suddenly everything seemed slightly dangerous, unpredictable, *American*. The lonely figure walking alone beside the darkening highway. The three black youths standing in front of the convenience store near the Aud. The whine of a police siren a few blocks away from the arena parking lot. Nothing he hadn't seen or heard before, of course, but here, having crossed over to the other side, the American side, things that nerved menacing more than the plain sum of their seemingly ordinary parts. And then, always the same relief of coming back after the hockey game to see the Halloween-orange BREWER'S RETAIL sign a mile or so on the northern side of the border. The state-sanctioned distribution and sale of all alcoholic beverages. Canada. Home.

"Interesting place," Bayle called over to Davidson.

Davidson gave a cursory turn of his head toward the rest of the bar behind him. "It's cheap," he replied, returning to his drink.

"You're standing in the server's area, sir." A wilting blonde waitress heroically grinning in spite of an overflowing tray of chicken bones and empty beer bottles and highball glasses waited for Bayle to move away from the bar, anxious to fill up anew. Bayle picked up his drink, scanned the seething room, hesitated.

Finally: "So what the hell is all this *doctor* business?" Davidson said, giving Bayle the reason he needed to hug close to the shore of the bar. Bayle carried over his drink and sat down on the black vinyl stool next to Davidson's.

"Philosophy. I'm working on my doctorate in philosophy."

"Jesus H. Christ," Davidson said, crushed ice clinking colliding with upper row of teeth as he finished off his drink. "You better let me get another one of these first."

Absolutely, Bayle thought.

"You about ready?" Davidson asked, pointing to Bayle's half empty glass.

"Absolutely," Bayle answered.

Bayle the drinker: how? Swift and thorough, all or nothing. A two-beer buzz not in the least appealing (for the infinitesimal intoxicating action that occurs, better off staying straight and doing what can only get done clear-headed and quick), Bayle, when drinking, drank. On average, three one-and-a-half-ounce shots of Canadian Club whiskey per hour, a bottle of any brand of beer regularly substituted for one of the shots from about the fourth hour of continuous drinking on.

Bayle the drinker: why? Not to accentuate a good time, certainly (what could booze do, after all, to make better the already enlivening effect of a few hours of good hard work?). Nor to simply pass the time (too crude a solution to such an enduring human dilemma). And, most definitely, not to blot out a bad time (facile hedonism to think that five or six hours of hurried slurping could somehow cancel out the remainder of that day's and the next's accumulated uneasy minutes).

So, again: why?

Larry's, one forty-three a.m., Bayle sitting perfectly upright on his bar stool holding his fifth glass of bourbon. More precisely: Bayle sitting perfectly upright on his bar stool holding with slightly bloodied right handed knuckles his fifth glass of bourbon.

"Don't get me wrong," Davidson says, "that loudmouth you decked, he's been asking for it for years. But that woman he was going on about: that really is his sister and she really is a crazy bitch, especially when she gets into the sauce. Not as bad as him, but still, pretty bad. And don't take this the wrong way, but you don't exactly strike me as the violent type."

"Harry," Bayle answers, "if I was a book and God was a book critic, the pretentious sonofabitch just might call me a flotsam on life's jetsam. But do you know what, Harry? Do you know what? He just wouldn't be reading between the lines. Because if He did, if He really, really did, He'd see I'm trying to get upstream on every page. On *every* fucking page."

"Okay."

"And Harry?"

"Yeah?"

"One more thing?"

"Yeah?"

"A family is like a hockey team. When one member is in trouble, it's up to all the other members to help out. Especially if it's your sister."

"Okay."

Bayle and Davidson drink from their drinks.

"Hey, what time is last call around here?" Bayle asks.

"I don't think last call is an option for us tonight. That I keep this place in the black is the only reason we're still sitting here."

Bayle and Davidson nurse their drinks.

"How do you feel?" Davidson asks.

"I feel ... I feel great!"

"Just like the tiger, huh?"

"Yeah," Bayle answers, "just like the tiger!"

Bayle, sipping, looks at his dried-blood-blotched knuckles over the top of his glass, smiles; over the top of his knuckles looks at a familiar but not-placed black female face coming his way.

"In that case," Davidson says, "grab your coat."

The woman, Gloria, arrives and sticks her scarf into her purse, leans over, and kisses Davidson full on the mouth. Davidson does the introductions.

"Peter, Gloria. G., Peter."

Hello, hello.

"You got everything, Bayle?" Davidson asks.

"Yep."

"Any questions?"

"Nope."

"All right, then. Let's get this show on the road."

"Absolutely," Bayle says.

13

"A LITTLE overcast for sunglasses, isn't it?"

The slumping figure at the back of the bus once again his only passenger, the bus driver was beginning to recognize Bayle's face.

"Not used to all this Big Sky country," Bayle replied.

"Montana is Big Sky country."

"What do you call the Midwest, then?"

"Nothing. We don't call it nothing."

It was nearly one in the afternoon. Davidson had dropped Bayle off at The Range sometime after four a.m., the conscientious nine-thirty wake-up call he had left with Ron before setting out for Larry's the night before coming and going. Just like old times, he thought. He touched with his left hand the scabs beginning to harden on the knuckles of his right and grimaced, though not entirely from physical pain. Just like old times.

The bus pulled up immediately adjacent to the arena's front entranceway.

"See you in a few hours?" Bayle said.

"Where else am I going to be?" the driver answered.

An hour later Bayle was coming out of the rink just as Davidson was going in. The awkwardness of encountering in sober daylight what was essentially a stranger who, only the inebriated night before, had been alcohol-established as a faithful confidante and lifetime comrade kept both men uhming and ahhing at the arena entrance. Although cloudy and only a little after two, it was already sticky and warm. And getting warmer. The partially opened door of a pickup truck belonging to a service man repairing a broken lamp in the arena parking lot emitted the I.M. Wright Show loud and clear.

"Gotta get some quotes," Davidson said.

"Yeah, I just talked to them."

Look at it this way, folks. If the liberal rabble rousers at the *Eagle* manage to brainwash City Hall into forcing Bunton Groceries to spend a million

dollars on so-called arena "improvements," there are only two things they can do: move the team out of state, or raise ticket prices, prices at the concession stand, prices —

"How's the hand?"
"Oh, fine. Fine," Bayle said.

....just another case where liberals in love with big government like to stick their noses in somebody else's business and make it harder and harder for regular citizens like you and me to get our fair share of the American Dream.

"Well, I better get in there before they're all gone," Davidson said.
"Yeah, I gotta get going too."
"If you want to wait around for half an hour or so I can give you a lift home."
"That's all right, the bus should be here any minute," Bayle said.
"Okay."
"But thanks anyway."
"Sure."

.... safeguard that Dream, folks, fight for it with your every drop of energy.

"I'm usually at Larry's by about ten if you feel like grabbing a drink later tonight."
"Thanks," Bayle said, "but I really think I better try to take it easy from here on in. I mean, I've got a lot of work to do if I'm ever going to write this article."
"Okay."
"Thanks anyway."

Until tomorrow then, folks, I.M. Wright.

"Sure."

Bayle wasn't the only passenger this time; Jefferson, the janitor he'd spoken to for his article, managed to get the driver's and Bayle's attention (arms waving and lunch box flaying) an instant before the bus pulled away from its highway stop. On board, "Thanks a bunch for stopping," he said, "the old Chevy decided she wasn't going to go with me to work this morning." He dropped his coins into the steel slot next to the driver and took a seat across the aisle from Bayle in the middle of the bus. Bayle returned Jefferson's smile and cheerful good afternoon but gave his attention over to Davidson in the parking lot climbing into his truck, slamming the door shut, and speeding away. Couldn't have talked to anybody that quickly, Bayle thought. Must have changed his mind about the quotes.

The hours he'd spent as Davidson's late-night guest a little more than twelve hours before played themselves out before Bayle's still alcohol-fogged mind: the house-subdivided one-bedroom apartment (hardwood-floored, military sparse, hospital clean); the several drinks he and Davidson had kitchen-table shared (Gloria — identified by now by Bayle as the helmet-hidden, smooth-skating silver Warrior mascot of that night's game — sharing the table but not the bourbon, mostly silently keeping pace with cup after cup of hot lemon tea); the continuous Glen-Goulded Bach playing on the boombox sitting on the kitchen countertop; the twenty years of newspaperman anecdotes Davidson had perfected through what were probably just as many years of barroom rehearsal (Bayle laughing heartily throughout, Gloria still essentially silent but grinning deep at all the right places); Davidson's sudden announcement that it was time to call it a night and dutiful putting away of the bottle in the cupboard; the ride back to Bayle's hotel through the deserted back streets of the unfamiliar town.

And later, back in his room at The Ranch on his back, blood sugar level falling, surety of spirit shrinking, energy of all sorts of just half an hour before ebbing: Bayle fitful for a place to go, a job to do, a thing to Be. None of these apparently in the offing, however: seven quarters in the pay phone at the end of the hall. Five rings later:

"Hi, this is Jane. I can't come to the phone right now, but I'll try to get back to you as soon as possible if you leave your name and message after the beep."

The beep.

"Therefore he who suspends judgement about everything —"

"Peter?"

"Therefore, he who suspends judgement about everything which is subject to opinion reaps a harvest of the most complete happiness."

"Goddammit, Peter, you're drunk."

"Complete happiness."

"Goddamn you and your Goddamn Greeks anyway, Peter. I can see you've really made a lot of progress —"

"Complete happiness."

Click. Uhmmmmmmmmmmmm ....

Immutable Empiricus ring-ring remedy done, Bayle walked back to his room, brushed his teeth (twice), pissed (prolonged), and went to sleep.

"He sure got a lot of nerve showing his face around these parts," Jefferson said. Nodding for Bayle's puzzled benefit in the direction of Davidson's truck stopped at a red light in front of the bus, "Don't matter to him none if we all lose our jobs if the Warriors got to leave town," he said. "He gets his name in the newspaper all the same anyway. He gets his check every week."

"Roy, what the hell are you talking about?" Bayle's adopted journalistic civility had dissipated in the wake of his hangover and the inevitable post-purpose psychical flatness that necessarily accompanied his every morning after. Bayle the next morning was no longer ennui impermeable or even ass-kicking Tony the Tiger; was, in fact, simply Bayle again. And all that that implied. And, worse, didn't.

"I'm talking about what you call a liberal rabble rouser,

sir, that's what I'm talking about. One of them big government lovers."

Making the radio connection, "Don't tell me you listen to that crank," Bayle said.

"What you talking about, 'crank'?"

"What's-his-name, I don't know, the radio guy, Wright."

"Mr. I.M. Wright?"

"Yeah, right."

Jefferson put his lunch box on top of his lap, sat up straight, and looked across the aisle and over Bayle's head at the flying-by farmland. "I think it be a good idea if you be careful about who you be calling a crank," he said. "Lots of people round here appreciate the job Mr. Wright does looking out for the interests of everyday folk like myself."

"C'mon, Roy, you don't really believe that crap that he —"

"Scuse me," Jefferson said, picking up his lunch box. He walked to the very back of the bus before finally sitting down, as far away from Bayle as he could get.

The bus moved towards town. As the simple shock of Jefferson's Wrightian defence began to somewhat diminish, Bayle more than once tried to make conciliatory eye contact with the janitor, but with little success. Each time Bayle would catch him looking in the direction of the front of the bus Jefferson would quickly turn his head to look out the window beside him, a hard expression of obvious distaste on his face.

Finally Bayle gave up, settled on watching the bland prairie farmland repeat itself past his own window. His mind, however, stayed stuck on the infuriating contradiction of a working-class guy like Jefferson playing dupe to, and even defending, such an obvious big business mouthpiece as Wright. Empiricus knows, Bayle wasn't even remotely political — what kind of card-carrying sceptic was? — but it just didn't make sense. And it bothered Bayle like hell that it didn't. Worse, it bothered him like hell that it bothered him so much that it didn't.

Eventually, and meant to be fortifyingly said only in his

head: "He who suspends judgement about everything ..." Bayle said, attempting to calm himself, voice trailing off. "He who suspends judgement about everything ..." he said again, getting no further the second time than he did the first.

"What's that again?" the bus driver asked, seeing Bayle sitting alone now, assuming his moving lips were meant for him at the head of the bus to hear.

"Nothing. Just talking to myself," Bayle said.

14

"επιοτημη or δοξα?
I mean, of course, if you don't mind me asking."

The impact of being addressed in Classical Greek here at Larry's — women's tag-team wrestling live from Rochester, New York, on each of the room's four big-screen televisions — was nearly that of the effect of the three rapidly administered shots of Wild Turkey. Bayle was back, but by himself this time, and only on the condition of just one quick one, and only then because he thought the change of scenery from his small room at The Range might alleviate his soul-searching procrastinating. He turned around from the bar to find a black-suited minister grinning good-naturedly and offering Bayle a duplicate of what he was drinking, vodka on the rocks.

Seeing that both of Bayle's hands were full with a glass of bourbon and a bottle of Budweiser — Bayle's condition of coming already broken almost as soon as he had come — "Oh, dear, I see that you're already fully occupied," the minister frowned. "Not to worry," he said, broad smile of before promptly reappearing. He emptied the contents of one drink into that of the other and placed the empty glass on the bar top. "A double play!" he said, clinking Bayle's glass, expertly sipping down a good third of the three fingers of alcohol in his own. Bayle cautiously sipped his own Wild Turkey without saying a word and seriously considered whether he had only imagined the Greek.

"So what's it going to be then?" the minister said, his face now suddenly serious, even stern. "Knowledge or belief? Which one is it that rules your tender soul? And don't try to sell me any of that Hegelian dialectism nonsense. As they say in my business" — he tugged at his white clerical collar — "you can't serve two masters. Which is it?" He drank again, eyes slightly narrowed and never leaving Bayle's. Bayle, more than a little baffled, could only sip.

"Oh, what a bloody ass I am," the minister said, all affability again. He wiped his free hand on his black trousers before presenting it to be shaken. "Charles Warren. Actually, the Reverend Charles Warren, but I'd be very happy if you would just call me Chuck."

Still a little overwhelmed, Bayle, by instinct, offered over his beer-holding hand.

"Ah ha, putting your best hand forward!" Warren said. He took the bottle of Budweiser from Bayle and put it on the bar beside his empty vodka glass.

"Bayle," Bayle said, shaking-hand free now and meeting Warren's. "Peter Bayle."

"Oh, I know who you are, Peter. You don't mind if I call you Peter, do you?"

"No, no, not at all ...." Bayle said, shaking his head no, as puzzled-looking as before.

"Oh, I get it," Warren said. "I know you but you don't know me. Gotcha. Just like poor old Job down there on the farm. Let's grab a seat, shall we? It's really not as mysterious as it all might at first appear. Which, incidentally, is just what Job found out in the end, isn't it?"

"Yes, but what *did* Tillich mean, exactly, by Ultimate Concern? Collecting baseball cards? Sniffing women's used underthings? Belief in an omniscient, all-powerful Being? I mean, really, Peter, let's narrow down our terminology here a little bit, what?"

The Reverend Warren, in his part-time capacity as the Warriors' team minister, had heard through Samson about Bayle's philosophical background almost as soon as Bayle arrived in town and hoped that he and Bayle could, "You know, banter on a bit about the Ontological Argument and what not" because "one does get a bit starved out here in the territories for really meaty conversation."

St. Louis-born one year after Bayle, Warren had attended Christ's College, Oxford, on a full scholarship and almost completed his doctoral thesis on Aquinas after an outstanding undergraduate career at Washington University when he was called back home to Missouri during his father's fatal battle with leukemia. His mother falling infirm shortly after her husband's death, Warren, an only child and his mother's sole

99

benefactor, entered the local Baptist ministry because, as he explained it to Bayle, "First, I thought I could get paid to talk about Aquinas and Anselm all day long — Wrong! — and second, the Catholics, my first choice, though impressed by my academic background, wanted me to go to school for another five years. No could do. Health insurance for a sixty-three-year-old woman with a history of heart problems does not come cheap, let me tell you."

After an unprecedented five-month accelerated stint at a local seminary ("I could have done the whole thing in two weeks, tops, no exaggeration") he was ordained by G.A.R.B. — the General Association of Regular Baptists — a rigidly fundamentalist sect, and sent off to tend to his present flock, a medium-sized church in a medium-sized conservative town in the Midwest that in its beer-with-a-shot-on-the-side, working-class heart, appeared willing to close its eyes to Warren's public disregard of his G.A.R.B.-ordained order of abstinence.

His mother, now an invalid in a nursing home in the suburbs of St. Louis, although well-served by the monthly cheques Warren made sure paid for the best health care she could receive, no longer seemed to recognize him when he visited, and for some reason would only talk about a torrid love affair she claimed to have had with Don Ho when she was a WAC serving in Hawaii during World War II. Warren confessed that he could not watch "Hawaii Five-O" re-runs on television without being overcome by waves of overpowering sadness of "nearly Kierkegaardin proportions."

When not at the church, he read like a demon at the local library most evenings ("demon" being his choice of expression), usually stopped in at Larry's afterward in order to "wind down a little bit," and eventually hoped to get a congregation with "a little less ... literal interpretation of the Bible," preferably on the east coast. He also, Bayle observed, chain-smoked unfiltered Kents, lapped up his drinks with an intensity not even matched by Bayle at his own swinish worst, and, after a certain intoxicated point, would occasionally affect the English *what?* at the end of his sentences. Within an hour Bayle couldn't be sure if Warren was a liberal Protestant in a conservative church, a closet atheist, or something in between. Warren was, most certainly, an alcoholic mess of a mass of contradictions. He was a man after Bayle's heart.

"So it's agreed then that Kant's entire theory of the Categorical Imperative — his whole system of ethics, in other words — can be clearly and indubitably attributed to the fact that he never got his rocks off."

"Okay," Bayle said.

"Right, then. So. On to less abstruse, but no-less-significant matters. Married?"

"No."

"Alternative lifestyle?"

"No."

"Girlfriend?

"Yes."

"Ah ha. Name?"

"Jane."

"Jane. Hmmm. Dark and solemn, or fair and winsome?"

"A little of both."

"Dark and winsome?"

"The other one."

"I see."

A short break in the exchange while more drinks are ordered and served and Warren explicates his understanding of Plato's theory of love as contained in *The Symposium* and Bayle once again agrees without qualification to whatever Warren says. (Bayle, when soused, believing that talking about sensation-hating Plato when one was good and loaded was only slightly less obscene than arguing about the existence of God when a beautiful woman was in the room.)

Bayle was:

> (a) a crude materialist with a longing for subtler notions;
>
> (b) simply drunk;
>
> (c) all of the above.

"Politics?" Warren continued.

"None."

"Religion?"

"None."

"Hobbies?"

"Nope."

"How fascinating. Breast fed, by any chance?"

"You mean recently, or as a baby?"

"Your call."

"No."

"No to which?"

"No," Bayle said.

"I see. Right, then. Mother and father both still alive?"

"Just mother."

"Brothers or sisters?"

Bayle didn't answer.

On the television, the redhead in the Supergirl costume pins, and then bites on the forearm and refuses to be detached from, the stocky woman in the Daniel Boone coonskin hat, cheekless leather chaps, and pink thong. The bartender asks, "Another round for you and slugger here, Rev?" and a vodka on the rocks and Jack Daniels arrive though both are, at the moment, not yet needed.

"To repeat," Warren said. "Brothers or sisters?"

Bayle didn't answer.

Warren finished his drink. "Don't worry, you always get a second chance with all the really important questions."

Bayle looked up from his own drink. "Really?"

"Maybe. I don't know. I just made that up."

A little before eleven Bayle suggested they cut out for somewhere else, having remembered Davidson saying that was when he usually dropped by Larry's. Bayle felt a little guilty for having turned down cold the old man's afternoon invitation for a drink later at the bar and then showing up there just a few hours later. "Any other places around here worth checking out?" Bayle said.

"No need," Warren said. "Ample refreshments back at my

place. Vehicle's in the lot out back. Just let me settle up my tab with Jake, what?"

Paying Warren as little notice as he did anyone else in the bar, Jake, the bartender, presented Warren with a white slip of paper which Warren only perfunctorily scanned over before hastily initialling and handing back. Warren turned to Bayle beside him at the bar. "Are we off, then?" he said.

But in the three or four minutes it took them to leave the air-conditioned bar and make their way through the parking lot's maze of mostly pickups red, white, and blue and reach Warren's red Ford Ranger, they both decided it was pretty late and to call it an evening and promised to get together again before Bayle left town the next week. Warren sat inside his truck but didn't turn on the ignition, both hands hanging loose over the wheel, staring straight ahead at Kellog Avenue and the blue neon of the Bunton Grocery store across the road. Bayle stood beside Warren's driver's side window.

"Bake sale at nine a.m. for the Christian Women for the Restoration of Capital Punishment Fund," Warren said. "Counselling at eleven." Bayle didn't know whether to say he was sorry or simulate some sort of interest. Instead, he watched with Warren the traffic on Kellog roll by through the evening muck of warm black damp.

"It wouldn't be so bad, you know — the counselling, I mean," Warren volunteered. "It's just that ... I mean, everybody carries around their own pain, God knows I know that. And talking about it can sometimes help, I know that too. It's just that, well, it's just that's it's, well ... *so fucking boring.* I mean, if there was something I could really sink my teeth into, just one person I could really reach, one person I could really help ...."

Whoosh, a passing automobile on Kellog. The air conditioner sticking out of the side of the cinder block cement wall of Larry's hummed and dripped. The "B" in the Bunton Grocery sign across the street flickered and buzzed. As if with reluctance, Warren started up the truck, put it into gear, and slowly backed out of his parking space. He stuck his head out the window.

"I say, Peter," he said. "Kept meaning to ask you all night: What's all this slugger business Jake referred to?"

For a second or two Bayle honestly didn't know what Warren was talking about. Then, remembering the evening before with Davidson, "Oh, that," he said. "Just had too much to drink and took a swing at some guy when I was here with Harry last time."

"Because?"

"Because?"

"Because why?" Warren said, head still hanging out.

"Nothing. Because nothing. Hey, listen, I'll give you a call before I ship out back north, okay?" Warren waved goodbye and left Bayle to the short walk back to The Range he said he needed to clear his head.

Walking alone through the dark, unfamiliar streets, Bayle wondered about nothing. Wondered about nothing all the way home.

15

A WEEK after Bayle and Patty had gone downtown together to the library they never made it to, Bayle's mother called him up wanting to know what had happened. Bayle thought she was talking about Patty and him staying out all night and Patty not coming home until the next day, so he reminded her that they'd called to say she was staying over at his place and not to worry.

"I know that, Peter," his mother said. "I'm the one you woke up at two in the morning and told, remember? But what *happened?*"

"Nothing."

"*Something* happened."

"What do you mean? Nothing happened," Bayle said, moving the cursor up a paragraph on his computer screen. He was basically done his final paper for his seminar and just needed to go over it one more time before presenting it tomorrow morning at nine.

"All I know is that maybe she wasn't one hundred percent herself before then, but since that night with you she's ... *it's like she's not there*, Peter. And she won't see me. She won't. She must go to the bathroom when I'm in bed asleep because I swear I haven't ... I haven't seen my baby girl in ...."

Bayle's mother lectured, cajoled, harangued, hectored, and told-you-so'd, but she didn't cry. Bayle's mother did not cry. That just wasn't something she did. It was one of the things Bayle had always liked about her.

"Look, I've got to go," Bayle said. "Patty's going to be fine. I'll come out and see her soon."

"When?"

"Soon."

"When, Peter? There's something's wrong with her, something's —"

"I've got to go. I'll come as soon as I get this essay I'm working on done."

"Something's wrong with your sister, Peter."

"Quit saying that. I've got to go."

"Come and see her, Peter."

"I'll come as soon as I can."

Bayle's nine o'clock seminar the next day came and went with him being granted a twenty-four hour extension. Upon re-reading his paper after he'd gotten off the phone with his mother the night before, the section on Hume had seemed to him a little confused. He spent the next thirteen hours in the Robarts cafeteria drinking bad coffee and reading and making

106

notes on Hume's *Dialogues Concerning Natural Religion,* and then another eight more at home drafting pages of new material he eventually decided not to use. He finally made it to Etobicoke two days after his mother's phonecall, but Patty wouldn't let him in her room to see her.

Bayle came into the kitchen, a cold pot of tea sitting on the table in front of his mother. He sat down.

"Well?" she said.

"She told me to go away," Bayle answered.

"I told you. She won't see anyone," his mother said. "She's been like this for over a week now." Looking up at Bayle, "Peter, I don't ...." The choke in her throat cut her off. For the second time in three days Bayle's mother was on the brink of doing what she didn't do.

Bayle got up from the table and stormed down the hallway, pounded on Patty's bedroom door.

"Cut this shit out, Patty, and open up the damn door."

Patty didn't answer and the door didn't open so Bayle pounded again, harder and louder. His mother came down the hall to see what was going on.

"Go back in the kitchen!" Bayle yelled.

His mother put her hand to her mouth and suddenly looked every one of her fifty-nine years. "Peter, what's —"

"Oh, just go back," a weary voice, Patty's, managed from behind the still-closed bedroom door.

Bayle put his arm around his mother's waist and walked her back down the hall to the kitchen. He poured her a cup of tea and kissed her on the top of her head.

Back at Patty's door he could hear the lock in the bedroom door turning. He waited for it to open and Patty to let him inside. And the door did open. But Patty stood in the doorway with arms folded across her chest in her housecoat, bare feet, and with hair so dirty it positively gleamed in the light of the hallway. Bayle's scalp itched just looking at it.

Forcing a smile, and as cavalier as he could, "So what's with the hibernation act, sis?" he said. "You've got your seasons mixed up, you know. Winter is for sleeping. Summer is for going boy crazy and hanging out at the mall all day."

"Do you want something, Peter?"

"As a matter of fact, yeah, I do. I want to sit down. I come all the way out here to deepest, darkest suburbia and you don't even offer me a seat on your messy floor."

Patty blocked his way into the room.

"Go sit in the livingroom," she said. She went to shut the door but Bayle stopped it with his hand.

"Let go of my door," she said.

"Not until you tell me what's going on," Bayle said.

"Nothing's going on. *One hundred percent absolutely fucking nothing's going on.*"

"Don't tell me that, something's going —"

"What's going on is I'm trying to shut my door!"

She threw herself against the door and Bayle didn't resist, door slamming shut in his face. He heard the lock snap back into place.

Bayle stared overhead at a long ugly scar of a crack in the plaster ceiling. He knew that the plaster was white, but the hall light gave the entire corridor a jaundiced yellow glow. He knew she was on the other side of the door listening.

He rested his head right against the wood. Softly, "Have you had a chance to do any painting yet?" he said. "God knows you bought enough stuff that morning to keep you in paint, varsol, and brushes for the next ten years." Bayle knew she was listening. "Don't forget: you promised to let me have the first self-portrait."

He waited for an answer that didn't come and walked back to the kitchen. Flicked off the hall light when he'd reached the carpeted end.

His mother looked up from her cup of tea.

"Nothing," Bayle said.

The two of them sat at the table staring off in their separate directions.

Finally, "Has she been painting?" Bayle said. "I mean, I

know she hasn't come out of her room to do it, but have you smelt any paint fumes or anything like that?"

"Patty's never painted," his mother said.

"I know," Bayle answered, before going on to describe to her the early morning shopping spree at Picasso's on Spadina the week before and Patty's sudden enthusiasm for all things artistic. Jackson Pollock, Frank Stella, Helen Frankenthaler: all names Bayle had never heard Patty mention before, and the closing of the subway doors at St. George the only thing that had finally managed to shut her up.

"Now it makes sense," his mother said. Bayle looked up from his hands.

"It was last Monday," she said. "The afternoon after Patty stayed over at your place. She finally came through the door a little after one and sat herself right down at the table and got out a bowl and spoon and the container of milk and ate nearly an entire box of Corn Flakes. When I asked her where she'd been — because when you'd called you said she was coming home early the next morning — she said she fell asleep on the subway and when the subway man woke her up at the Kennedy station it turned out she'd been riding the car back and forth for close to an hour. Well, naturally I was upset. And when I told her that that was a good way for a young woman to get herself violated, she said she already had. She said that while she'd been sleeping someone had stolen all the parcels she'd bought downtown that morning with you. When I asked her what had been in them, what had gotten stolen, she just keep on eating her cereal. But after she was all done eating and had put away the milk and cereal and had washed and dried her bowl and spoon, just before she went to her room — the last time I've seen her since then, now that I think of it — she said, 'Well, it looks like nobody is going to be doing any self-portraits around this house after all.'"

16

TOLD NOT to think of a pink elephant, one thinks of a pink elephant, the stronger the insistence not to, the larger and pinker the animal imagined.

Already two days into his trip and commanding himself to cut to the chase, to put his cards on the table, to tell his lifeless life to himself like it was — the clock ticking, he knew, on when he had to return to Toronto and give Jane the good news that he was more than just literally back — Bayle did no such thing.

Lingering over his complimentary breakfast of glazed donuts and black coffee every morning in The Range's lounge, The Breakfast Corral, only made for a nervous stomach and, because of all the donuts he was eating, a small red pimple on the tip of his nose. Every time Bayle touched his nose it hurt. Naturally, he couldn't stop touching his nose.

Solitary walks up and down Main in the afternoon heat generated nothing but sweated-through underwear and an apparent allergic reaction to the car fumes from the busy street. The pharmacist told him to use the eye drops three times a day and to quit going for walks outside. Hadn't Bayle ever heard of a treadmill?

And the extended baths he took at the conclusion of each day gave Bayle wrinkled fingers and toes but no important breakthroughs as to why he was so disinclined to become Dr. Bayle. He was disappointed but not really surprised. Patty had always been the reflective one.

Bayle's sister had had her enthusiasms; Bayle, His Place. Bayle-sized cardboard boxes as a toddler. An off-limits-to-everyone-but-Bayle tree fort in the backyard in the summer and snow fort in the winter as an adolescent. A makeshift "study" in the basement laundry room as a just-turned teen (a small, fake walnut desk and neat row of incomplete World Book Encyclopedias behind him sharing the tiny room with his mother's washing machine and humming, three-speed dryer). Bayle in His Place was what Bayle liked best. A place, to be sure, of not intense self-scrutiny, but that wasn't the point of His Place. Patty did enough of that for everyone. More than enough.

Patty at age 7 would put on magic shows with the whole family for her audience and then mope around the house for days afterward because card tricks and find-the-peanut-under-the-shell games, no matter how successfully executed, were not nearly the same thing as sawing a lady in half and making thirty-two handkerchiefs of as many different colours emerge from your beautiful assistant's mouth. Bayle at that age had liked to sit inside a cardboard box.

But Bayle was running out of boxes to sit in. And runny eyes and a throbbing red nose were only a couple of the occupational hazards of a man without a box.

17

A CHANGE in the weather, if not the actual weather. Still hot and humid, the radio weatherman sorry to say he still couldn't hold out any hope for relief from this unseasonably warm October, relief for Bayle, at least, in the form of the discovery of his thesis advisor's fax, still stuck in his suit jacket pocket three days after his arrival in town.

By Monday, two days later, Bayle hadn't been in the least enticed to visit Larry's, had been a good-boy journalist and forced himself to talk to as many strangers as was possible, and had generally attempted to behave like a conscientious correspondent should (staying sober, doing interviews, reading articles, taking notes, making a first draft for about the first third of the projected hockey piece). He wrote in the evening, in his room, on his bed, his laptop fittingly positioned on his lap. The writing went fairly easily, mostly just quotes, facts, and figures arranged in agreeably journalistic order, the occasion to work welcome if not entirely absorbing.

Still, he persevered, an honest buzz of energy humming throughout his body and brain, the fax he'd taken to carrying with him everywhere pulled out and read over every time the informational banality it was his job to process bored him to temporary distraction or the sweltering five minute walk from The Range to the bus stop seemed as if it might liquify him down to nothing more than a messy puddle of blue jeans, suit jacket, and a few of his more basic elements.

Remember the fax, Bayle thought. Help is on the way. Read the fax.

> Thomas Smith
> 371 Huron Street
> University of Toronto
> Dept. of Philosophy
> #129
> 16 October

Bayle,

Needless to say, the message you left on my voice mail at school about your little trip south was unexpected. No matter. Your propensity for unexpected vacations from your responsibilities are, by now, getting to be almost expected, aren't they? I hope this letter finds you and your hockey team mutually edifying.

116

I've shown my friend Hunter at Saint Jerome's College in Waterloo a draft of your thesis and he's very interested. They have a tenure-track position in post-Plato Greek opening up and he would like to talk to you in person. They'll have to advertise the job nationally and conduct interviews at APA in January, but it's basically his decision as to who gets the job.

I informed him that you will have defended your thesis by the end of the winter session. This was what we had agreed upon at our last meeting. But then again, who knows? These dates that we periodically set for your getting on with your career always seem to be more like interesting suggestions to you than actual deadlines, don't they?

Call Hunter now (519-396-6789) and have your thesis on my desk by courier no later than Friday next. Your oral is at ten a.m. at the School of Graduate Studies, November 14. We should meet in advance of then.

Smith

Waterloo ... Not Toronto, no, but not ... this, either, Bayle concluded, eyes moving from the framed singing-cowboys-at-the-campfire print hanging on the wall over his bed to the copy of today's *Eagle* strewn across the wall-to-wall carpeted floor.

And the admittedly blunt prospect of spending his working life teaching the intricacies of the syllogism and the cosmological argument to row after row of bored freshmen and serving on faculty committees set up to decide whether white or off-white wallpaper should cover the staff washroom walls? The very academic vapidness of spending all day talking about things he no longer burned bright to talk about? Yes, but not ... these, either, he also concluded, mind moving from his two most recent attempts at honest employment — overeducated proofreader and underqualified journalist — to

117

the not entirely implausible notion of a committed colleague
or two to goad him back into thinking about high-minded
thinking.

Waterloo also wasn't much more than an hour's drive
from Toronto. The prospect of the fully employed and once
again altogether purposeful Bayle spending his weekends
back in the city not making philosophically sophomoric crank
calls from the pay phone outside the filthy men's room at
Knott's Place but, instead, being once again desirous of
ploughing with regularity the once-again sated Jane was not
an insubstantial cherry to be added to the already appetizing
prospect that would be his return to the world of the happily
engaged. As erotically anaemic over the last year as Jane had
grown steadily impatient with his lack of between-the-sheets
interest, Bayle looked forward to once again being a fully
realized woman-pursuant maleman. Where his desire for
performing his delivering duties had disappeared to he didn't
know, only that he wanted it back and that perhaps having a
grown-up life to call his own might just be the thing to restore
the thing that was keeping him from wanting to once again
wield his Jane-seeking thing.

That Bayle hadn't even been able to manage an erection
in more months than it pained him to remember allowed him
to generously overlook the fact that putting him down in her
date book for Wednesday and Friday night intercourse was
just the sort of amorous automation on Jane's part that at one
time had begun to pique Bayle so very much. From where he
was standing right now, Wednesday and Friday nights
sounded just fine. Sign me up.

Gingerly, Bayle fingered his recovering but still-red-
scabbed knuckles. Waterloo, he thought. St. Jerome's
College. Professor Bayle.

18

"HEY, GANG!"

"Theodore. How's half of the best play-by-play team in the entire South Central Hockey League doing this evening?"

"Just fine, Mr. Samson, just fine."

Game two of the Warriors' young season found Bayle back in press box row, against what he considered his better interests slightly anxious watching for Davidson's arrival. Warm-up was already over, the zamboni beginning its final pre-game circling of the ice.

"I can only stay a minute, we're on a station break, pre-game stuff, but I just wanted to see if we're going to have a special guest in the broadcast booth tonight." Able cut his eyes hopefully Bayle's way.

"What a wonderful idea," Samson said. "Get the boy right in on the action and away from us old fuddie-duddies."

As if on cue, the peak of Davidson's felt hat could be spotted coming up the arena steps. He carried his customary can of Coke and computerized tools of the trade, but looked even more sotted-slow than usual, the methodical steps of before seeming almost cautionary this time. Eventually managing to make it to row fifteen, he collapsed himself onto the nearest stool behind the press box.

Stationary at last, Davidson took a deep breath, exhaled. Blankly staring over the ice surface he slowly wetted his bloodless lips several times, weakly popping open the top on his Coke can, the long fizzle of escaping carbonation his only explanation for his sorry-looking state.

"Well," Able said, breaking the silence, "if you're game, Petey, we really should be getting a move on. Bob tends to get a little antsy when I'm late coming back from a commercial."

Bayle stood up but didn't move from his spot. Staring at the end of the press box counter at the still catatonic and pasty-faced Davidson, "Is he going to be all right, you think?" he said.

"Oh, I'll be sure to keep a careful eye on Mr. Davidson, Mr. Bayle," Samson said. "You and Theodore run along now and enjoy yourselves."

Bayle nodded, slowly gathering up his laptop and pages of notes, yet still staying where he stood. He continued to watch the feebly sipping and staring Davidson.

"Mr. Samson's right, Petey," Able said, "we should already be up in the booth by now."

"I guess," Bayle said.

"That's the spirit. Grab your stuff and follow me. You're going to just love the view we've got up there."

"And I do the play-by-play and the Bobster here handles the colour end of things and that's about that. This is our fifth year working together for the Warriors and no one's caught on to us yet, have they Bob?"

"A minute and a half to air."

"Bob gets the signals from Doris back at the station about commercials and the like. He's the technical brains of the partnership."

Bayle sat between Able and Munson in the small broadcast booth overlooking the Bunton Center ice surface. The fit was a little bit tight and the company less than ideal, but he was determined to keep his mind on the journalistic job at hand.

"But to answer your question," Able said, "to tell you the truth, no. I did football for more years than I want to admit up at the state college — just I-AA stuff, you understand, but it looks good on the old résumé, you know. And Bob and I did boys basketball at the junior college in town for, oh, how long would you say we worked those Cougar games, Bob?"

"One minute."

"So neither of us did any hockey before we started up with the Warriors. I can't speak for Bob, but I'd never even seen a hockey game in person until I called my first one, an exhibition game against Oklahoma back in '92. We did a few practice broadcasts working from NHL games on cable, but let me tell you, it was nothing like calling the real thing. Let's just say that the tapes from those first couple games are never going to see the light of day, if you know what I mean."

"Fifteen seconds to air."

"Excuse me while I put this thing on," Able said. He pulled on a bulky black headset identical to the one Munson was already wearing and clicked a couple of silver switches on the lighted control board in front of him to the ON position. "But, hey, when you get right down to it, it's really not that different, is it?"

"Five seconds."

"At least that's what I tell myself everytime I go on the air: It's really all the same game."

"We're on," Munson said.

Good evening, everybody, this is Ted Able. Greetings from the beautiful Bunton Center and welcome to the second game of the Warriors' march towards their first South Central Hockey League championship. Tonight's opponent is the Tulsa Tumblers, last year's champs, and it looks like we've got a good one for you tonight, gang. As I said before the Wichita game a few nights ago, Bob Munson and I are just thrilled to be back for another year of fast-paced, hard-hitting Warrior hockey and we hope you'll be with us every step of the way. But before we get to tonight's starting line-ups, the Warriors would like to thank the following sponsors of Warrior hockey: McNally's Home Furnishings, J.P. Brown Tailoring, Fatty's Burgers, Sanderson Pharmacy, Burger King, Sparky Jensen Motors, The Sandwich Shop, Sassy New You Boutique, Esposito's Chain of Fine Family Restaurants, Southside Towing, The Men's Corner, Wal-Mart, Anderson's Gag Emporium, The Church of the Holy Redeemer, Waigle Liquor, The Sound Shop, Yarn N' Stuff, Coca-Cola, Boone Chiropractic, Elson Landscaping, Billie Joe-Bob's Barbecue and Ribs, You're Safe Storage, Rankin Insurance, The Muffler Guy, B.J.'s School of Dance, Jack Gibson — Attorney at Law, Tuxedo

Junction, Whitby Flowers, Watson Hearing Aids, Franklin Air Conditioning and Heating Repair, Judd Trust, Windsor Apartments, Donuts Galore, Westfall Construction, Noyes Boys Mobile Homes, G.M. Trucks, Jeanie's Houseware, and Big Jim's Pawnshop. The Warriors would also like to give a very special thank you to the following Warrior boosters: CDH Security Services: we're not selling protection, we're selling peace of mind; Simpson Audio and Video Rentals: buy it or rent it, just make sure you get it from Simpson's; Happy Day Cable: Happy Day cable for all your cable needs; Bunton Family Grocery Stores, where freshness is next to Godliness; and radio station WUUS, the voice of America's heartland, featuring the I.M. Wright show every weekday from two until five. We'll be right back, gang, right after these important commercial messages.

"We're off," Munson said.

"Yes, sir, Petey," Able said, taking off his headset, wiping clean the lenses of his glasses with a pocket-produced tissue, "when you get right down to it, it's all really the same game, isn't it?"

19

BAYLE WATCHED the entire five to three Warrior loss from the broadcast booth but still managed to find himself between every period on the periphery of the press box checking up on Davidson. The old man didn't look any worse than he did before the game began, but certainly hadn't improved any over the course of the contest, either. Davidson's cloudy, confused eyes were as much on Bayle's mind as the game.

Has probably looked a lot worse, though, Bayle persuaded himself at last. As soon as the final buzzer sounded, he thanked Able (acknowledged) and Munson (not) for the chance to see the game from up high and made his way down towards press box row to get a copy of an official game summary sheet.

The counter was deserted but for a young female intern emptying off a game's worth of accumulated debris into a green garbage bag — half-finished coffee cups, knocked-over boxes of yellow popcorn, ripped up, scribbled-on game programs — and Davidson printing out a copy of his game report. Bayle wondered how he could have already visited the locker room and gotten quotes from the players for his piece. Between the tips of his forefinger and thumb Bayle lifted a cold, coffee-soaked game report off of the table and stood considering whether to ask the chin-on-hand, hunched-over Davidson at the other end of the counter if he knew where he could find a clean copy. The older man sat motionless watching his story slowly emerge out of the printer.

Forget it, Bayle thought, letting the sopping piece of paper fall back where it came from, he probably doesn't even know where he parked his truck. Also: Remember this, he thought; let this be a lesson. (Upon consideration, Bayle sure that the drooping-over Davidson was simply too alcohol-ill to go downstairs to do any interviews, Bayle himself feeling suddenly thankful at the prospect of the enforced equilibrium and general state of well-being that being Professor Peter Bayle was surely going to restore to his life.) He picked his laptop and notepad up off the counter and started off down the cement steps.

"Do you drive?" Davidson croaked. Bayle turned around. Davidson hadn't moved, still stared at the still-printing printer.

"What, you mean like a car?"

"A car, a truck. Are you licensed to operate a motor vehicle?" Davidson's voice was coarse but intelligible.

"I guess so, yeah. Why?"

"You sure do a hell of a lot of guessing, you know that?"

Bayle knit his brow. "To tell you the truth, I've really never thought about it." He scratched his pimple-inflamed nose. "Why do you want to know?"

"I need you to drive me to Larry's," Davidson said. "I get a little lightheaded from time to time. It's all the damn smoke in here. Do you realize that this is the only building in the entire league that still allows smoking in the stands? It's like a Goddamn refrigerated pool hall. I wouldn't put it past Samson to be stocking gas masks at the concession stands before long."

The final page of Davidson's story fell out of the printer. He shuffled and evened up the pages on the countertop before standing up, putting on his suit jacket as he did so.

"Let's get a move on," he said.

"Look, don't take this the wrong way," Bayle said, "but I really should make it an early night tonight. I've still got a ton of articles left to look at."

"Don't worry, I'm not asking you to suffer through the horror of having to share a drink with me. I only need you to give me a lift. It's a ten-minute walk to your place from Larry's. Think of the bus fare you'll save."

"It's not that, it's just —"

"Just what?" Davidson demanded. Like Bayle standing on the arena steps facing him, each of Davidson's hands hung occupied at his sides with computer and notebook.

"Why doesn't Gloria give you a lift?" Bayle asked.

"She doesn't get off work until about one. Part of her job this year is helping Lefty wash the players' jerseys and socks after every game and getting the dressing room clean for the next day's practice. She'll meet me at Larry's when she's done. Like I said, you don't have to hang around."

"I thought she was just the team mascot."

"The fancy word for it is downsizing, son. More work, same pay. Coming to your town soon."

Staring straight ahead as usual, Davidson stood absolutely motionless, both hands still dangling and full. Apart from the false body odour of bourbon he gave off and the chalky facial complexion, Davidson could have been anybody's slightly irascible father waiting for a tardy son to pick him up at the bus station.

"Where are you parked?" Bayle said.

"The team lot, south side of the building. At least they haven't taken that away from me yet."

"Taken what away?"

"Nothing, forget it," Davidson answered. "Let's get going." He held up the pages of his story. "I've got to fax this thing over to the *Eagle* first. They've got a machine downstairs, only take a couple minutes."

"All right," Bayle said, "but try to make it quick, okay?"

"Don't worry. You'll be snug as a bug in your little bed in no time."

The stands were almost empty of spectators by now, five black men and one Hispanic in workman's clothes and glowing orange *Probationer at Work* vests beginning to sweep up aisle after aisle of concession-stand garbage. Fifteen downward rows later Davidson and Bayle were at ice level travelling the bureaucratic corridors of the Bunton Center. They stopped before the closed door of Samson's office, loud voices and laughing audible within.

Davidson knocked on the door. The office went quiet.

"Who is it?" a voice, Samson's, said.

"Davidson."

"Oh, Mr. Davidson, come right in."

Samson, Duceeder, Able, and Munson sat silently about the room, shit-eating grins on all of them.

"I just need to fax my article over to the newspaper," Davidson said. He walked to Samson's desk and slipped the pages of his story into the machine. Duceeder and Munson sat with crossed arms on the edge of the desk on either side of the fax, continuing to beam from ear to ear. The machine sucked the paper down and in. But just before Davidson could push the flashing green START/SEND button, "The fax isn't working tonight," Munson said.

Davidson looked at the machine, then back at Munson. "It took the pages," he said. "It says it's ready to send."

"Maybe that's what it says, but it's still not working tonight."

Davidson again surveyed the machine in earnest, an old man's confusion spreading over his face. "It says it's ready," he repeated.

"It's broken," Munson said. "Ask Duceeder."

Davidson looked from Munson to Duceeder, stared into the eyes of the smirking-strong latter. In on the joke now, "I think I'll risk it," he said. But before he could put finger to button Duceeder slid off the desk and stood between him and the machine.

"That probably isn't such a good idea," Munson said, still sitting. "You and your story just might mess up Mr. Samson's machine even more. And you wouldn't want to do something like that to Mr. Samson, would you?"

Davidson looked to Samson behind his desk. Samson offered back only upturned palms and a frowning shrug of not-very-well-feigned compassion. Able with swelling cheeks in a chair by the wall looked as if he would either explode or begin giggling uncontrollably at any moment. The other two carried on with their tag-team tough guy act. Bayle, not having moved from his spot in the doorway since entering, heard himself say, "Let's go, Harry. We'll drop off your story at the newspaper on the way to Larry's."

Davidson jammed the pages of his article into a folder under his arm and broke from the room quicker than he'd managed to move all evening, a non-stop flow of under-his-breath expletives trailing right behind him. The others kept on as they were, grinning triumphant at the fax-foiled newspaperman. Bayle shook his head a few disappointed times at the human contents of the room — if only with eyes on the floor in front of him — and turned to go.

"Mr. Bayle? Please relay to Mr. Davidson my regrets regarding the players' boycott, will you?" Samson said. "I'm afraid that I've spoken with several of them on an individual basis and they seem quite adamant about their new no-quote policy. And as far as league regulations go, there's really nothing I can do to change their minds. Let's just hope this doesn't come to affect Mr. Davidson's status as the *Eagle's* correspondent for the hockey team in any way."

"The players' new what?" Bayle said.

"I'm sorry, Mr. Bayle, but I'm afraid that I've been keeping these gentlemen waiting long enough," Samson said, open palm taking in Duceeder, Able, and Munson. "We have a whole slate of hockey-related issues that simply must be attended to this evening and here it is almost 11:30 already. You must excuse us."

"Okay, but what's this —"

"Good evening, Mr. Bayle."

Bayle briefly considered responding but didn't; left the room without saying a word, someone shutting the door after him. Halfway down the hallway he could still hear the laughter.

20

MAYBE BECAUSE he needed and appreciated Bayle's help in getting him to the bar, Davidson answered each of his puzzled driver's questions as best he could. Yes, the players had stopped talking to him, Robinson, the team captain, informing him before practice on Friday that for reasons he refused to go into none of the Warriors would be available to Davidson from that day forward. Of course not, Davidson said. There was nothing he could possibly imagine that might have brought about such a rift between himself and the team. A few times he had lashed out in his column at the placement on the Warriors' roster of Dipper, the squad's acknowledged enforcer, as an out and out "goon" move, but it was hard to imagine the entire team giving him the cold shoulder for that and that alone. Besides, he said, he'd been railing against violence in hockey for as long as he'd been writing sports for the *Eagle*.

Flipping on the turn signal and pulling Davidson's truck into Larry's parking lot, "And how long has that been," Bayle said.

"Twenty years this month," Davidson answered. Each undid his seat belt and locked and shut the truck doors. "Twenty Goddamn years to the month that I was stupid enough to ever leave Alberta and come back down here."

Bayle handed over the keys to the truck. "Wait a minute. You're from Alberta? You're Canadian?"

Davidson took a few seconds before answering. "I spent a few years up that way." Saying nothing more, sensing Bayle's confusion, "I came back down here in '76," he said.

"That's funny," Bayle said. "Did you know that Duceeder is from Alberta? I think he even said he moved down here about the same time as you did."

"Huh. What a coincidence."

Each man stared at the opening and closing door of the bar. The air-conditioning unit sticking out of the side of the building droned out the possibility of any other noise. "Let me buy you a drink for driving me down here," Davidson said.

"I should get going."

"Just one."

"No, thanks, I've really got to go."

A pause. "Okay," Davidson said.

His tie taken off and stuffed into one of his coat pockets, the old man stood with his hands in his wrinkled jacket. Beads of sweat were visible on his brow and upper lip. Poor old bastard, Bayle thought. How can he write a game report without any quotes from the players? Poor old bastard. Okay. Just one.

"Okay. Just one," Bayle said.

"Sure," Davidson answered, his hand almost immediately on the bar door. "Just one."

132

Six Wild Turkeys and four beers on Davidson's tab later it was decided that they'd leave the truck at Larry's for Davidson to pick up tomorrow and that Gloria, who'd finally arrived from work, would drive the three of them in her own car back to Davidson's house for a nightcap.

There, the bourbon was poured out and the Bach was put on and the kettle was set on the stove boiling. Fifteen minutes later Davidson was leaning back in his chair at the kitchen table, eyes closed and snoring. Deciding that this was for her probably not an entirely uncommon experience, Bayle worked at his drink and waited for Gloria to make the first move, to acknowledge her open-mouthed boyfriend, to at least say something about what should be done. No such luck.

Bayle tried to empty his glass of liquor as quickly as he could, but the three fingers of bourbon Davidson had given him before nodding off were taking a steady number of sips. Gloria sat at the table and sipped her cup of tea as if Bayle and the dozing Davidson were back at the bar and she was in the music-filled kitchen by herself.

"Should we put him to bed or something?" Bayle said.

"He's all right," Gloria said. "Gonna feel bad in the morning one way or another anyway, sleeping in that chair there for awhile won't make it that much worse than it already is. Never has yet."

Bayle tried to appear assured; slowly nodded.

Gloria lifted her tea cup and gave the defenceless Davidson extended clinical consideration. "Still, I can't say I've seen him lap it up like this in a long time," she said. She didn't finish the thought.

Bayle nodded again, took another drink. Three more extended pulls, he figured, and the glass would be empty enough that he could tactfully be on his way. And then what? he suddenly thought. How the hell am I supposed to get back to The Range? He took an earnest swallow and considered the equally painful prospects of a long walk home through strange streets and having to ask his drinking buddy's companion for a two-thirty in the morning lift. Needless to say, being Professor Bayle was going to mean never being the sort to end up shit-faced in the economy kitchens of alcoholic journalists while begging for rides home from their mascot girlfriends.

"You want another, the bottle's in the cupboard," Gloria said. "Help yourself."

"Thanks, no, I'm just going to finish this up and I'll be on my way," Bayle said, holding up his glass and the inch and a half of bourbon that remained in it as some sort of evidence that he really was almost done with his drink and really would soon be going.

Gloria took a sip of tea and turned her attention to the the room-permeating Bach. Bayle attempted to fill in the time it took him to finish up his drink by similarly disappearing inside the music, but was not nearly as successful. Classical or classic rock, song had never been that undefinable something capable of soothing Bayle's occcasionally savage breast.

It was one of the first disinterests Jane and he had discovered they shared in common. Over drinks on their phone-arranged first date — at the top of the T.D. Tower, Jane's choice, dry martinis and a fifty-fourth-floor view — somehow over the course of the evening Bayle had come to disclose how at the pitch of his sister's brief fling with bebop jazz she'd taped to the front of her bedroom door a quote she'd found in one of his German philosophy textbooks, "Life without music would be a mistake." Jane immediately replied that since she and Bayle did not care for music and, at the same time, she found it hard to see at least her own life as a mistake, the statement was obviously false. Bayle attempted to gently defend Patty by saying that he thought she'd meant it not so much as an unqualified truth claim but more as an overall attitude toward life. Jane said that in that case it sounded like his sister had a lot to learn about life.

In the few seconds it took for a passing jet to move out of their shared sightline Bayle quickly considered just what the fuck he was doing drinking a fucking martini and who the fuck this pretentious yuppie germalist was to say his sister had a lot to learn about life.

But by the time all that remained of the departed airplane was the exhausted trailing phantom of its plane self, Bayle had willed a return to his outwardly amicable first-date manner. In time, several more drinks, a shared taxi ride back to Jane's place, and mutually satisfying intercourse — orgasms effectively achieved on both sides — were all accomplished without incident.

Bayle thumb-tapped a simple, repetitive beat on Davidson's tabletop altogether antithetical to the twisting melodies of Gould's rendering of Bach's *Goldberg Variations*. Spying the room for some kind of distraction, he was slightly startled to be reminded of Davidson's drowsing presence. A thin string of bubbling saliva had begun to spider down the right side of the journalist's mouth.

"Are you sure we shouldn't do something for him?" Bayle said.

"What do you suggest we do?" Gloria answered. Leaning against the kitchen counter, she held her cup of tea in both hands in front of her face, softly blowing away the rising steam. An almost smile crept over the lip of the cup.

"I don't know, but ...."

A raised eyebrow; a sip of tea.

"But *something*. Are you telling me that this" — Bayle gestured toward the drooling Davidson — "doesn't bother you?"

"I didn't say that."

"Well, then?"

"Well, then, what?"

"If it bothers you so much, why don't you do something about it?"

"Now we're back where we started. What exactly do you suggest we do?"

Bayle picked up his glass, took a long, final drink, and emptied it. He looked at Davidson then back at Gloria. Since they'd arrived at Davidson's place she'd changed into an oversized man's black sweater and a pair of loose grey track shorts, no socks. Standing there in front of him with legs crossed, naked foot over naked foot, Bayle couldn't help but notice the sharp lines of muscle through her skater's thighs and calves, the here and there shoots of pulsing blue veins.

"I've got to go," he said. "I'm doing an interview with Duceeder at 1:30 tomorrow and I'll be lucky to get six hours sleep as it is." He stood up from the table and looked at Davidson again. "Tell Harry thanks for the drink. I'll see myself out."

"You're giving up that easy?" Gloria said.

"What?"

"It's just that it seems like, what with you so concerned about Harry and all, you might want to stick around and, you know, try to do *something*."

"I guess I came to the conclusion that that would probably be more your job than mine."

"And how do you figure that?"

"Well, you're his girlfriend, right? Maybe you should keep a little shorter leash on him. You might want to try and get him to cut back a little on the booze, for starters. You also might discourage him from bringing back guests to his house after the bars close down. I'm sure I'm not the first person to take advantage of Harry's hospitality."

As if testing out the idea aloud, "You think I should tell Harry not to drink anymore," Gloria said matter-of-factly. She went to the stove to top off her cup.

"Does that sound like such a bad idea to you?" Bayle said. "Look at him. Do you think that the amount of drinking he does is somehow good for him?" Bayle set his laptop down on the floor.

"It's not that," Gloria said. "It's just that I'm a little bit confused about what I'm supposed to be telling him to do instead."

"Instead of what?" Bayle said.

"Instead of drinking."

Gloria slowly steeped her tea bag in her cup and watched Bayle's face.

Bayle threw up his hands. "Fine. Whatever. Whatever works for the two of you. I've got three days left in this crummy little town and then I get on with my real life. Believe me, a year from now I'll be in my little office at St. Jerome's quietly doling out As, Bs, and Cs, and the last thing that'll be on my mind will be Harry Davidson's drinking problem." He picked up his computer by the handle. "Like I said, tell Harry thanks for the drink. I plan to be pretty busy for the next couple of days, so if I don't manage to see him again before I leave town, let Harry know it's been a pleasure and that I was sorry to hear about him and the team."

Gloria stiffened to attention. "What do you mean you're sorry about him and the team?"

"About the boycott," Bayle said.

"What boycott?"

"Harry didn't tell you?"

"We don't talk about each other's work. What boycott?"

Bayle looked at the clock hanging on the wall over the stove. "Look, it's nearly three and I've got to be up by eleven for my interview. I should start walking right now if I want to get to sleep before five. I'm sure Harry'll tell you all about it in the morning. I'd appreciate it if you could just point me in the direction of Main."

"I'm gonna drive you home and you're gonna tell me all that you know about this boycott business," Gloria said. "Tonight."

"Look, it's late, I can walk," Bayle said.

"Nobody's doubting the fact that you can walk, but right now you're getting a ride home in my car. Let me get my keys."

Still in Davidson's driveway, Gloria's well-travelled yellow Volkswagen Bug taking its time deciding whether or not it wanted to run, Bayle turned on the radio and flipped to AM 590, WUUS, in the hope of catching the tale end of the I.M. Wright show and coming at least a little bit closer to understanding his inexplicable hold upon the local populace. Maybe it's like Hegel, he considered, no one really believing a word of what he says, but people continuing to read him faithfully anyway just because it's fun trying to figure out what the hell he was talking about.

The car finally coughing and shaking to her satisfaction, Gloria snapped off the radio.

"I'd appreciate it if I could just listen to this for a couple of minutes," Bayle said. "It's sort of like a hobby for me."

"You start talking," Gloria said, putting the car in gear, the radio staying off. "And you go nice and slow now and tell me all about this boycott. You can listen to that foolishness some other time. Right now, we've got more important things to discuss."

21

NOT QUITE sobered up enough yet to be technically hungover, hatless and not the umbrella sort, Bayle clanked two quarters into the newspaper box next to the bus stop near The Range in search of cheap cover. A hard, warm rain set the tone for the 1:30 interview with Duceeder he was late for.

Newspaper folded in two, halo-like over his head, the bus hissed to a stop in front of him, door opening inward as it was still slowing down.

"You live in a cave or something?" the driver said. "They've been calling for this rain for nearly two days now."

"I didn't get a chance to look at the paper yesterday," Bayle said, steeping up and dripping into the bus. "Busy. Working. You know."

The driver cranked the door closed behind him and shifted into gear. Looking in the round mirror hanging above his head at the image of Bayle with his pimple-provoked red honker head-back applying his eye drops, "Looks like you had a busy night," he said. "Busy, working, I mean. You know."

Bayle blinked several times like the pharmacist had instructed him to and briefly considered whether he could possibly look as bad as he felt. Fuzzy teeth. Sour stomach. Mushy head. Not a chance.

"What line of work you in again?" the driver asked.

"Journalism. For the next seventy-two hours, journalism."

"You write for the local paper, do you?" the driver said, looking again in the mirror suspended high over his seat.

"No. Out-of-town assignment."

"That's good," the driver said.

"Why's that?" Bayle said.

Windshield wipers flapping, drip, drip, drop after drop of rainwater fell off Bayle's nose and chin onto the front page of the unfolded *Eagle* lying across his knees.

"You haven't looked at your paper yet today, have you?" the driver said.

"No, actually the only reason I bought it was for ...."

Bayle's voice trailed off, eyes falling on today's headline — *6 INJURED AS EAGLE BUILDING IS ROCKED BY BOMB BLAST-Local Militia Group Claims Responsibility* — mind made quick to discover that C.A.C.A.W., Concerned and Armed Citizens for the American Way, had sent six *Eagle* staffers to the hospital late the night before because of its spread of "poisonous liberal lies," Harry's articles about the safety infractions at the Bunton Center arena a prime example of "anti-free-enterprise propaganda concocted by the socialist media."

Bayle set the newspaper back down on his lap and stared out the bus window. Football-field-sized puddles swelled the surrounding farmland with more of the steady afternoon rain. A farmer in overalls and a Warriors baseball cap stood with arms crossed underneath the awning of his porch watching the afternoon traffic and a full day of plowing pass him by. The small advertising board sitting in the middle of the muddy front lawn of a U-Haul company promised free coffee and friendly service. Three cows in a small fenced-in field chewed their cud, ignoring the sound of the passing bus. Bayle looked down at the paper again, the violence of the headline he read over and over utterly belied by the simple scenes outside his window that were all that he could see.

Bomb blast. Building is rocked by bomb blast.

Giving or taking a few minutes, one hour later last night and he might have been one of the injured. Or worse.

Undergoing the sort of earnest existential stock-taking that the falling of the Canadian dollar or a fierce winter wind coming off Lake Ontario never could have inspired, Bomb blast, Bayle thought. Building is rocked by bomb blast. One hour later last night and maybe me no more, he thought. Me no more. Me. No more. Me. No.

"Okay."

Bayle looked up. "Okay?"

"Okay, this is your stop," the driver said. The bus was idling in front of the arena entrance.

"Sorry, I ...." Bayle gathered up his newspaper and folders of notes and shambled toward the bus's front exit.

The driver rested his hand on the handle to the closed door, looked Bayle up and down. "You all right?"

"Yeah, thanks," Bayle said. "Just ... yeah, I'm fine, I'm fine." He rubbed his pimple-inflamed nose; winced.

"Maybe you shouldn't be working so much."

"I'm fine, really, believe me."

"Don't worry about me," the bus driver said. "You're the only one you've got to convince of that." He pulled open the bus door. Rain pounded against the walkway in front of the arena so hard it bounced straight back up.

"It's still raining," Bayle said.

"It never stopped."

22

HE MANAGED to get the information he came for.

For thirty minutes Bayle kept his head lowered to the notepad on his knee, writing down everything Duceeder said about the necessity of educating the public in a non-traditional hockey market about the very rudiments of the game itself. Every time he felt his attention to the task at hand begin to waver, his mind a messy montage of the *Eagle* cover shot of the bomb blast, Davidson's pathetically drooling snoozing, even Duceeder's own fax-denying smirking face of the night before, Bayle told himself to keep his eye on the puck. Get the quotes, do the article, go home, get the doctorate, get the job, get the girl, get a life.

Duceeder's voice filtered back into consciousness. Bayle patted his suit jacket where he kept Smith's folded fax. He pressed his pen harder to the page. Keep your eye on the puck, Bayle.

"Take our fifth or sixth home game back in '88, our first season down here," Davidson said. "One of our players gets his third goal of the game, the first hat trick in Warrior history. Naturally, somebody in the crowd who knows a bit about the game throws his hat onto the ice. Pretty straightforward stuff, right? Except that our security staff had been given strict guidelines before the season started about immediately removing anybody from the rink if they started acting up. You know, the usual stuff: fighting, drunken behaviour, throwing crap onto the ice, that sort of thing. So of course what does security do but run right down to row seven and cart this poor guy off, probably the only guy in the stands who knew what a hat trick was. And we just tossed him into the street on his behind like it was nobody's business. Anyway, we gave this fella free passes to the next five home games, a Warrior baseball hat, and the whole Warrior organization's sincerest apologies."

Taking it all down, Bayle said that that was good, that that was a funny story. Just the sort of thing his editor was looking for. Thanks, he said.

"No problem," Duceeder said, sipping from a large WUUS coffee mug. "Glad to be of help."

Interview apparently over, Duceeder stood up and clicked

on the radio sitting on top of his filing cabinet while Bayle busied himself with gathering up his things. A commercial for a local steakhouse that offered in-house action movies and all the hot towels you could use saw Bayle almost to the door. Advertisement done, over the suddenly familiar music beginning its slow fade:

> Welcome to today's program, folks, my name is I.M. Wright. I want to start up today's show by answering a question that a caller put to me before we actually came on the air. Yes, caller, it *is* a sad thing that the liberal media has once again decided to portray well-meaning Christians as somehow the problem with our society and not, as it should be doing, trumpeting it as the only real answer.

Bayle's ears and eyes stuck to the little white radio. Back behind his desk now, Duceeder put on a pair of black half-moon reading glasses and noted Bayle standing there listening, but eventually gave his attention over to some paperwork on his desk.

> In making C.A.C.A.W. out as an extremist group when you'll never read a mention of those baby-killers uptown at Planned Parenthood, you once again get to see the *Eagle*'s true agenda come shining through: Christian bashing, plain and simple.

"They tried to blow up a fucking building!" Bayle said, open left hand gesturing toward the radio. Duceeder peered over his reading glasses at Bayle, the radio, then back at Bayle again. Bayle's hand stayed extended as he stood there oblivious and motionless, continuing to listen. Duceeder's eyes stayed on Bayle.

> I tell you, folks, it's real difficult for an ordinary Joe like me to understand how a group of God-fearing

Americans — a little misguided, perhaps, a little overzealous in their desire to stand up against the socialist threat and do the right thing, maybe — but avowed Christians and patriotic citizens nonetheless, can be labelled extremists, while the baby butchers downtown get off scot-free.

"Avowed Christians, my ass," Bayle said. "The last time I read the Ten Commandments it didn't say, 'Thou Shalt Not Kill — Unless Those Murdered are Those You Happen to Disagree With, In That Case Bomb the Hell Out of Them.'" Arms folded tight across his chest, Bayle shook his head slowly but firmly from side to side, steady ready for Wright's next oral assault.

Duceeder cleared his throat, didn't get Bayle's attention, did it again — louder — and finally did. Bayle shook himself free of the radio and looked at Duceeder looking at Bayle over the top of his reading glasses.

"Anything else?" Duceeder said.

Bayle seemed stunned by the interruption.

"I said, 'Anything else?'" Duceeder said.

A moment's indecision, but only a moment's. "You see this?" Bayle demanded, unfurling today's newspaper, pointing to the headline on the front page.

"Yeah, so?"

"I could've been there. An hour earlier and that could've been me."

"What were you doing at the *Eagle* at that hour?"

Bayle had to think for a second. "Dropping off Davidson's story."

Duceeder's face suddenly filled with smile. "Oh, that's right," he said. "That old fax machine just didn't seem to want to work for Harry last night, did it?"

"I could've been killed, Duceeder!" Bayle yelled, shaking the paper. "I could be flying back to Canada right now in a fucking body bag!"

"Okay, okay, but —"

146

"But what?" Bayle shouted. "But what?"

"But why the hell are you telling all this to me?"

Bayle didn't have an answer.

A streak of swift silver passed by him in the hallway heading in the direction of the front door of the arena.

"Gloria!" Bayle said, taking off down the hall. "Wait up!"

23

GLORIA DIDN'T know any more about the players' boycott than what Bayle had told her the night before. Samson couldn't tell her anything other than "Apparently the players have conducted a vote of some sort and decided they aren't speaking to Mr. Davidson anymore. Naturally, I'm very sorry." She knew he wasn't lying, knew that the players had held a meeting to prohibit team contact with Davidson, but she also knew that there had to be more to it than that. In her experience, hockey players couldn't be expected to spell "puck" even if you spotted them the P and the K. Obviously someone must have put them up to it.

"Duceeder," Bayle said.

"Duceeder," Gloria seconded. She was also just as positive about why Duceeder would be behind the boycott.

"He's always had it in for Harry," she said. "Throw in those articles Harry wrote about the Bunton Center that have got the owners so upset and threatening to leave town and Duceeder's just got to be the one. Besides, he's the G.M. He can do anything he wants to the players."

"That bastard," Bayle said.

"But at least we know what's going on now," Gloria said. "And the truth shall make you free."

"New Testament?" Bayle said.

"Harry Davidson," she answered.

Gloria asked Bayle if he wanted a ride back to The Range and Bayle said that he guessed he wouldn't mind, but only if it wasn't too much trouble. Gloria told him that if it was too much trouble she wouldn't have asked, so Bayle said, Yes, in that case then he would, he would like a ride. They pushed their way through the arena doors, the one on the left aluminum-covered from shoulder to shoe, the one on the right in tweed jacket and blue jeans. The rain had relented slightly during the hour or so Bayle had spent inside the arena; it was still coming down, but only steadily, not in a torrent anymore.

Gloria started up the Volkswagen, flipped on the windshield wipers. "You want to, you can put on the radio if you like. Wouldn't want to be the one to stand between you and your hobby."

"Thanks anyway," Bayle said, "but I think I've had about all the I.M. Wright I can handle for today."

"Then I expect you wouldn't mind if I ...." Leaning across him, the tips of her braless breasts underneath her costume just touching, faintly dragging across his knees, Gloria took a cassette out of the glove compartment and slipped it into the tape deck. A burst of airy strings flooded the small automobile like the pleasant shock of sudden sunlight on an up-to-then overcast day.

"I know this," Bayle said. It was the sort of hummable piece of classical music even the non-musical like Bayle had heard a hundred times before. "Mozart? No, Brahms. No, wait. Vivaldi? *The Four Seasons?*"

"Bach. Concerto number five in F major."

Bayle pursed his lips, nodded his head a few rapid times as if recognizing the obviousness of his mistake. Recognizing no such thing, "That was your music at Harry's place?" he said.

"I keep my portable stereo over at his apartment. It keeps me from just having to cart it back and forth all the time."

Bayle wanted to ask how a woman who drove home from her job outfitted in a B-movie alien outfit and who made her living inciting frothing farm hands at hockey games to cheer louder and louder for the home team had managed to cultivate an appreciation for Bach concertos. While he was at it, he would have also liked to ask where she'd learned how to figure-skate. His own mention of the harassed Harry, however, pushed Bayle's mind back onto more weighty subjects.

"Did Harry tell you how close we came to being at the newspaper last night when that bomb went off?" he said.

"No," Gloria answered.

Bayle couldn't tell if the expression of intense concentration on Gloria's face was the result of the wet highway in front of her, the swirling music on the tape player, or the significance of Bayle's question.

"Well, the way they described it in the *Eagle,* it sounds like his own office might have gotten torched. I'm sure he'll tell you all about it when he gets back from the paper."

"Harry's not getting back from nowhere. Harry's been at home all day, sick. And I know what you're thinking, but what Harry's sick with isn't from drinking."

"Oh, yeah?" Bayle said, doubtfully. "What ails Mr. Davidson, then?"

Gloria ignored both the question and the insinuation in Bayle's voice.

Instead, "What sort of relationship you got with the players?" she said.

151

"Not much," Bayle answered. "I've spoken to a bunch of them a few times for my article. Nothing outside the arena. Why?"

"Whatever it is that Duceeder's done to get the players to brush Harry off like they're doing is wrong. Harry isn't the easiest man in the world to get along with, but those players don't hate him like they're seeming to. If you found out what it is that Duceeder's done to put the fear into them then you could threaten to write it up in that article you're putting together and things could get back to like they was before."

Bayle considered the honest impulse to do Davidson a good turn; in turn, found the inclination toward helpful Harry-intervention quickly countered with even greater force by Empiricus directive number two declaring loud and clear in Bayle's wavering ear that not involving oneself in the conflicts of others is an essential step toward freedom from conflict within oneself. Victory, then, to the compulsion toward non-conflict. Bayle, mind your own business.

"I'd like to help, Gloria, I really would, but it's not that kind of an article," he said.

"Oh, what kind of article is it?" she spat out.

"Look, I think it's just as terrible as you do what's been going on between Harry and the team, but it's not that kind of journalism and I'm not that kind of journalist. In fact, I'm not any kind of journalist."

"No?"

"Believe me, no. The only reason I'm even here is because a friend thought I needed a vacation. And the article I'm doing is not about anything more than how a Canadian sport gets played in middle-America and how a team like that goes about conducting itself down here."

"Seems like they're conducting themselves pretty badly if you ask me. Isn't that worth you writing about?"

"It's bad, all right, but I'm pretty sure that my editor wouldn't find it within the scope of my article."

"Oh, well, your editor wouldn't find it within your scope. Why didn't you just so say in the first place."

The car turned silent but for the Bach. Unit upon unit of virtually indistinguishable track housing declared that they'd hit the perimeter of town, each new brown-roofed hive proudly proclaimed as a *Selective Living and Deluxe Recreational 24-Hour Secured Community.*

"I don't know how Harry's doing financially," Bayle said at last, "but maybe it wouldn't even be the worst thing in the world right now for him to leave the *Eagle* for awhile. Getting away from Duceeder and the all the rest of those bastards might be just what he needs to get his drinking under control."

"What Harry needs is his job back. He gets his job back, he'll be fine."

Abandoned tennis courts and rain-pocked swimming pools drifted by Bayle's window. A large roadside billboard reading, *Come Join the Crowd and Get In on the Fun at Windsor Estates*, forced itself upon him and then was gone.

"Do they know about the boycott at the *Eagle* yet?" Bayle asked.

"If they don't, they will soon enough. Man can't do his job if the players don't talk to him."

Bayle didn't have an answer; wished he did — really, truly wished he did — but he didn't.

"Besides, the Warriors are leaving for their road trip tomorrow and I'm going home the day after," he said. "Plus, I've already got pretty much all the information I need to get from the players and everybody else that I needed to talk to."

"You say you're leaving Friday?" Gloria said.

"That's right."

In a small, hard voice, "Fuck," she said. Gloria turned the car onto Bayle's street with a violent whip of the steering wheel that shook Bayle in his seat nearly as much as did hearing the normally profanity-free Gloria so wholly profane. Gravity-pressed against his door, Bayle looked at Gloria's face for an inkling of explanation.

Recovered, the car back on course and making its way down Main, "Sorry," Gloria said.

153

"No problem," Bayle replied, unrumpling himself from the interior of the Volkswagen.

"It's just that I'm leaving town with the team tomorrow," Gloria said. "I was hoping you might check up on Harry. I don't want to leave him all alone as sick as he is."

Gloria pulled the car in front of The Range, the wipers still working and the ignition still running. Each sat without speaking, watched the specks of rain on the windshield get erased and return, only to be erased then return again. The music, not lively as before, almost matched the day in its melancholy strokes of cello and violin. Bayle knew he was free to say his thanks and be on his way any time he liked.

"How did you and Harry meet? Through the team?"

Gloria gave Bayle a tired look across the front seat of the Volkswagen. "Some other time, okay?"

"Come on, I'm interested," he said.

She looked at him a few seconds before speaking. "Thought you said you had an article you got to work on."

"The article can wait. I want to know. Really. Was it when you started skating as ...."

"The Warrior?"

"Right."

"Harry's the one who helped get me the job skating for the team. We knew each other a good while before" — Gloria pointed to her costume — "this."

"How then? How did you know each other?" he said.

Although Jane's NOW classified had, for their first year and a half together, anyway, more or less delivered on its implicit promise of a hassle-free relationship, Bayle had, in time, grown interested in how other couples managed to find each other. He hadn't yet but still hoped to come across someone who had embarked upon a shared life with another just as ... logically as he had.

The tape, with a loud click, ended before the music did. For a long moment Bayle and Gloria sat without speaking, watching the wipers squeaking away the rain. Finally Gloria turned her head Bayle's way, the smiling upturn of one corner of her mouth seeming to say that she was either looking forward to or was almost anxious about seeing Bayle's reaction to what she was about to tell him. Either way, Bayle decided he liked what he saw. Bayle liked the way Gloria smiled.

"I car-jacked him," she said.

Bayle tried to comprehend the announcement. Toronto didn't see too many car-jackings. "You mean you broke into his truck while he was in it?"

"Something like that."

"Okay," Bayle said.

Pause.

"Do you mind me asking why?" he said.

"I needed money and he looked like an easy target."

"Okay."

"And before you ask me why I needed the money, it was because I was a drug addict who needed money. For drugs."

"But I didn't though," Bayle said with emphasis. "I didn't ask."

"No," Gloria said, "but you would've." Bayle didn't answer.

"And," she continued, "how we got to how we are now is none of anybody's business but me and Harry's. Enough for you to know that we've been together now for just over four years and I been clean for three years, six months, and twelve days, and Harry hasn't been car-jacked since."

Gloria silent now, the rain on the roof of the car seemed almost deafening. Bayle was surprised to see the Reverend Warren appear from behind The Range, his black trench coat unbuttoned and flapping open, his shirt and white clerical collar unshielded from the sheets of falling rain. A look of joyful indifference radiated from his face. Bayle and Gloria both watched him casually stroll down the front yard's curling stone pathway leading to the street. He got inside his truck and patiently waited for the wipers to clear the windshield before pulling away.

"I guess I could stop by for a few minutes after you leave town tomorrow and check in on him," Bayle said. "If Harry's actually sick."

"Thank you. I'd appreciate that."

The rain kept coming and going, appearing then disappearing with each fresh pass of the window's black rubber blade.

"And I suppose there's no reason why I couldn't come by before my plane leaves on Friday. It's a late flight. I should have time."

"That would be good. Thanks."

"But he's not really that sick, is he?" Bayle asked.

"He's sick, believe me. Harry's not the sort to be stuck inside if he doesn't have to be."

"Well, I'll come by tomorrow and stop by for as long as I can on Friday, but after that, he's on his own. After that I've got to go. After that I've got to get back home."

"It's two less days I have to worry about. I appreciate it."

Bayle opened his door a crack, readying himself for the dash from the Volkswagen to The Range. After his time in the dry car, the few drops of rain that managed to hit his face were colder than he had expected. Goose bumps shot up his arms.

Staring through the downpour at his destination, the front door of his home away from home, "That's the best I can do," Bayle said.

"About all anybody can," Gloria answered.

24

NOT EXACTLY sure why he was doing what he was doing, and definitely not having the time to spare to be doing it, that's not what Bayle was thinking. Instead, West Wing 347, where the hell ....

The wall-to-wall carpeted hallways of the *Executive Suites Living Apartments* twisted and turned, would not yield to him the sought-after West Wing. Every few minutes, it seemed, he re-encountered vaguely familiar red EXIT signs and the same gleeful announcements for *Wednesday Night Movie Night!*, *Pizza Thursdays!*, and the *Monday Night Football Watching Club!* He checked and double-checked the room number he'd written down in his notepad and for the most part successfully resisted the usual sort of too-obvious Kafka comparisons that inevitably come to mind when one is likewise building bewildered.

Bayle figured he'd start with Robinson and go from there. Being the team captain, he seemed more likely to be made directly privy to the particulars of Duceeder's scare tactics than any of the other players. Bayle finally found the West Wing and took the stairs to Robinson's room on the next floor.

The halls of the building were like the downtown streets: clean, quiet, but singularly deserted. None of the usual signs of apartment living — personalized door fronts, arriving and departing residents, delivered newspapers wrapped in plastic covers lying on door steps — were evident. Bayle had the eerie sensation that the entire building had been evacuated for some ghastly health reason without his or the players' knowledge (the players' significant others and children, he later learned, gone for the day on a "Shop Til You Drop" bus excursion to the outlet mall). He could just see the headline in tomorrow's *Eagle*: *DEADLY CHEMICAL LEAK AT LOCAL APARTMENT COMPLEX-Twenty-Plus Canadians Go to Their Grisly Deaths.* For an irrational instant he even felt the spectre of C.A.C.A.W. somehow hanging over the seemingly deserted building. He longed for a wailing pre-schooler or a den full of stereo-thumping teenagers to prick his paranoia. Following the line of indistinguishably unadorned doors to Robinson's apartment, neither these nor any other noises announced themselves. He kept walking.

Anticipating having to spend the heart of that afternoon shaking down whatever clues he could about the boycott and a good portion of the evening looking in on the alone and ailing Davidson, Bayle had worked as long and hard as he could the previous rainy night on his article, but with little progress. Every time he came to a spot in the story where a quote from the Warriors' hierarchy would have been appropriate he became dispiritedly stuck, unable to muster the concentration necessary to complete the paragraph. Even the previously guileless lines of the players now seemed coloured by Davidson's expulsion from the team locker room.

Shutting down his computer a little after one, Bayle promised himself that tomorrow he would settle down to work and finish up the hockey article no matter what. He would revise the article on the plane and have a passable story for Jane when she picked him up at the airport in Toronto. Bayle the new. Coming right at you.

Toward this very end, then, Bayle had finally telephoned Hunter in Waterloo to let him know that he'd be back in Toronto in a few days and that he was very much looking forward to speaking with him in person about the opening in the St. Jerome's philosophy department. Bayle felt greatly relieved to have finally made the phone call and, at last, gotten his future into gear. He also felt greatly relieved to have only gotten Hunter's answering machine.

Bayle knocked on Robinson's door but got no answer. The sounds of a loud television set and scrambled voices coming from another room several doors down gained his attention. He knocked a last fruitless time at 347 and then went to see if those at the end of the hall knew where he could find the Warrior captain. He rapped at the half-open door.

"Leave it!"

"Fuck you, I'm not watching fucking 'Family Ties.'"

"Hey! Michael J. Fox. He's Canadian."

"Turn it!"

"Did Robinson leave? Is Robinson still around?"

"What is this shit?"

"The third Superman movie."

"Turn it!"

"Hey, leave it, leave it, I remember this part, you get to see Lois Lane's tits."

"Bullshit. Turn it!"

"No shit, leave it, you get to see —"

"Lois Lane, she's Margot Something. She's Canadian."

"I'm not watching the fucking news, I'll tell you that fucking much, I will not watch the fucking —"

"Hey! Anybody know where Robinson is? That reporter guy is looking for him."

"What reporter guy?"

"Yeah, what reporter guy?"

"The guy from back home."

"Oh."

"Oh."

"Just stop flipping it around for a second and leave it somewhere long enough so I can — Hey! Turn it back, I think that's — No, no, the other way. No, one more. Yeah, I think that's — No. Forget it. It's all right. You can turn it. I thought it was something else, I thought it was 'Baywatch.' It's just a commercial."

"'Baywatch'. Pamela Anderson. Canadian."

"Can we please just watch something from the beginning? Please?"

"Is Robinson here or not? That reporter wants to talk to him."

"Who?"

"Robinson."

"No, fuckface, who's looking for him?"

"Him."

"Oh, him. Okay."

"Not MTV!"

"Let's just see what's —"

"Who wanted to know where Robinson is?"

"Him."

"Who?"

"Him. That guy."

"Oh. Robinson's not here. Try Dippy's room."

"Hey, put it back."

"Turn it."

"Hey, 'Gunsmoke.' That's Lorne Greene. He's Canadian."

"Who the fuck is Lorne Greene?"

25

"IT DOESN'T make a lot of sense, I know," Bayle said, "but it's all I could get out of him."

Davidson nodded, didn't say a word, didn't shift his gaze from the small black-and-white television set sitting on the footstool in front of him. For the first time to Bayle's eyes suitless, in an overstuffed armchair and outfitted in a white t-shirt and boxer shorts with black-stockinged feet resting on top of the stool in front of the T.V., Davidson, if not looking desperately ill, didn't, at the same time, look well. His face, beached-whale grey, was tight to the bone, the few strands of thin black hair still left on his head uncombed, scattered, greasy. Steam from the mug resting on the arm of his chair surprisingly testified to its non-bourbon contents. Bayle thought he could smell lemon tea.

Bayle stood in the middle of the livingroom running down his findings from that afternoon. He tried to recount to Davidson as faithfully as he could the conversation he'd finally managed to have with Robinson, but couldn't keep from wondering at the black-and-white T.V. Bayle had never seen one before. Did they even still make such things? And if so, who buys them? The sound was turned nearly all the way down; a blizzard of static made it difficult to distinguish between Hogan's Heroes and the Nazis.

"It took me a while to get it out of him, but Robinson claims that it was the players on their own who decided not to talk to you. The only mention he made of Duceeder at all was a meeting he'd had with them a couple days before they decided to start the boycott. And that was just to discuss all the rumours about the Warriors' moving and what would happen to the players' contracts and benefits if the team really did decide to move."

"And what would happen to them?" It was the first full sentence Davidson had put together since letting Bayle in the front door. He still didn't look away from the television.

"From what Robinson said, they would all become null and void. Everyone would more or less become a free agent."

"Well, that pretty much explains it then, doesn't it?"

"Not to me it doesn't. Even when I pressed him, Robinson couldn't find one bad thing to say about you. The only reason he could come up with as to why they stopped talking was because the team just wanted to distance itself from you and your articles as much as possible to try and show their solidarity with team ownership. But it just doesn't add up. Somehow Duceeder is behind this, I just know it. I don't know how, but he is. I wish I had more time to get to the bottom of it all, but I'm leaving tomorrow. Gloria told you I have to leave tomorrow, right?"

Davidson didn't answer the question, didn't seem to even consider it. "You've been talking to Gloria too much," he said. "Her and her Goddamn conspiracy theories. Isn't it plain enough that those boys are just sore at me for putting their jobs on the line? Bunton Groceries isn't going to put a million dollars of renovations into that dump the Bunton Center. One way or another they're going to have to either move or sell, the players and their families spilt all over the damn place in the process. Hell, I don't even blame them for being mad at me. What right have I got to be jeopardizing their livelihood like that? Half of them will probably be out of hockey by this time next year, right back where they were before in their lousy home towns stuck selling used cars on commission." Davidson shook his head and drank from his mug of tea, his raised, mug-holding arm momentarily improving the television reception. Drink drunk, tea returned to his side, a fresh storm of electric snow once again made it nearly impossible to tell the heroes from the villains.

"Correct me if I'm way off base here," Bayle said, "but I got the impression that you wrote those articles to help some people out — namely the people who pay their ten bucks to get in the arena every game and expect it not to fall down on top of them — and not to force anybody into retirement. You've got nothing to be ashamed of. Your intentions were good."

"The best laid plans, blah, blah, blah. Here," Davidson said, handing Bayle his mug, "you're supposed to be looking after me. Reuse the same tea bag that's on the counter. And make sure the water's hot. The only thing worse than this damn dishwater is when it's lukewarm."

"If you don't like it, why do you drink it then?" Bayle said.

"I promised Gloria I would until I started to feel better."

"Gloria's not here. I won't tell."

"Are you going to make the Goddamn tea or do I have to get up and do it myself?"

Bayle made the Goddamn tea.

Living up to his pledge to check in on Davidson didn't, in the beginning, entail much more than Bayle resoaking the older man's tea bag every half hour or so and managing to watch along with him the same brain-pickling, late-sixties television sitcoms on the only channel the black-and-white was capable of pulling in ("The Brady Bunch," "My Three Sons," "Petticoat Junction"). Only when Davidson began to throw up repeatedly and violently at a little after nine o'clock, disturbing specks of blood red blood flecking the bubbling pools of watery disgorge, did Bayle feel like he was doing anything but keeping the more-than-usually cranky Davidson company for a few aimless hours.

After the vomiting had stopped Davidson agreed to lay down for the evening and let Bayle stick around for a couple of hours just to see if things remained stable. Bayle even went so far as to suggest that a trip to the hospital might not be a bad idea, but Davidson wouldn't even discuss it. Bayle didn't press the point. While Davidson in the bathroom readied himself for bed, Bayle in the kitchen steeped one last mug of hot bedside tea without being able to shake the stubborn image of his cancer-recovering father just as television-bewitched as Davidson had been before the vomiting had finally forced off the black-and-white. Bayle ended up soaking the bag for so long and making the cup of tea so strong that he had to pour it down the drain and put the kettle on again and begin all over.

Cancer was cancer and never to be slighted. But except for experiencing an understandable degree of anxiety over having to learn how to live with the partial incontinence and impotence, the dreaded "Double Is" of successful prostate removal, Bayle's father fresh from the hospital seemed fine, at worst simply irritated at not being absolutely one hundred percent while the Leafs made their first real run at the Stanley Cup in fifteen years. Although it was mid-April and there were exams to take and papers to get done, Bayle came home from the city every chance he could, every night that he'd sit and watch the playoffs with his dad in the livingroom the Leafs that much closer to a classic all-Canadian showdown with Montreal in the finals.

Even with a three-inch plastic catheter inserted inside his penis and a urine bag taped to his thigh, Bayle's father had never seemed to his son more alive. Grabbing hold of what he dismissively refered to as his "piss sack" whenever he lurched to his slippered feet to celebrate another Leaf goal by Andreychuk or Gilmour or another game-saving stop by Felix "The Cat" Potvin, from where Bayle was sitting on the other end of the couch his old man resembled nothing so much as some battle-scarred soldier heroically cheering his blue and white comrades on, oblivious to the pain in his body and the nasty looking purple incision just above his belly button that the doctor had made for the backup catheter. Naturally he was worn down a little by the operation and with less energy than he would have liked, but with undersized, overmatched, but unrelenting Captain Dougie Gilmour leading the way, the Leafs mowed down the Red Wings, the Blues, and then took a three games to two lead on the Kings in the Western Conference Final, one step away from winning the right to go to war for the Holy Grail of hockey, Lord Stanley's Cup.

"Can you believe that the last time we won that thing was '67?" he'd ask Bayle nearly every time his son came to visit and the Leafs were playing. "'67! Christ, that's longer than you've been alive, Peter! Think of it! Think of that!"

Bayle knew his old man was going to be all right the night the Leafs finally went down to Gretzky and Los Angeles in the seventh and deciding game. Two hours later his father still

H E R O E S

refused to admit defeat. They were sitting side by side in lawn chairs in the darkness of the backyard, a Labatts Blue Light in each man's hand, the only sound besides the occasional bark of a neighbourhood dog the odd mosquito-slap of an unprotected bare arm.

"Number one," his father said, looking straight ahead into the inky night, the game still right there before his eyes, "Gretzky should have been kicked out of game six for that high stick on Gilmour. Whether he meant to do it or not is irrelevant. Just read the rule book, that's all I'm saying, just read the damn rule book. You use your stick and you draw blood and you're out of the game. Period. So let's just tell it like it is, all right? That's all I'm asking. Because anybody else does that and it's a five-minute major and an automatic ejection. But because it's Mr. Wayne Gretzky he only gets let off with a warning, it's really as simple as that." His father swatted a mosquito dead on his arm and absently adjusted the urine bag on his thigh.

"Number two, if Gretzky gets tossed like he's supposed to, not only does he not score that winning goal in overtime, but the entire Kings team collapses when he gets kicked out. Los Angeles is basically a one-man show, Peter, you know that as well as I do. So without him they're finished, caput, game and series over, hello Les Canadiens and here comes Canada's real team in the blue and white with the leaf on the front to kick your sorry asses."

Bayle's father took another sip of his beer. The alcohol was a definite post-op no-no, but given the post-game solemnity of the occasion and his basically problem-free recovery, well worth the risk of Bayle sneaking the two beers up from the downstairs fridge without his mother or sister's seeing. Bayle and his dad sucked at their cans in the dark like two nervy teenagers trying to cop a buzz without the parentals finding out. The beer tasted all the better for it.

"Losing like that, that isn't really losing," his father said. "I'm sorry, but it's not. If you want to call it anything, call it forfeiting. What you saw out there tonight was a Leaf forfeit.

And I'll tell you another thing, Peter," he said, Bayle able to make out the can of beer in the dark being pointed his way for emphasis, "I wouldn't put it past those American bastards in New York who are calling the shots in the NHL these days having something to do with this."

"C'mon, dad," Bayle said, laughing.

"You c'mon," he said. "You think those pencil-heads weren't just dying to see Los Angeles in the Stanley Cup final? Think of the media coverage. Think of the T.V. markets they're going to get. Think of all that exposure. Now I'm not saying that *every* referee in the league is in the direct payment of those corporate whores down in New York, but that sonofabitch Kerry Fraser and a few of those linesmen, well ...." Bayle could hear the beer can being crunched in his father's fist.

Patty headed off to Quebec a couple of days later on a French immersion program she'd delayed until her father was safely out of the woods. Bayle himself wondered if it wasn't too late to squeeze into a summer class or two.

But as the summer of his recovery warmed on and the catheter was finally removed and a daily supply of Depends adult diapers took its place and a pretty young female nurse came by the house every day to clean and disifinfect the six-inch stapled-closed surgery wound, Bayle's father began to slowly, then rapidly, lose interest in his recuperation, the spirit of determined healing of April, May, and early June disappearing along with the end of the hockey playoffs and the onset of an unusually scorching Toronto summer.

Except for Bayle's mother's faithful but generally fruitless round-the-clock repeating aloud of the doctor's various instructions and warnings, the livingroom television was now the one chattering constant in the house, Bayle's father from morning until night horizontal on the couch in front of the tube, two months after the operation still not having graduated beyond his red housecoat and slippers. Previously his father had been only a hockey watcher with maybe a quick peek at the late-night news to check on the weather to see if it looked liked rain the next work day. But now, just as long as it was on, whatever played on the television never appeared to matter — soap operas, sitcoms, game shows, afternoon talk shows, even previously insufferably boring baseball — Bayle's father's attention never seeming entirely focused on the program at hand anyway, never expressing preference for one network banality over that of another. His eyes, however, more and more lingered on the set, the shallow gaze never really leaving, only steadily fading with summer's increasing weeks and heat.

When Bayle's mother's badgering best couldn't get his father to commit to his exercises or to start thinking about when he wanted to go back to work or even to change out of his housecoat, she called Dr. McKay, who'd performed the operation. When he assured her that it wasn't unusual for some patients to experience slight depression during the recovery period, even after they've shown initial signs of doing well, his mother temporarily quit calling Bayle up every other day to report on his dad's gloomy condition. But Bayle knew something wasn't right.

Bayle would sit with his father in the livingroom like before but that was all that remained the same. When Bayle would try to encourage him to do some of his exercises or just get up and start moving around, his father would say he was too tired and flip the channel. When Bayle would ask if he wouldn't feel better if he changed out of his night clothes and got dressed, his dad would say no, he liked wearing his housecoat because you didn't notice the diaper. When Bayle said that that didn't matter, that that wasn't what was important, his father said, "When you're fifty-three years old and have to wear a baby diaper, then you can tell me what does and doesn't matter." When Bayle asked if he wasn't getting sick of just sitting around the house all day and didn't he feel like going back to work, his dad said, "Do you think Fred or Billy or any of those other guys down there are going to want to pull the truck over everytime I piss myself?" Bayle said a lot of things, but his father always had an answer.

Eventually they settled into an uneasy truce and silently watched T.V. together whenever Bayle would come to visit. It was like when Patty was on the downside of one of her enthusiasms. All you could really do was wait it out and hope that whatever was next would come along sooner and not later. Bayle watched T.V. with his dad and waited.

Bayle began to dread making the trip out to the house just like he hated being around Patty whenever she was between obsessions and the slightest breeze could knock her over, the sappiest song on the radio set her off weeping, her standard answer to anything that was asked of her a listless "Whatever." Bayle wished his father had had his operation in the middle of winter and had the Leafs to wake up to every day to help keep his mind off a future filled with not knowing whether a cold can of beer on a hot summer day after cutting the grass was going to soil his pants or whether or not he was ever going to be able to make love to his wife again. But all he had were summer reruns and the sound of the gasping livingroom air conditioner trying its best to keep up with the rising thermometer.

Soon Bayle started making up excuses why he couldn't come home to visit as much as he knew he should and began spending more and more time at the library putting in exhausting ten-, sometimes fourteen-hour days on his single summer course, more often than not barely having enough energy left over to call his mother to see how his dad was making out. By the end of blazing August, chest pains and problems arising from recuperating negligence that couldn't be treated at home demanded a short but critical stay in the hospital. Bayle's father never came home. He died in his bed at Toronto General two weeks later, eighteen days before the Maple Leafs opened training camp.

Bayle packed a gym bag and moved back home for the rest of the summer, but mostly stayed with his mother and sister at the hospital, they in two chairs on either side of his father's bed, Bayle in the bigger, softer chair in the corner of the room by the window where he'd try to concentrate on the book in his lap. Although thinner, his father wasn't in much pain because of the drugs and usually slept. The few hours a day he was awake he was dozy and didn't say much, mostly just looked at the television, but now with the sound turned off.

Once though, near the end, when Bayle was sitting on the bed and holding his dad's hand, his father opened his eyes and, looking right at him, with perfect clarity said, "They were so close, Peter. How often do you get that close? The last time they won it all was in '67, you know. That's longer than you've been alive. Think of it. Just think of that."

The official cause of death was explained to the family as basically heart failure. For months afterward Bayle explained it to himself and others that way too. But one bitterly cold Saturday night in November, back at his parents' house in Etobicoke helping his mother and sister move some of his father's clothes and shoes from the upstairs bedroom out to the garage, it suddenly occurred to Bayle that his father had simply given up.

Halfway through the livingroom on his way to the back door, three boxes full of shoes, socks, underwear, and work shirts piled high in his arms and up to his chin, Bayle stopped. "Hockey Night in Canada" was playing on the livingroom television to keep everyone company during their upstairs-to-outside trips, and Bayle stood in the middle of the room, staring at the game.

Hockey-indifferent Patty used to like to say that this room, and the hockey game that seemed to be ceaselessly playing in it, was "An empty place, as empty a place as any room with this much meaningless racket coming from it can be." Now Bayle knew how wrong she'd been. Now — their father no longer squirming away on the edge of his easy chair yelling out for the Leafs to "Forecheck, boys, forecheck!" and for the referees to "Open up your Goddamn eyes, you idiots!" regardless of whether the room was family-full or empty but for him and Freddy, the family cat — the room really was empty.

Bayle's mother came downstairs with her own smaller load and told her still-staring son that they were almost done and that he could watch the game later. Bayle didn't share his revelation with his mother.

Bayle moved himself and all that remained of his cardboard-boxed father through the livingroom and out to the garage. There, he placed the boxes on top of a lidless other full of some of Patty's old things, the British Flag with the baseball-sized bleach spot in one corner that she'd brought home with such excitement from a yard sale years before neatly folded in four on top.

When he came back inside Patty was sitting staring at the bowl of plastic fruit in the middle of the the kitchen table. Her own box of their father's clothes sat on the chair next to her. Just recently post-radical-environmentalist but still pre-converted Catholic, between their father's still-fresh funeral and the death of her most recent reason for living, Patty these days was into monosyllabic answers and sleeping a lot.

"That the last of the boxes?" Bayle said.

Patty stayed focused on the phoney apples and oranges.

"Hey, sis," Bayle said, "is that —"

"Ask mum," Patty said.

Bayle looked at Patty looking at the bowl of fake fruit. Looked and waited for his sister to break her stare. Waited, then waited some more. Eventually yelled upstairs to his mother that he had to go.

When she came down and asked him what was the rush and why he wasn't going to stay and watch the third period like he'd planned and have some of the McCain's chocolate cake she'd defrosted for all of them, Bayle said he'd forgotten all about some very important work he had to do for one of his classes. Tonight. He kissed his motionless sister goodbye on the cheek and his puzzled mother at the back door and went out to the garage. He stuck Patty's British flag under his coat and went and stood and waited alone by the freezing bus stop.

For years afterward the flag remained where he put it that night when he got home, folded in four, under his bed. Bayle would occasionally spot the thing there when searching after a pair of underwear or an errant sock. Down on his knees, picking up the piece of clothing, Bayle would promise himself that one of these days he really needed to do something about all of those dust balls underneath there.

Davidson's bathroom door opened up. A little unsteady, but at least with his head out of the toilet bowl, he stepped out pyjamaed and ready for bed. His face was red-cheeked scrubbed, his stringy hair parted neatly to the side, but still, Bayle thought, someone who looked like he could use some immediate medical scrutiny. But what was he supposed to do, throw the old man over his shoulder and carry him to the hospital? He told himself that the time he would be sitting in Davidson's livingroom instead of in front of his computer back at The Range working on his article was sacrifice enough.

"Stupid for you to sit out here while I'm just going to be sleeping in the other room," Davidson said, "but have yourself a belt if you want. You know where I keep the bottle."

"Thanks," Bayle said, "but I've got a lot of work to do later tonight after I leave here. I'm way behind as it is and I want to stay on the ball."

"So go home and do it then, nobody asked you to stay. I already told you it's just a damn flu bug that I've got. Probably picked it up from one of the players." Davidson shuffled across the hardwood floor hallway to his room and shut the bedroom door behind him, leaving Bayle by himself.

Bayle by himself, first he tried the T.V.

But the plot of "I Love Lucy" could not drag him in, the horrible anxiety Lucy seemed to experience over the expensive new hat she had bought and the prospect of inflaming Ricky's unpredictable Cuban temper simply unable to generate even the minimal amount of empathy needed for even half an hour of imbecilic escapism. He brought a dish towel back from the kitchen and hung it over the T.V. screen, changed the channel to complete snow, and turned up the volume. He closed his eyes and leaned back in Davidson's armchair hoping for stormy soothing. He received only a static-smudged television station with the volume turned up. Wide opened eyes scoped the small room.

Bayle by himself, he picked up today's *Eagle* off the coffee table.

A fresh round of explosive destruction, this time inflicted upon the local art museum, had once again been claimed responsibility for by C.A.C.A.W., the justification this time being that "the American people have been slowly bled to death long enough so that the cultural elite of this country can indulge their appetite for outright moral depravity." Bayle wondered who would get it next and how badly. More than the actual bombing, it disturbed him just how easily he assumed that there would be more attacks. He put the newspaper back down on the coffee table. Although no new retching sounds filtered down the hallway from Davidson's bedroom, at only a little after ten-thirty it was still too early to assume that he was out of the woods and head home.

Bayle by himself, he pushed eleven long distance numbers, leaned back on the couch, and waited for the other end to pick up.

If Bayle couldn't with all sincerity say that he'd missed Jane over the last week — that sort of Romantic idealization simply not the sort of thing their relationship was based upon, she never hesitated to point out — he couldn't even remember the last time he'd dialed up Jane's number with full intentions of actually speaking to her. For a change, he hoped he wouldn't get her answering machine.

He put his feet up on the coffee table, shoes covering up the C.A.C.A.W. story on the *Eagle*'s front page, and listened to the throbbing ring tone. His own feet in front of him unexpectedly leading to Gloria's feet in his mind — the long brown toes, the healthy cords of blue veins — Bayle surprisingly felt himself throb a little and then just a little bit more, the first time in who knew how long that that particular piece of equipment had itself managed to pick up.

Good: not the familiar clicking beginning of Jane's answering machine.

"Hello?"

Not so good: not Jane's voice, not even female, in fact. Male, young, almost yelling, trying its best to be heard over heavy beated dance music slowly pounding away in the background.

Obviously Bayle had misdialed. Apologizing, hanging up, he dialed again.

"Hello?"

Options. Bayle could: slam down the receiver, immediately followed up by broken-hearted wailing about the room; roar into the receiver (succeeded by identical broken heart and wailing); or, politely ask the young man who answered for Jane, patiently waiting while she got called to the phone.

"Yeah, just a second. Jane! Phone!"

An eared explosion of plastic colliding with wood said that the receiver had been dropped onto the night table beside Jane's bed where he knew that the phone was kept. Bayle's ear still smarting, the phone was picked up and more carefully set back down. A garbled conversation between a man and woman punctuated by the woman's throaty laugh and promise to "get back to this subject later, *much* later" floated above the music.

"Jane Warriner," Jane said.

"Hi."

"Hello?" she said again, louder.

"I said, 'Hi'."

"Hello? Peter?"

"Christ, Jane, of course it's me, who did you think it was?"

"I'm sorry, it's just that it's a little loud here right now and ...." The man's voice muttered something Bayle couldn't make out but of which he imagined the carnal worst.

"Are you having a party or something?" Bayle asked. He attempted to appear as casually informational as possible.

"What's that again?"

"Are you having a party?" Bayle shouted. He sounded like an angry parent.

"I'm having a friend over, Peter, if that's what you mean, yes. Is that all right with you?"

"No, no, I was just wondering if —"

"I take it it's all right for you to wake me up at two o'clock in the morning anytime you're drunk and feel like it, but if I decide to have someone over from the magazine for a few drinks to talk about next month's issue, I suppose that I need your permission."

Bayle didn't answer, wanted the long distance hum between them to mend the misunderstood moment, to dissipate the thousand miles, to suck up the accumulated strain and mixed connections of the last year and a half. There was no hum, however; the loud music in the background would not allow it.

"Look, I really just called to let you know that my plane's supposed to be getting in tomorrow night around ten."

"You're kidding. Has it really been nine days already?"

"It'll be nine days tomorrow, yeah. You sound like —"

"August, no! I am *not* having another Jagermeister! Oh, all right, put it down over there. I know I'm going to regret all this tomorrow. I'm sorry, Peter, what was that again?"

Bayle couldn't remember what he was saying, could only dizzyingly conjecture what a man named "August" might look like and what Jane's use of *all* implied. Instinctively he pulled out all the big guns he'd been saving up for when he was triumphant-news home-returned and once again Jane-entwined. He let her have it all, unloaded the whole smiling story of his rosy professorial prospects and future, even briefly considering bringing up the long-awaited return of his below-the-belt reawakening (on second thought, though, deciding that the idea of announcing, "Hey Jane, guess what? There's this really hot woman down here who's given me my first boner in over a year!" probably not such a great idea after all).

Bayle's appropriately edited tale told, "That's wonderful, Peter," Jane said, "it really is. I'm happy for you. I really am."

Bayle thanked her, told her that he understood when she said she had a late editorial meeting the next night and couldn't pick him up at the airport, and agreed to bring in his draft of the hockey story to the office sometime Saturday afternoon. Before hanging up, over top of the thumping music, Jane once again told him how happy she was that the trip south had worked out so well for him, that it sounded like he really was finally back on track. Bayle once again thanked her for saying so.

Resting the receiver back in place, the sound of plastic clicking to plastic the room's only sound, Happy for me? Bayle thought. Happy for us.

Davidson coughed twice from the other room.

Except that Jane couldn't stand loud music.

Davidson cleared his throat.

Except maybe a little reggae music when she felt like getting laid.

Davidson coughed one more time.

But —

The ring of the telephone drove Bayle's heart. He whipped the receiver back to his ear before it had a chance to shrill a second time.

"Hello?" he answered.

"Bayle?"

"Yes."

"Bayle, it's Gloria. I've only got a minute. How's Harry doing?"

"Gloria. Where are you?" The sound of Gloria's voice kept Bayle's heart pounding.

"San Antonio, we just got to the hotel. Is Harry sleeping? Is that why you're answering the phone?"

"Harry. Right. Yeah, Harry's in bed. He turned in about an hour ago."

"How's he doing? He drinking his tea?"

Bayle looked down the hallway at Davidson's closed bedroom door, his pair of worn, old man slippers set outside the room, side by side. The sound of static coming from the television set filled up the small room.

178

"Bayle? You still there? Bayle?"

"I'm here," Bayle said.

"How is *Harry*, Bayle? You're not giving me any answers. What's wrong? Is something wrong there? I want to know if there is. I want to *know*, Bayle."

"Nothing's wrong," he said. "And don't you worry about Harry. Harry's going to be just fine."

"You sound pretty sure."

"Well, I guess I am."

"You guess you are?"

"I mean I am. I am sure."

"Uh huh."

"Don't worry, you'll see."

"Uh huh."

"I am," Bayle said, "you'll see. Nothing bad is going to happen to Harry. I'm going to make sure of it."

Part Two

26

THE ROUTINE was, at times, tiring. Returning home to Davidson's place in the settling dim of early evening after finishing up at the *Eagle* whatever assignment he'd been given that morning by Wilson, the paper's sports bureau chief, and before getting around to making Davidson and himself a simple supper (scrambled eggs and toast, fish sticks and fries, grilled cheese and tomato soup), Bayle often found it necessary to take a short nap. He dozed for usually no more than half an hour in the same place where he slept at night, on Davidson's livingroom couch, too exhausted to dream, but one whole country and a million miles away from having no dreams at all. The difference was incalculable.

Taking over the old man's job until he was well enough to return had been Bayle's idea. "Well," Davidson said, "at least if you're filling in for me I know I'll get my job back."

Wilson and Davidson had started off as entry-level field reporters at the *Eagle* twenty years before and had been, up until seven years ago when Wilson married a local Baptist girl with two small children from another marriage and uncompromising teetotalling ways, fairly regular drinking companions. Energy heretofore given over to boozing it up with Davidson was rapidly transformed into dedicated *Eagle* ascending, the end result being Wilson becoming head of the paper's sports department by age forty and Davidson becoming one of his employees.

Wilson was also probably Davidson's only friend at the newspaper and had said nothing about the curiously quote-less Tulsa game report Davidson had turned in just before taking ill. He gave his former drinking buddy until the Warriors came back to town from their eight-day road trip to find out what was wrong with him and decide whether or not he thought he could continue on as the team's beat reporter, not to mention handle his other duties as one of the sports department's two full-time writers. Wire reports could suffice until the team returned home, but if he wasn't back on his feet by then, Wilson wasn't going to have much choice but to start looking around for a permanent replacement.

Hell, yes, Davidson said. Of course he'd be ready and able by the time of the team's next home game. No problem. Just some damn bug he couldn't seem to shake off. No problem at all. Bayle wondered at Davidson's sudden amnesia about the team's boycott but never brought it up. Whenever Davidson mentioned covering the team again Bayle would just nod right along. Talking about working again always seemed to lift the old man's spirits.

Not that they did much talking. Dinner done, the dishes by Bayle's hands washed and left soaking in the sink, Davidson's take-with-meals medication taken (to combat the less-intense but still-existing fever, dizziness, and nausea), a

184

cup of lemon tea set steaming on the arm of his easy chair, the two men quietly passed the evening until Davidson went to bed around eleven listening to the Warriors' game on the radio or, on the nights the team wasn't playing, watching T.V.

Game nights they spoke more than others, but not so much to each other as to the radio, Yes!-ing when the Warriors scored a goal, Goddamn!-ing when they let one in, here and there throughout the contest each offering Coach Daley strong counsel about player match-ups and general points of hockey strategy. And when, as was inevitably the case one or two times a game, Dippy and the opposition's tough guy dropped their gloves to mix it up, Davidson would huff off down the hallway and announce over his shoulder that he had to go to the crapper and to "give me a holler when the circus leaves town." Waiting until he heard the reluctant wooden scrape of the bathroom door being pulled shut, Bayle would elbows-on-knees lean into Gloria's boombox on the coffee table and silently urge Dippy on, guided along by Able's sure, AM radio voice and a former livingroom rugrat's memory of a thousand bloody hockey fights, his father's eager blow-by-blow account of each battle hovering above his little-boy head, each excited deliverance drowning out Bob Cole's tame CBC report.

"C'mon, Tiger," his father would yell, Dave "Tiger" Williams, the best pure fighter the Maple Leafs had ever had taking to task some gutless sonofabitch dumb enough to mess around with Salming or Thompson or any of the Leafs' other bread and butter players. "Make that bastard pay, Tiger, make him pay! Get in there, boy, get in there tight! Use your right! Your right! Let him have your right!" And more often than not Tiger *would* find a way to unload that wicked right hook of his and give the K.O.'d player one more good reason to think twice the next time he contemplated taking advantage of one of Tiger's smaller teammates.

When the fight was finally over, the linesman picking up the discarded gloves and sticks and sometimes even sweaters, Bayle's father would smile and lean back in his easy chair and nod his head with the satisfaction of knowing that at least for tonight — at least at Maple Leaf Gardens tonight — fairness and justice ruled the world once and for all, that the bad guys weren't going to get away with anything they shouldn't, and that the good and honourable were guaranteed the standing ovation they so rightly deserved.

And in spite of Able occasionally falling behind the play Bayle decided that he called a pretty good hockey game. Munson was nearly as surly and uncommunicative on the air as he was off, but Able's lively delivery more than compensated. The Warriors managed only two wins on their road trip, but by Bayle's count Dippy ended up undefeated in nine fights, including two hard-earned ties, again with the Wichita tough guy, Bladon, Dippy's only real competition for the league's penalty minutes lead.

Pugilistic inebriation aside, Bayle only drank an occasional can of beer during his time at Davidson's, and even then, only when preparing dinner. Coming home half-dehydrated after spending a good portion of the blistering day covering some businessmen's over-50 softball tournament or a Boys and Girls for Christ Back in the Classroom charity soccer game (the weatherman bewildered as ever by the lingering heat wave now into its second week, of late given over to delivering nightly updates on the rapidly dropping aquifer level), Bayle, for a change, actually tasted what he drank.

Days he worked, evenings he spent with Davidson. And after the old man had gone to bed and Bayle had ironed and set out his work clothes for the next day and made and packed away his lunch, Bayle would sit in Davidson's worn easy chair and hate Duceeder and what he'd done to Harry.

Because life no more for Bayle a baffling kaleidoscope of confounding colour necessitating the careful construction of a sceptic's brick-solid breakwall to keep the entire tidal-waving mess at comfortable arm's length away. Uh uh. Black and white everywhere Bayle looked now — everything he heard, touched, tasted, smelt, too. Cops and robbers, you see. Good guys and bad guys. Us versus Them.

Although what he was actually going to do about getting even with Duceeder and getting Harry his job back Bayle wasn't sure. Nor what more could be done for Davidson's failing health. Nor, now that he thought about it, how he was going to explain to Jane his non-existent hockey article and the nearly maxed-out *Toronto Living* credit card he'd been entrusted with and which should've been returned by now, Bayle along with it (the card easily converted to a handy cache of instant-teller cash).

But most problematically of all, Bayle wasn't sure what he was going to do about not being able to fall asleep at night until Gloria's long, skater's body had been squeezed out of his restless flesh by the necessary sweet pulling free of himself by his own guilty right hand, the first time in Bayle couldn't remember how long that even the slightest urge to spank his monkey had seemed like anything more than just a good idea he should probably get around to one of these days. Sharing Davidson's morning *Eagle* with him over coffee and toast before heading out to do the job the old man could no longer do, Bayle really wasn't sure. But his job kept him busy. And in the evenings there was usually hockey to listen to.

Nights — the livingroom air conditioner working overtime to take out the room's warm stale air and replace it with what was cool and fresh and new — Bayle lay on his back on the fold-out couch and hated. Hated Duceeder with an intensity that rivalled the deep-gutted spite he still felt for Donald Comiskey, Etobicoke Collegiate's starting quarterback and Patty's student council president and one of his sister's last ever dates.

After Patty with smeared mascara and a torn sweater at three a.m. through intermittent tears and over an entire carton of Loblaw's neapolitan ice cream finally managed to tell Bayle the whole story of what had happened — at the Scarborough Bluffs and in Donald's parents' red Trans-Am after he for the thousandth time said he really, really wanted to and Patty just as many times insisted that she didn't — Bayle helped his sister finish the ice cream, saw her off her to bed, and waited up all night at the kitchen table with a pot of coffee for company for what everyone knew was Donald's customary nine a.m. tee-off at nearby Indian Creek Road Golf and Country Club.

When Bayle came stomping out of the trees near the second hole a little after nine, choirs of birds chirping away their Saturday morning salute, Donald did his best to try and look simply annoyed that a non-member was on the course until Bayle grabbed a driver out of Donald's bag without stopping and kept on coming. When Bayle had to tell himself to stop hitting Donald or he might just kill him, he dropped the golf club to the ground and jogged back into the trees and then all the way home.

Later, sitting at the kitchen table again, waiting for the police to show up at the front door and take him away, Bayle wondered whether, if he went to jail, he would remember today as the worst or the best day of his life. The police never came and Bayle never had to decide. Common sense to the contrary, pros and cons on both sides, it seemed.

27

"JUST GIVE me the damn thing back and I'll go myself."

"I'll go," Bayle said. "I just don't know why I can't mail it on my way to work tomorrow."

"Because you aren't going to work tomorrow morning — I am," Davidson said.

"So you've said."

"Yeah, and what the hell is that supposed to mean?"

"Nothing, forget it. So mail it yourself tomorrow. It'll get there the next day. What's the hurry?"

"Just give it back and I'll go myself," Davidson repeated.

It was silly, selfish even, not to straightaway agree to do Davidson the simple favour when the old man had casually asked him to after dinner, but the thought of leaving the house and travelling the three or four blocks to hand-deliver the small, crudely gift-paper wrapped package left Bayle clammy on the outside and churning within. In the week that Bayle had stayed at Davidson's — the road trip over now and the Warriors' team bus due home any time — he'd never once ventured out after coming home from work.

Where this sudden anxiousness came from he didn't know, only that in the last week he hadn't felt anything of this stomach-tightening sort. Being asked to drop off the package — "Just something for somebody you don't know and that doesn't have a damn thing to do with you other than you delivering it," Davidson had told him — Bayle felt the same way he did every time he flew and the stewardess's voice over the intercom calmly announced that it was now okay to take off your seatbelt. Hurling through the sky at five hundred miles an hour in two hundred tons of steel thirty thousand feet above the earth and now it's suddenly okay to freely move about the cabin. Thanks for the invitation, Ms., but the seatbelt stays on.

Still, he knew Davidson couldn't go. The medication was helping and he wasn't that bad off if he didn't move around too much and got plenty of rest, but even just from the front door of the house to the truck and then to wherever he wanted Bayle to go through the evening's still-considerable humidity and heat was simply out of the question. If the thing had to be dropped off tonight Bayle was going to have to be the one to do it. He took the house key off its hook by the back door.

"If I've gotta go out in this muck the least you can do is tell me what it is I'm delivering," Bayle said, holding up the package.

For a few seconds Davidson seemed to consider whether or not he should answer Bayle's question. Then, without expression, "My autograph book," he said. "Nearly every hockey player worth his jockstrap over the last forty years is in there." He took the cup of tea Bayle had made for him and slowly moved from the kitchen to the livingroom without another word.

"And I guess I'm supposed to believe that this person you want me to give this to is actually expecting your, ah, autograph book?"

Davidson eased into his chair in the other room with a soft, settling groan that sounded part-pain, part-relief. "Of course not," he said, his left arm slowly rising, the remote control pointed as if in wrathful accusation at the unawakened television set. "It's for his fourteenth birthday. And don't give it to anybody but Billy, you understand? Nobody. And for Christsake, don't be a damn fool and let the cat out of the bag about what it is, either."

The captain turned off the seatbelt sign and Bayle was free to roam around the plane. He stuck the key to Davidson's place in his pocket and said he'd be right back.

28

BUT FOR the pair playing road hockey in the driveway, 66 Maple was like all the other houses along the street, each ranch-style residence outfitted with an attached garage, small yard, and tiny cement porch. Bayle parked and locked up Davidson's truck and walked to the foot of 66's driveway.

"Excuse me," he said. "Is there a Billy that lives here? I'm sorry, I haven't got a last name."

The teenaged shooter, hockey stick raised hip-high and ready to slap the tennis ball at his feet in the direction of the net at the other of the driveway, looked back over his shoulder without lowering his stick. The goalie untensed, rose from his ready crouch.

"I'm Bill," the boy said. He turned around to face Bayle. "I'm Bill Duceeder."

The boy wore the requisite three-sizes-too-big blue jeans and two-hundred-dollar running shoes, but topped the whole thing off with a beaming white t-shirt with PROPERTY OF THE WARRIORS stencilled across the front and an equally new-looking Warriors baseball cap with the bill pointed backwards, the very cool way it wasn't intended to be worn. Bayle wondered how the paunchy-looking older guy outfitted in the goalie regalia managed to remain standing. Had to be ninety degrees out, he thought, and then with all that protective leather gear on top of everything else .... Ah, probably just like a million other fathers who would rather be anywhere else than sweating through their eyeballs and risking taking a tennis ball to the nuts, Bayle guessed; probably because his kid asked him to. Bayle smiled remembering his own old man going through the exact same torture for him in their driveway.

"What do you want, Bayle?"

Bayle immediately recognized the voice from behind the goalie mask. "Duceeder?" he said.

The boy looked in confusion from Bayle to his father, then back at Bayle again. "I'm Bill Duceeder," he repeated.

Duceeder peeled off the white goalie mask and shovelled back onto his head the wet mat of hair temporarily sweat-stuck to his forehead. He placed the catching glove, blocker, and goalie stick on top of the net. Fat goalie pads still attached to his legs, he waddled down the driveway's blacktop toward Bayle like some kind of obscene penguin. "Go on inside, Bill, and pour us a couple iced teas before the game comes on, okay? I'll be in in a minute. And see if you can talk your mother into cutting us some more of that birthday cake."

"But he said he's looking for me, Dad."

"Go on inside, Bill."

"But Dad, he said —"

"*Now*, Bill."

The boy gave Bayle a disappointed last look before turning around in the driveway and slowly walking toward the house, hockey stick disappointedly dragging along behind him. He hesitated at the front door, taking his time in taking off his hockey gloves and throwing his stick on the lawn, but eventually went inside.

"What are you doing here, Bayle? And what do you mean by asking for Bill?"

Pudgy and soaking, a sopping strand of displaced hair hanging over one eye, Duceeder almost looked like everything Bayle had made him out to be. But somehow the goalie pads and chest protector saved him, gave him even a certain paternal dignity. Bayle reminded himself who Duceeder was and why he'd come and handed over the package.

"What's this?" Duceeder said.

"It's for Billy. For Bill, I mean."

Duceeder considered the wrapped package. He looked back at Bayle. "He sent you over with this, didn't he?"

"Who?" Bayle said.

Duceeder made a face. "You're telling me that this isn't from Davidson?"

"I didn't say that, I just ... I mean, yeah, it's from Harry. He hasn't been feeling too well lately and he asked me if I could drop this off. But I didn't know that Billy was Bill. I mean —"

"You mean you didn't know Bill was my son."

"Right."

"Right." Duceeder bounced the thing up and down in his hand a few light times. He gave it a last look and then handed it back to Bayle. "Return to sender."

Bayle slowly took the package from Duceeder's outstretched hand. Looked at it. Looked back at Duceeder.

"Don't make this a bigger deal than it has to be, all right?" Duceeder said.

"Look," Bayle said, "Harry said to give this to Bill. And if I told Harry I would, then I —"

"Go home, Bayle. This hasn't got anything to do with you. You did your job, you're off the hook. Just tell Davidson that that jerk Duceeder wouldn't let you make your birthday delivery, all right? That's all he wants to hear anyway." Duceeder turned around and bow-legged and goalie-padded moved away. He stopped halfway up the drive, seeming to contemplate whether or not to keep going. He turned around and faced Bayle again.

"I know you think he's Mr. Sincere and everything, but he's full of shit, you know that? If you haven't already found that out for yourself, you will soon enough, believe me."

Bayle knew this was where he was supposed to jump to Davidson's defence. Duceeder continued.

"Friend of the common man, right? Defender of the down and out. Writes a few articles in that rag of his and all of a sudden he's Joe Public's best buddy. The next time you see Mr. Martyr ask him about Dan Fenton. Ask him how much all his whining about piss-poor washrooms and old arena wiring at the Bunton Center did for Dan."

"C'mon, Dad! The Chiefs won the toss! They're getting ready to receive!" From behind the screen of the aluminum front door, an enormous plate of chocolate cake and vanilla ice cream in each hand, Duceeder's son had apparently gotten over the mystery of Bayle's presence. "C'mon, hurry up!"

"Who's starting this week?" Duceeder asked.

"Grbac," Bill answered.

"Oh, boy. Feast or famine with that guy. Well, let's see what he's got tonight."

Duceeder unlaced the goalie pads and threw them on the lawn beside his son's discarded hockey gloves and stick. Taking one of the plates of cake and ice cream, father and son disappeared inside the house, closing the door behind them, leaving Bayle standing by himself in the driveway.

29

BAYLE DIDN'T see Gloria's yellow Volkswagen parked out front of Davidson's place until he almost slammed into it. In the interval it had taken him to return from Duceeder's, the evening's light had been replaced by a thickly damp, almost physical blackness, only occasionally punctured by an infrequent streetlight. Truck safely parked and recognizing Gloria's car now, coming around the side of Davidson's house, fishing in his pocket for the key to the backdoor, Bayle whistled; whistled how interesting it was that he'd never noticed until now just how well-lit Canadian streets were compared to those in the United States.

Whistling done, house key out, quick swipe of sweat from his face on his arm accomplished, the graveyard that was who was on the other side of the door remained as terrifying as pre-whistling before.

The voyeur exposed.

The spy spied.

The peeper meets his prey.

Bayle turned the key to the left and hoped it would break off in the lock.

It didn't. But his sudden appearance in the doorway did draw Davidson up from his chair at the kitchen table quicker than Bayle had ever seen him move, even before taking ill.

"Look, Bayle!" he said. "Look who's back!" Beaming at the younger man, Davidson kept thumb-pointing over his shoulder at Gloria sitting at the table (slack-limbed lovely long Gloria; loose grey sweat-shorts and black sleeveless t-shirt, flesh-bare legs crossed one over the other, much-much-skin-exposed sandled foot airborne happy tapping to tunes only to her ears heard: Gloria as Bayle had lustily nightly conjured her). "Look who's back in town!" he said.

Except for noting how many days it was before she was to return home, Davidson had barely even mentioned Gloria's name over the last week; now he was like a squirming teenager whose only aim in life was to share the wonderful news of her arrival with the rest of the world. Bayle frankly found the whole display more than a little bit embarrassing. Bayle also saw that Gloria wasn't wearing a bra.

Davidson turned away from Bayle and stood before Gloria. He offered opened hands for her to hold in his and she took them and did, she and he eye-to-eye smiling. And smiling. Bayle thought he felt a little bit sick to his stomach.

Without breaking eye contact with the blissful Davidson, "Gotta say I'm a little surprised to still find your face around these parts, Bayle," Gloria said. "Thought you'd be handing out all those As, Bs, and Cs at — where'd you say you were going again? — Saint Something or Other College."

Bayle and Gloria hadn't spoken since that first night on

the road when she'd called home to ask after Davidson's health, but Bayle had always assumed that Davidson, who'd talked to her on the phone almost every other evening, had told her he'd moved out of The Range and in with him. Why wouldn't he have?

"I guess Harry told you I've been kind of hanging around here since you left," Bayle said. He still hadn't met Gloria's eyes. Not that that would have been easy if he'd wanted to. Davidson and Gloria's hands were their own again, but their faces only mirrored that of the other.

"As a matter of fact, no, he didn't."

"How come you didn't tell Gloria I was staying here, Harry?" Bayle said. Davidson didn't answer, apparently didn't hear, just stood there staring at Gloria. "Harry?" Bayle repeated.

"Hmm?"

"Why didn't you tell Gloria I was staying here with you?"

"Didn't I tell you Bayle was sleeping on the couch, G.?" Davidson softened his voice, though not enough that he could have intended Bayle not to hear. "Kid was between a rock and a hard place. Girlfriend back home gave him a Dear John letter over the phone and he really didn't have anywhere else to turn. We got along fine though. No problemo."

No problemo? Davidson went to the sink counter to unplug the whistling kettle.

"Why, that was real nice of you, Harry, real generous. Good to have friends in times of need like that." Gloria cut her eyes Bayle's way, but Bayle was looking hard at Davidson.

"Did you take your medication tonight, Harry?" Bayle said, knowing he had. "You know that the doctor said it wasn't going to work properly if you didn't take it three times a day."

"What medication?" Gloria said. She uncrossed her legs and looked at Davidson's back as he poured the boiling water from the kettle into her tea cup. "What medication, Harry? You didn't say you were taking any medication on the phone."

"Harry's not been well, Gloria. In fact —"

"You mind, Bayle, I'm talking to Harry," Gloria said. Arms crossed, eyes narrowed, waiting for Davidson's answer, "Well?" she said.

Davidson finished getting the tea ready and walked it over to the table. "It turns out I had some kind of virus, that's all. But the doctor gave me an antibiotic for it and now I'm fit as a fiddle. Nothing to worry about." He placed the cup of tea on the table in front of Gloria. "Can I get you some honey for your tea, G.? Maybe some toast? You sure you're not hungry? You've had a long trip."

"I'm fine," she said. Davidson shrugged his shoulders and smiled okay and began to energetically wipe down the countertop. Gloria spooned the tea around in her cup and kept a close eye on him as he finished up the job and wrung out the yellow dishcloth and hung it over the sink's faucet.

"Gotta make a pit stop but I'll be right back," he said, sprightly moving off down the hallway. Bayle and Gloria heard the bathroom door close.

"Well, he sure looks better than before, you gotta admit that," Gloria said.

"It's just because you're here and he's excited," Bayle said.

The sound of running water came from the bathroom. The clock over the kitchen table ticked ticked ticked slow ticking seconds.

Breaking the silence, "Look, you don't know what he's been like," Bayle said. "I guess you didn't know I've been working his assignments at the *Eagle*, either."

"No. I didn't." Gloria set down her cup of tea. "I thought you had your own job waiting for you back in Canada. How come now you're working Harry's?"

This time Bayle did look in her direction, even if not exactly meeting her eyes.

"I came to be working it because Harry was — I mean, *is* — too sick to do it himself. I was doing him a favour. Just like I was doing him a favour by staying here and cooking his meals and badgering him to take his medication and making his Goddamn lemon tea every night. Just like I thought I was doing you a favour, too. You seemed pretty keen on the idea of me hanging around here before you left town."

"I said I hoped you'd look in on him once in awhile, not take away the poor man's job. It's bad enough he can't be covering the hockey team no more because of that sonofabitch Duceeder, but now I've gotta come home to find out you've been writing all his other stories too?" She picked up her cup but set it right back down.

"*He needed me*, Gloria, you don't understand, you weren't here. You never saw him sitting in that chair in the other room like a T.V. zombie every night when I'd come home from work. You never saw what a chore it was just to try and get him to eat a little something at dinner every night just so his medication would work. You don't know. I do. I was here."

"Well, those things don't seem to be the way they are now, do they?" she said.

Bayle didn't know what to say, had seen the suddenly animated Davidson just as well as Gloria had.

"Maybe it was you that needed someone," Gloria said.

"Now what the hell's that supposed to mean?"

"It means, what with your girlfriend cutting you loose and all, maybe you were the one needing —"

"What happened between my girlfriend and me's got nothing —"

"Maybe it's got everything —"

"People, people," Davidson said, coming into the kitchen, holding up conciliatory hands. "What's with all this ruckus? You'd think we weren't all good friends here." If anything, Davidson looked even better than he had before he'd left the room.

Gloria leapt up from her chair and into Davidson's arms.

"Hey, what's this?" Davidson said, talking to Gloria but looking over her shoulder at Bayle.

"This is someone who's glad to have her old Harry back," she said, "that's who." Gloria nuzzled her head between Davidson's shoulder and neck. Davidson grinned off into space.

Bayle brushed by the clinging couple.

"Just give me a couple of minutes to throw my stuff together and I'll be out of your hair," he said.

Gloria gently broke free of Davidson's embrace. Taking his hand in hers she followed after Bayle into the livingroom. "You don't have to rush off just because I'm here, Bayle," she said. "I expect I'll be staying the night, but I don't think Harry's gonna be so mean as to make me sleep on the couch, are you, Harry?" She squeezed Davidson's hand. Davidson just smiled. "Are you, Harry?" she said again, slight pressure of fingernails applied to the flesh of Davidson's palm this time finally doing the trick.

"Hell, no," he said. "Bayle can stay here for as long as he likes. Damn couch is starting to show his imprint from sleeping on it for this long now, anyway." Davidson chuckled at what he thought was a pretty good attempt at lightening the mood of the room. Gloria frowned, dropped his hand. Bayle continued piling his belongings onto the couch.

"Look, it's no big deal," Bayle said, going to the closet and pulling out his suitcase. "I mean, I was planning on moving back into The Range sooner or later anyway. It's closer to the *Eagle* and I can use the extra twenty minutes sleep in the morning." He folded his few articles of clothing on top of the rest of his stuff in the bag and zipped it shut, surveyed the room for any forgotten items.

"But today was your last day at the paper, Bayle," Davidson said. "I'm starting back up tomorrow, remember?"

Bayle looked down at his packed suitcase. "I guess you are ready to go back now, aren't you?"

"Like I said, fit as a fiddle," Davidson answered, smiling widely, slapping hard his tiny pot belly twice for emphasis.

"What are you gonna do, Bayle?" Gloria said.

Bayle picked up his bag and laptop. "I don't know," he said. It wasn't the kind of honesty any of them wanted to hear.

Lowered heads; silence.

"You need a ride, Bayle?" Gloria asked, looking up.

"Christ, yes, of course the kid needs a ride," Davidson

joined in, the second head to lift. "It's the least we can do for you for covering my ass down at the paper when I was on the sidelines. Kid did a damn good job, too, G., you should see his stuff. Solid. Real solid. Surprised the hell out of me, actually. Kid writes just like an old pro."

"No thanks," Bayle said, completing the suite of raised eyes. "I think I'll just walk for awhile. I'll catch the bus when I get tired."

Gloria and Davidson stood looking at Bayle. Bayle stood in front of the door looking at his shoes. No one moved or spoke until Davidson put out his hand. "Okay then ..." he said.

Bayle set down his suitcase and computer and shook the old man's hand. He picked both items back up and turned around for the door.

"Bayle?" Gloria said. Bayle turned around. "Your nose looks better," she said.

"My nose?"

"I mean, it used to be sort of red. Now it's ...."

Bayle smiled. "Right." He touched his nose. "Clean living and good company," he said. He winked at Davidson. Davidson winked back.

"Thanks, Bayle," Gloria said. "Thanks for taking care of my Harry so good."

"Sure," Bayle said, "my pleasure." He took a last look around the room. "My pleasure."

30

SPRUCE, DAVIDSON'S
street, down to Oakview; to the end of Oakview to
where it turned into Evergreen; all the way down
Evergreen as it met up with Main; Main for three
quarters of an hour and still no end in sight. Bayle
walked and walked but couldn't seem to tire. Then he
walked some more and still felt restless. Doubling
back along Main Street, he moved in the direction of
Kellog without ever once thinking of stopping in at
Larry's. Never thought about it, but that's where he
was going. Not a decision; a destination.

R a y   R o b e r t s o n

It was a little after nine and the room fairly throbbed. Heavy clouds of cigarette smoke and the surprisingly almost sweet stink of urine and male sweat saturated the air. The effect of the A/C unit was instantaneous and, to the purely physical degree it could be, rejuvenating. But the muffled fury of the men in the bar kept Bayle from feeling any less unsettled than he had been before he came in, cool air to be preferred over the hot and hummy variety, but, inevitably, weather only weather, not something capable of assisting in the answering of such suddenly pressing problems as: What now? Why? And just exactly where?

In place of tackling these and other likewise questions Bayle pushed to the front of the bar, ordered a double Wild Turkey with a Budweiser chaser, and wrestled with that. He won the match easily, in fifty-seven seconds flat. He ordered another two-ounce opponent and pulled at his bottle of beer while waiting for his next victim.

The bourbon ascended almost as quickly as it went down. Before he'd paid for and been served up his second drink thin waves of wellness coursed up his spine and settled into the top of his head. Finally he could breathe. Bayle sipped at his beer and was almost ready to begin asking himself why he felt like nothing so much as someone who, miraculously saved from a sinking ship, has just discovered that his beloved lifeboat has a slow leak. Or a quick leak. Anyway, sinking. Again.

"I say, what's a nice sceptic like you doing in a place like this?" The Reverend Charles Warren carried his usual straight vodka and just-as-usual unflappably affable expression (if with eyes, Bayle noticed, streaked a fatigued red, and with a runny nose).

"That's a damn good question, Chuck," Bayle said, turning around from the bar. "A damn good question." The sudden sting of embarrassment Bayle felt at having altogether forgotten his nearly two-week-old promise to get in touch with Warren was almost immediately eased by both Warren's utterly warm way and Bayle's simple joy at having someone to talk to.

"And you would agree, of course," Warren said, "that a good question is infinitely more valuable than even the most ostensibly satisfying answer."

"Of course," Bayle said. Good old Chuck.

"All right, then. Shall we get a table?"

"Absolutely."

Table got, drinks drunk — and, in Bayle's case but not Warren's, got more and more of — Bayle, as the evening progressed, began to do most of the talking, Warren gradually slipping into a silent pattern of distracted listening and nervous nodding, more than once even accompanying these with an undisguisable yawn.

And like a storm-formed, swift-moving current rushing and gushing for as long as it gets fed by something bigger than itself — twigs, leaves, and all sorts of other errant matter caught up in the surge of water going faster and faster than it ever has before — Bayle picked up the slack by torrenting on and on about Duceeder and, occasionally, for variation, C.A.C.A.W. and I.M. Wright. One table leg an inch shorter than the others, the small table between the two men rocked with each of Bayle's table-whacking declarations of Duceeder's Davidson-destroying heinousnous and the generally evil right-wing agenda lurking amidst them.

At one point, after Warren had excused himself to make a phone call, it occurred to Bayle as he sat at the table by himself with no one to lecture at that he was carrying on just like one of the religious nuts at the corner of Yonge and Dundas back in Toronto. All he needed were a few free pamphlets on how to go straight to heaven and a cheap tambourine to keep the beat. He jumped up from the table and with far too much enthusiasm asked the bartender who was winning the strong-man contest playing on the television set above the bar. The bartender responded by asking Bayle if he wanted another round. His own glass had just been refilled and Warren had barely touched his first, but Bayle without hesitation answered yes. When Warren returned and inquired over the unnecessary drinks, Bayle answered that he'd won a bet with the bartender.

"What was the bet about?" Warren asked.

"I don't remember," Bayle replied. "I never gamble."

Except for the clearly unimpressed head or two that would periodically turn the way of their corner table whenever Bayle would loudly preface Duceeder's name with "that mother-fucking-fascist-bastard," Bayle's rare garrulousness almost seemed to suit Warren's mood. Even in all his bourbon-fuelled franticness — made even more frantic by the simple fact he'd been almost entirely abstentious while staying at Davidson's — Bayle could see that Warren was behaving less and less like himself, not so much tired as uneasy and detached, nervously distant. Bayle began to worry that he was boring Warren and would soon be left to his own devices and have to go home. Not having any home to go to, Bayle attempted to interest Warren in something other than the watch on his wrist he'd taken to looking at every few minutes.

"Hey, you said you did your thesis on Aquinas, right?" Bayle said.

"Aquinas ... yes." By this point it seemed a tremendous effort of concentration on Warren's part just to string together a complete sentence.

"And I think I also remember you saying that you were pretty close to finishing it. How close? I mean, you ever think of dusting it off and finishing it up? No burning desire to be Dr. Warren?"

"Dr. Warren ...." Warren consulted his watch again. Bayle started to slightly panic.

"Well, speaking for myself," he said, "I've always thought that Aquinas was never much more than watered-down Aristotle with a little Christian mumbo-jumbo thrown in to hide the influence." Drink in hand, Bayle leaned back on two legs of his chair and smiled at the wide sweep of conversational expanse he'd cut.

"Mumbo-jumbo ... yes ...." Warren looked at his watch and abruptly rose from his seat expressionless and stiff, like a departing spirit shooting straight up from the body of the deceased as depicted in one those pamphlets the Yonge Street proselytizers stick in your hand while waiting on a red light.

"I say, Peter," Warren said with great effort. "I say, Peter, it's been grand, really, but I've really got to ...."

Bayle stood up too.

"C'mon, Chuck," he said. "You're not really going, are you? It can't even be eleven o'clock yet. You know I was just joking around about the Aquinas. I mean, you've got to understand that I've got the greatest amount of respect for him, Anselm ... *all* the great thinkers of Mother Church. In fact, I'd be really curious to find out what your opinion is on how all this Death of God theology fits in with the medieval idea of ...."

Warren left Bayle talking to himself at the table.

Bayle flung a handful of *Toronto Living* money at the bartender and caught up with Warren at the door.

"My sister was a Catholic, you know," Bayle said. "Did I ever tell you that? My sister Patty? She converted. She wasn't born Catholic, but boy oh boy, when she converted to something, let me tell you, it meant something, it was the real thing. No in-between with my sister. My dad used to say, One thing about our Patty, when she sets her mind on something, by God, she does it with body and soul. The old man, he never really understood Patty. Mum not much either. But the old man ... the old man, he pretty much hit it right on the head right that time, though, yeah, that's for sure, that was our Patty all right, yeah, the old man, he pretty much hit it on the head that time."

Warren gently attempted to peel Bayle's white knuckles from the lapel of his black suit jacket. Smiled weakly.

"Mum never really talked much about Patty after she'd been gone awhile. But not too long afterward I'd get these phone calls from her at the weirdest times — weird for my mother, anyway — at, like, one or two in the morning, and she'd ask me if I thought she hadn't paid Patty enough attention when we were kids like Dad always did with me and my hockey and us both being Leafs fans. I'd tell her not to be silly and that of course she didn't have anything to do with what Patty did. And I wouldn't be just saying it to make her feel better, either. Because Patty always knew exactly what she was doing. She wasn't perfect — who the hell is? You tell me, who the hell is? But she always knew what she was doing. That's why she didn't leave a note. She didn't have to. What would be the point? Doing what she did, doing it the way she did it, she let everybody know exactly what she was thinking. I mean, *I* knew what she was thinking. I *always* knew what Patty was thinking."

Warren received the weeping man.

"My place," Warren said. "See someone there first and ... and then we can talk." He put his arm around Bayle's shoulder and guided him through the door of the bar. "Talk then all you want, Peter."

31

WARREN TOOK care of himself as soon as he'd buzzed Ron up to his apartment and the syringes had made their way out of the deep pockets of the boy's leather jacket.

The effect of the morphine on Warren wasn't as sudden as it was on Bayle, but within a few minutes of pulling the needle point out of his arm the Reverend had become his old amiable self again, listening with fixed attention as Bayle monologued on and on throughout the night, even asking for clarification at certain points or nodding in firm agreement or frank understanding at others. Only by showing little interest in verbally contributing anything of his own to the evening did the drug's impact show itself.

When Bayle saw what was going on and insisted on having whatever it was that Chuck was having, Warren made only short protest before asking Ron if he would fix Bayle.

"On your tab, Rev?" Ron said.

Warren sat in his enormous red-leather reading chair, dwarfed by a long wall of philosophy and theology titles lining the length of the entire livingroom behind him.

"My boy," he said. "Do I look to you like the sort of man who invites another gentleman into his home and then asks him to outlay for his own refreshments?"

"No sir, Rev." Ron smiled agreeably at the ball of shrunken pale Bayle sweaty plopped sitting silent with downcast eyes on the couch beside him.

"You can't get morphine anymore, you know?" he said to Bayle. "I mean, you simply cannot get it. It's like, stone age, right? The shit they used to geeze in the fifties. But I take care of the Rev. The way he talks when he's high, man, it's like ... he just *murders* me." Ron tapped the toes of his Nike hightops non-stop as he spoke.

"Entirely too much killing going on in this world, young man, so enough of that sort of talk, what? Let's take good care of my friend here, shall we? Half the regular dosage, a quarter grain should do, I think."

Ron, after being immediately assured by Warren upon being let into the apartment that Bayle "was a trustworthy chap, not to worry," had dropped his initial unease around the man he recognized as his aunt's former lodger and hung around long enough to drink the can of Coke Warren always had on hand waiting for him in his refrigerator whenever Ron "was kind enough to make a housecall."

"Ron doesn't do drugs," Warren remarked to Bayle, the boy feeling up and down Bayle's forearm in search of a good vein.

"Oh, a nice fat juicy one," Ron said, taking the syringe off the coffee table and without warning expertly sliding the needle in, Bayle's blood filling up the hypo in equal proportion to the morphine going into Bayle.

"Ron's going to be a cable mogul, Peter," Warren said. "He's saving carefully and living clean so that one day he can make all us poor unhappy citizens purchase the ultimate drug from him instead of these mere pharmaceuticals. Isn't that right, my boy?"

Ron smiled and nodded. He pulled up the arm of his leather jacket and looked at the second hand on his Rolex, checking Bayle's pulse.

"Tell him your unoffical motto, my boy," Warren said.

"Television: the drug the whole family can enjoy."

"Wonderful," Warren said. "Just wonderful. McLuhan couldn't have said it better, lad."

"And the best part of it all," Ron said, untying the bandanna from Bayle's arm, "is that it's all completely legal. No cops or gangs to fuck with your operation, and, like, it just makes sense. I mean, not every family's got a drug addict in it, but you just name me one that hasn't got a television."

Because he'd imagined that, like booze, the morphine would go straight to his head, when the drug first hit him in the back of his legs, Bayle almost laughed. Just my luck, Bayle thought. Or maybe he said it aloud. But when it started its steady spreading climb through his back and neck, muscles everywhere along the way seeming to separate from the bone like fine brown meat hanging from a perfect Christmas turkey leg, he knew the morphine was doing its job. The centre would not hold. And geez, was that ever just fine.

Weightless, careless, almost Bayleless, Bayle talked; talked right through the night with the faithfully heeding Warren stoned cosy in his immense red armchair the entire talking time; talked right through until morning with Warren still listening intently but standing in front of the bathroom mirror carefully shaving. Talked talked talked. Talked so much that the next day his tongue was literally sore.

And then, suddenly, Warren announced that he had to go to work.

"Of course you're welcome to hang around here for as long as you like," Warren said. "But I'm afraid that if I'm going to make my nine o'clock counselling I'd better be moving along." Warren's words, and the irrefutable fact that there he was, freshly showered, cleanly shaved, and utterly respectable-looking, standing at the door with briefcase in one hand and mug of steaming English Breakfast tea in the other, cleared Bayle's head of what little pleasing obliviousness remained from the effects of the nine-hour-old shot of morphine.

"You're leaving? Now?" Bayle said.

"Afraid so, yes. Mrs. Delong, nine sharp. And if the old girl *does* somehow manage to come to grips with the idea that Jesus Christ really doesn't have an opinion one way or another whether she and her husband sell the trailer home and move nearer to her sister-in-law in Salt Lake City, I'm sure there's some other faith-shaking issue that must be dealt with immediately."

Bayle didn't laugh, move, or blink. Warren could smell the other man's fear at being left alone.

"Go home and get some sleep, Peter. Put your head down in a familiar place and you'll be as good as new. And don't worry about our little business here last night with Ron. Just think of it as a little walk on the wild side among friends, all right?"

Bayle attempted a smile, meekly nodded as confidently as he could.

"That's the spirit," Warren said. Hands full, gesturing

with his head toward the locked apartment door, "I wonder, could you?"

Bayle unlocked the chain and opened the door, putting him on the inside and Warren on the other. Unshaven, exhausted, eyes equal parts terrified and unintentionally menacing, Bayle looked like a demented house-husband seeing his partner off for the day. The impression wasn't lost on Warren.

"Do you have any plans, Peter?"

Bayle squinted past him down the hallway. No one was coming or going.

"Do you?" Warren repeated. "Have any plans, I mean."

Bayle fixed his attention back on Warren but didn't say anything.

Warren waited for an answer. After an uncomfortable while, "Get some sleep, Peter," he said. "All you need is some sleep."

They both knew it was a lie.

32

THE RANGE was the only place Bayle thought to go. He was on foot, and the majority of the town's other hotels and motels existed on the highway outskirts, but most of all he craved the illusion of familiarity and sanctuary that his former lodgings provided. That he knew it was an illusion didn't make it any less appealing.

Stiffly informed by Ron's aunt that check-in wasn't until noon — bleary-eyed and wrinkled Bayle no Triple-A traveller poster boy to begin with, the ugly yellow hypodermic bruise on his forearm and the neat little stack of faxes Mrs. Franklin had been receiving nearly every day over the last week from a certain Ms. Warriner in Toronto and the several phone calls asking after his whereabouts from a snotty-sounding fellow by the name of Smith no doubt not helping his case — Bayle took Jane's correspondence and the news of his delay to clean-sheeted unconsciousness with exhausted resignation. He picked up his gear and slowly made for the front door.

"You can wait in the Breakfast Corral until your room is ready if you want," Mrs. Franklin offered, studying Bayle from behind the front desk.

"Thank you," he said.

"And there might be some coffee left over from this morning, you'll have to check for yourself. The donuts are all gone, though, I can tell you that much right now."

"Thanks."

Rarest of exchanges: he meant it; she could tell that he did.

"Isn't your work done here, Mr. Bayle? Shouldn't you be home by now?"

For a few seconds what, this morning, passed for thought; then: "I was. I am. I mean, I will."

Mrs. Franklin silently nodded. "Go on in The Corral," she said. "I think I might recall seeing a glazed donut from yesterday lying around somewhere in the kitchen. I'll bring it out if Ron hasn't managed to get to it first."

Before she left, "Here," she said, taking the lid off the container of candies sitting on the front desk, "try one of these. You can only get them mail order from Vermont."

Bayle thanked her again, took the mint, and did as he was told, went into the dining room. I have so rarely depended upon the kindness of strangers, he thought. Also thought: I will not cry. Not over the prospect of a stale donut, a bad cup of coffee, and a mint, I won't.

Recalling with unfortunately increasing clarity the tears

he hadn't managed to hold back the night before at Larry's, however — these, as well as the unbroken all-night rant he'd subjected Warren to; because of the morphine, though, thankfully foggy on the content of the tirade — Bayle retrieved from the pocket of his dirty white t-shirt the several pieces of folded fax paper Mrs. Franklin had handed over. They were just about what he had expected. The worst.

Beginning casually enough, concerned yet congenial, asking after his well-being and only as a worried P.S. about his delayed whereabouts, Jane's inquiries quickly passed from this, to the cooly professional, to the frostily litigious. The most recent, dated the day before, declared in her signature antiseptic prose style that this was Bayle's last warning, that if he didn't within the next twenty-four hours refund in full the twenty-five hundred dollars he'd bilked from the *Toronto Living* credit card he'd been entrusted with legal action would proceed. No mention was made of her new main squeeze, August.

The coffee urn, fingerprint-smudged and cold silver to the touch, dripped him a third of a styrofoam cup of equally cold coffee. Bayle brought the cup to his lips but his distorted image in the urn stopped its progress. Me or the machine? he thought. The question wasn't entirely academic.

"They were a little stale so I microwaved them."

Mrs. Franklin held out a plate topped with two glazed donuts. Bayle put down the styrofoam cup and accepted the dish. "I put on a fresh pot of coffee that should be ready by the time you get settled in upstairs," she said. "I hurried up the girl. Your room is ready when you are."

He lugged everything up to the second floor and pushed open the unlocked door to his old room. Amazingly, it was exactly like he had left it. Why exactly he found this amazing he hadn't the faintest. Only it was. He laid down face-first on the freshly made bed and decided he'd never leave.

No post-morphine midday snoozing happening, however — sheep-counting, Gloria's-boombox-inspired Bach-humming, masturbating: each act discharged faithfully but without desired doze-inducing effect — a thought, an emotion, a feeling, okay, an ache: Nice if Gloria were here. Could remind her about getting Davidson to take his medication. Might talk about how to get Harry his job back. Could get a hug.

He looked at the clock on the bedside table. Twelve thirty-one. Wouldn't be home, would be at the rink, might be home, probably not home — she's home. He pulled on his jeans, no shoes or socks, and put a quarter in the payphone by the ice machine at the end of the hall, just a little uncomfortable with the idea of calling Gloria up in the very same room he'd just spilt his seed in just a few minutes before with her very own face and body dancing before his eyes in all manner of glistening positions and angles.

Halfway through the third ring Bayle hung up, ramming the phone back into place. Bayle's hand, however, appeared to be stuck to the receiver. He stood there staring at his fist wrapped tight around the offending piece of black plastic and wondered why, even with nearly eight years of higher education to his credit, such a presumably simple thing as staying on the line until the other end answered seemed beyond him. The sound of an avalanche of ice cubes crashing into a plastic bucket turned his head.

A fellow Range resident, a pudgy middle-aged man in circus-clown-enormous brown leather slippers with furry white lining peeking out around the edges and droopy blue pyjamas dotted with glowing white dollar signs, was intent upon building a tower of ice in his little white bucket, every time he pushed the red PUSH HERE FOR ICE button the cubed mountain rising another quarter-inch higher, four or five wayward cubes sledding down the pile and onto the floor in the process.

"The missus just gotta have ice with her Diet Coke, all right then, she gonna get it. Oh, she gonna get her ice, all right, by God, yes, she gonna get it." The man gave the button one last push and licked his lips with satisfaction while inspecting the teetering pyramid he'd managed to raise. "A.J. Simmons goes for ice, by God, yes, he gets ice. Period." He strutted down the hallway without losing even one cube, the swishing of his slippers on the carpet and the slight hum of the ice machine the third floor's only noise.

The sacrificed cubes scattered at the foot of the machine were already beginning to melt, their unsuccessful attempt at joining in with the happily bucketed others resulting in a steadily spreading pool of tap water tears of failed connection. Bayle thought he knew exactly how they felt.

Eventually Bayle slept. But the molar-rattling ring of the phone on the bedside endtable and its blinking red light flashing on and off would not go away. He picked up the receiver knowing this was a call he'd have to take eventually.

Except it wasn't the cold shower of Jane he'd braced himself for.

"Bayle can you come to Harry's right now?"

"Gloria? I just called — I mean, how'd you know I was here?"

"I mean *right now.*"

"I'm on my way."

Bayle walked, jogged, even flat-out ran two or three times in painful, pain-under-his-ribs spurts from bus stop to bus stop. He finally got picked up nearly a mile from The Range and had his hand on the cord hanging over his seat three blocks before they even got near Davidson's house. When he recognized the street he wanted and stepped down from the bus Gloria was waiting for him on the front lawn of Davidson's place. She didn't even give him chance to apologize for taking so long in getting there.

"Come on inside," she said, grabbing Bayle's hand and pulling him around the side of the building. "Only be quiet though. He doesn't know yet I know what's going on."

What was going on was nothing Bayle hadn't been witness to before: Davidson suffering from indisguisable vertigo, a face flushed from fever, even a few episodes of vomiting. But, unlike when it had just been him and the old man living in the house by themselves, this time Davidson all morning long explaining away his repeatedly bumping into the furniture or knocking over his coffee cup as him simply being "all thumbs today, don't know where my head's at, G.," and running the shower in the bathroom for five and ten minutes at a time to cover up the sounds of his occasional retching and fastidious cleaning up. Gloria and Bayle stood in the doorway to Davidson's apartment, just far enough inside to hear the shower working on the other side of the closed bathroom door down the hall.

"He's got to go to the hospital, there's no other way around it," Bayle said. "Except for that first night I told you about, he's never puked up like you say he's been doing today. He's *sick*, Gloria."

"You think I don't know that? Why do you think I called you?"

"Then tell him to get his ass in your car and let's go to the hospital." The sound of the shower suddenly stopped. They lowered their voices, Gloria's becoming a fierce whisper.

"You know I can't do that. I can't just drag the man off like he's some kind of sick baby or something. I can't do that to him. I won't."

"We don't know how sick he is, Gloria. He needs someone to have a look at him. And now, not later."

"You keep saying that like I don't believe you or something. I know it, Goddammit. But he's got to be the one to say it's time to go, not me."

"For Christsake, keep your voice down."

"You're the one raising your voice, you keep your voice —"

The sound of shattering glass and the stomach-turning heavy *ummph* of human flesh hitting hardwood floor sent Bayle and Gloria scrambling down the hallway.

His useless legs were in the bathroom, most of the upper half of his prostrate body spilt over into the hall. The water glass lay thankfully broken in five clean pieces beside the sink and away from the fallen body. Davidson struggled to lift his head up off the wooden floor a few difficult inches, nostril blood rivering down slowly, some of it dribbling over his

222

upper lip and into his mouth and onto his teeth. His disoriented eyes pleaded he be paid attention to.

"Get out," he said, voice hoarse, urgent. "Get out of here. *Now.*"

They heard him out before moving into action.

After making the call for the ambulance from the other room, Bayle returned with a glass of water and the pillows from the couch. Davidson's head in her lap, Gloria wiped his face clean with a wet washcloth and placed another cold rag on his forehead, over and over stroking the little hair on his head like a concerned mother would a feverish child. Davidson didn't attempt to protest his wellness anymore, simply lay there eyes-closed quiet and attended to.

"Here. Use these," Bayle said, offering over the pillows.

Gloria removed her thigh from underneath Davidson and — Bayle holding up the old man's head — carefully arranged the pillows. They slowly lowered his head back down together. Each remained there kneeling, watching Davidson rest, Bayle involuntarily sneak-peeking at Gloria's so-close eyes, lips, neck, and jutting collarbone, the expanse of brown chest above her black V-neck slope of t-shirt. Their faces not more than a foot apart, Bayle had never been this near to her before. He worried whether she could hear his heart hammering away through his chest. Also worried what kind of man it is that lusts after his sick friend's girlfriend.

"Gloria, who's Dan Fenton?" Bayle said, desperate to drag his mind out of the gutter of Gloria's body.

Still stroking Davidson's head, Gloria only looked up long enough to dismiss the name Duceeder had challenged Bayle to ask Davidson about by sharply answering, "Dan Fenton's nobody."

A moment of silence later, "He really is still sick," she said.

"Don't worry, the paramedics will be here soon."

"What did the doctors say when I was gone? Tell me what they said, tell me exactly."

"They didn't say much. Really. They thought it was just a virus or parasite in his system and that the medication should take care of it. But he's been taking it for over a week now and he should've been better in a couple of days, four, tops. I guess they'll just have to run some more tests. I'm sure they'll find out what it is this time."

Gloria stood up and began to pick up the pieces of broken glass off the bathroom floor. She worked slowly, like she was using the time to try and figure something out. Finally, "Harry doesn't need any more tests," she said. "What Harry needs is to be able to talk to those players again."

Bayle watched her carefully place each piece of jagged glass in the palm of her other hand.

"Look," Bayle said. "I've been thinking a lot about this boycott business since you've been away — thought about it a lot, actually — and I'm all for trying to do everything we can to help figure out some way of getting Harry out of this mess. But we've got to face facts. What Harry needs right now is a long stay at the hospital and some serious tests done on his condition."

"What Harry needs is his life back," Gloria said.

"Well, that's what I'm talking about. And that's why he needs to go to the hospital."

"That's why he needs to be back covering the team." Gloria punctuated the sentence by dropping the shards of glass into the plastic garbage pail under the sink. The small thud stirred Davidson awake.

"G.?" he called out, eyes opening wide. Gloria kneeled back down over him, entwined her right hand with his. All three of them could hear the ambulance whining their way down the street. Davidson closed his eyes again.

"The time for tests is over, Bayle," Gloria said. "The time for thinking about things too." Bayle's eyes locked with hers. "You with me, or not?"

Bayle heard Gloria's breathing. Heard the ambulance's siren so loud now it might have been parked right inside the livingroom. Wrapping his fingers around Gloria's free hand, heard both of them, each thing, distinct; one.

33

"WOW. THAT'S, like, a lot of powder. You'll have to give me a little time. I'll have to make some calls."

"How much time?" Bayle said.

"Like, tomorrow, noon?" Ron said.

"Where?"

"Here's all right for me if it's okay with you."

"See you at noon," Bayle said. He pushed back his black sunglasses further up his nose. He'd never made it a practice to wear sunglasses indoors before, but now it seemed like the right sort of thing to do. Watching Ron leave the restaurant and get into a black BMW driven by another teenager, Drug dealers making their getaways in BMWs, Bayle thought: I've been watching the wrong television shows.

After paying Mrs. Franklin up front for another week at The Range Bayle had about half of the twenty-five hundred of *Toronto Living* money he'd started out with, about a thousand of which he'd need for the cocaine. That left him about two hundred dollars in walking-around money. After that was gone he'd just have to wait and see. The combination of knowing exactly what he had to do each day and not having a clue where he'd be a week from now put Bayle in a permanent state of lightheadedness and nervous excitation, a sort of drunken giddiness of action.

And they still hadn't figured out a way to plant the cocaine in Duceeder's house. Bayle had argued for the much simpler plan of just putting it in the G.M.'s filing cabinet at the arena, but Gloria had pointed out that because of all the traffic at the Bunton Center it would be far too easy for Duceeder to claim it was somebody else's.

"It's got to be at his place. That way there's nobody else he can point his finger at."

"But how are we going to get into his house without him knowing?" Bayle said.

"Not we — *you*. Folks in that neighbourhood get a little jumpy when they see somebody of the non-white colour hanging around. I just show up there in my car and I've got half the Neighbourhood Watch dialing 911. It's got to be you that makes the stash."

So there was that. And Bayle still had to cover the Warriors for the *Eagle* on a day-to-day basis now that the team was back home until either Davidson got better or Wilson found a permanent replacement. As a favour, Wilson promised to advertise for the position for a full week before he brought anybody in for an interview, but after that he'd have to start talking to people with the intention of actually hiring someone.

And every evening between six and eight p.m. Gloria and Bayle would sit on uncomfortable wooden chairs on opposite sides of Davidson's starched white hospital bed. Davidson usually sleeping — when he wasn't, groggy and sulky and generally uncommunicative, as if betrayed into sickness by his two healthy friends — it was here, the day after the ambulance delivered Davidson to his temporary new home, that Gloria carefully laid out to Bayle her plan for getting Davidson his job back.

"And your friend, the guy who's going to impersonate the cop —"

"Dwayne," Gloria said.

"Right, Dwayne. He's just going to scare Duceeder enough for us to get what we want?"

"Soon as Duceeder calls off the boycott things go right back to like they was before. For everybody."

"By why real cocaine? Why not baking soda? Davidson won't know the difference."

"Because the only reason Dwayne's doing this is because he hates drugs like only an ex-junkie who's lost everything because of them and learned to tell about it can. He'll know the difference. I told him Davidson was a low-end dealer who's burned a couple friends of mine and we're trying to get back at him."

"But what am I supposed to do with a quarter ounce of coke after everything's back to normal?"

"Don't worry about that. If this friend of yours don't want to buy it back — and I never knew one that didn't if he came out ahead in the end even just a little bit — I can get rid of it myself."

"And nobody gets hurt, right?"

"Of course nobody gets hurt," she said. "Nobody gets hurt and Harry gets to go back to his hockey beat and out of this damn hospital."

Bayle felt less than convinced. A thousand dollars worth of cocaine. A break and entry. A false police arrest. It all seemed a little much, even for Harry's sake.

Through an opening in the white curtain set up around the sleeping Davidson's bed Bayle noticed the silver-haired man who shared with Davidson the small, starkly white room. About Davidson's age, maybe a few years older, one of the old man's eyes was open wide and unblinking at the ceiling, the other staying shut, hard and tight. He seemed neither awake nor asleep. His bony fingers were knotted in gnarled curls at his sides and his slightly opened mouth turned up at one corner just enough to promise imminent speech that never came. Bayle looked back at Gloria across Davidson's motionless body. A clear tube ran from one of the old man's nostrils to a large machine set up beside the bed for what purpose Bayle had absolutely no idea.

Looking up at Gloria, "Every time we'd make the trip to Maple Leaf Gardens my dad would leave the game kind of depressed," Bayle said, "even if the Leafs won. He never said anything, but you could just tell. I never really understood why and I never asked. My old man and me, we just didn't talk about things like that, that just wasn't the way we operated. But just before he died, when he was in and out of it all the time, he told me that the Bunker, the place where the Leafs owner Harold Ballad and his buddy King Clancy used to sit every home game, never looked as good in person as it did on television."

Gloria didn't say anything; didn't do or say anything that said to stop talking, though, either.

"But those old rinks," Bayle said, "like the Forum in Montreal, like the Gardens ... sure they were falling apart and the seats were too small and you couldn't see the ice half as good as you can in the new arenas, but they were the best. Like shrines, you know? Like fucking churches. And if you never had a chance to see Guy Lafleur, The Flower, racing down the right wing in one of them with that long blond mane of his flying in the breeze behind him, winding up for a slapshot pegged right for the upper left-hand corner, well, you just haven't lived. I'm sorry, but you just haven't." Bayle paused. "And the old man? My dad? He should have remembered that kind of thing after he had his operation, that summer he was supposed to get better. That's the kind of thing I should have got him to remember. I didn't, I know that. But I should have."

Gloria nodded, waited for more, but that was it. Sat there looking at Bayle looking at the elderly man in the other bed.

"I'll call my friend about the coke tonight," Bayle said.

34

BAYLE SAT cross-legged on his bed at The Range, the palm-sized peppermint tin of cocaine in front of him unopened since point of noon-day purchase — "No charge for the lid," Ron had said, handing it over under the table a few hours earlier at Fatty's, "one of my aunt's discards."

He stayed like this for several minutes, just staring down at the thing, before finally picking the container up and placing it on one knee, running through for what felt like the first and thousandth time his plans for tomorrow night's combined break, entry, and drug planting.

Bayle knew that Duceeder's wife and son accompanied him to every home game, so he'd picked tomorrow night, during the first period of the Wichita game, for when he'd make his move. Making his task easier, he remembered noticing that Duceeder's place was one of the few houses on the G.M.'s block without a CDH security sign planted out front. He'd get in the house as inconspicuously as possible, stash the coke, and leave without notice. When he got to the rink by about the end of the first intermission his story would be that he'd slept through his alarm clock.

He'd also taken the precaution of purchasing from the 7-Eleven near The Range a pair of brown garden gloves so as to avoid leaving any prints at the scene, and had laid out for tomorrow night all the black clothes he owned to provide for optimum night-time cover. He had it all planned out and there really wasn't anything left to think about. But Bayle thought about it again and again anyway, wished today was tomorrow, wished that the whole thing was over and done with. Three sharp knuckle raps to his locked-and-chained door put an end to any more thinking or wishing.

Bayle pounced on the container of drugs, heart gorging up into his throat in the process. Head whipping from side to side, he combed the room for a place to hide the tin, three more measured knocks at the door coming and going. "Who is it?" he chirped as cheerily as possible, hoping to buy a few more seconds.

"Charles Warren. I say, Peter, are you all right in there?"

"Chuck," Bayle said to himself. "It's only Chuck." He crammed the tin underneath the pillows on the bed and unlocked the door and undid the chain.

"Chuck," Bayle said. "It's just you." Warren wasn't high, but he looked like hell anyway; in particular, melting face tired and with a runny nose he continually wiped at with an ever-present hankie.

"Well, I wouldn't have put it quite like that, but, yes, it is me."

Bayle stood in the doorway looking visibly relieved; smiled, said nothing.

Eventually, "Is it all right if I ...?" Warren said, wiping his nose, motioning toward the empty room behind Bayle.

"Oh, sure, come on in," Bayle said, letting Warren through. "Sit over there in the chair. I'll sit on the bed. You're the first guest I've ever had in here so you get to sit in the chair. I'll just sit on the bed."

"All right, then," Warren said, watching Bayle closely. "I'll sit in the chair."

Bayle moved from door to bed in a hurried, artificial stride of stiff casualness, leaning back against the bunched pillows when he got there. He sent another long, exaggerated grin Warren's way.

Warren attempted to smile back but the effort was too much. He leaned forward on his chair. "How are things, Peter? How have you been?"

"Fine, fine," Bayle said; then, "Why? Does it seem like something's wrong to you? Not that I'd have any idea why you would. Think something's wrong, I mean. Because everything's just fine. Just hunky dory, in fact. Did you know I'm covering the Warriors for the *Eagle* now?"

"I believe I did hear something of the sort, yes."

Bayle nodded and leaned back into the pillows. Warren cleared his throat and got to the point.

"I say, Peter, I was talking to young Ron this afternoon, and —"

"Listen, Chuck, you can say that it's none of my business and I'd understand completely, but you really should try to go easy on that morphine stuff, you know? I mean, I've tied a few on in my time, but I can't even *remember* most of that night at your place."

Warren jumped at the opening. "No, no, you're quite

right to take an interest if you think a friend is in need of an encouraging word, Peter, you're quite right. In fact, the reason I dropped by here today was to offer you the same sort of advice in much the same spirit."

"Me?" Bayle sat up from the pillows.

"Come, now, Peter. A quarter ounce of cocaine? Really. I understand that you're going through a bit of a rough stretch right now, what with the breakup with your girlfriend and your failed academic career — not to mention your unresolved feelings toward your sister. And God knows there's no crime in a fellow finding a little comfort from life's little difficulties from time to time. Goodness, look at me and my own —"

"That little prick," Bayle said, looking away from Warren and shaking his head, imploding anger at his loose-lipped dealer overwhelming his surprise at Warren's mention of Patty.

"Now, now, Peter, blaming Ron isn't going to solve anything. What we like to say in counselling is that people like Ron are only symptoms, not the problem."

Bayle frowned. "Look, Chuck, I appreciate your coming over here, I really do, but I don't have a drug problem."

"Denial."

"What?"

"It's perfectly natural, Peter, it really is. It's what we in group like to call one of the essential steps toward recovery."

"Chuck, look, I told you: I don't have a drug problem."

"I know this isn't what you want to hear right now, Peter, but anyone who purchases a thousand dollars worth of cocaine most definitely has a drug problem."

"For the last time, I don't have —"

"I bet you haven't even left this room since you scored, have you?" Warren leaned back in his chair, crossed his arms tight across his chest. "Where is it, Peter? How much of your hard-earned money have you stuffed up your nose already?"

"I'm not high!"

"Yes you are!"

"Oh, for the love of —"

"My God, Peter, just take a look at yourself: agitated, nerves ground to the bone, and nearly as paranoid as these militia types we've got hurling their bombs around town now. I'm afraid it's as plain as the nose on your face, old man."

Almost at the point of yanking out the container of cocaine from underneath the pillows to prove he hadn't even touched the drugs, it suddenly struck Bayle that, thanks to Ron's big mouth, now that Warren knew he had the coke, letting him think that he was actually using was the only way he could possibly justify having it. He took a deep breath and ran both hands through his hair, attempting to look his most junkie-repentant-sincere.

"Okay," Bayle said. "Okay. Let's say I did have a problem and did want to get clean. What would be the first step? I mean, if I did have a problem." Bayle tapped what he hoped was a passable version of a cokehead's frantic tune on his thigh.

Warren stood up and put his hand on Bayle's shoulder. "The first step is always the most difficult, Peter. And by admitting to yourself that you've got a problem, you've already taken it." Warren didn't dab his nose as usual but blew it this time good and loud. He stuck the handkerchief in the inside pocket of his black suit jacket like he never intended to use it again.

Plans for Bayle to attend his first group counselling session tomorrow afternoon at seven p.m. sharp and the extraction of a promise to try and only do enough cocaine to get him through the night and the next day were made and given. Warren shook Bayle's hand firmly and reassured him for the third excited time that, with the right kind of professional help, anything was possible. Bayle tried to continue looking strung-out but cautiously optimistic. Warren looked like a man who loved his job and wasn't a problem drinker with a predilection for mainlining morphine.

The Reverend already at the elevator, Bayle suddenly remembered something. "Hey, Chuck?" he said, peering around his opened door. Warren turned to face him.

"Don't worry, Peter. We're going to lick this thing. Together. You'll see." Warren raised a clenched fist.

Bayle lifted a limp fist of his own. "I don't doubt it," he said, "I don't doubt it." The elevator dinged its arrival at Bayle's floor. "I was just wondering though," Bayle continued. "What did you mean by my unresolved feelings toward my sister?"

"Come again?" The elevator doors opened up.

"You said something earlier about my unresolved feelings toward my sister. Where did that come from?"

"Oh, that. You don't remember?"

Bayle didn't like the sound of where this was going.

Warren looked both ways down the hall, lowered his voice to a pointed whisper.

"The night you spent at my place enjoying Ron's ... little delivery," he said, looking up and down the hallway again. "Your sister. She was all you could talk about."

The news struck Bayle the way headlines, no matter how big the letters, never do. "But that's not ...."

Warren gave an enthusiastic thumbs-up and stepped out of sight into the elevator, remarking before the doors closed that he also did bereavement counselling and that that might be something they'd want to explore later on after first getting Bayle's more immediate problem under control.

Still half inside his room, half hanging out, "But that's not true," Bayle said.

Nobody heard him, though. Nobody.

35

HE KNEW it would take nearly an hour to walk to Duceeder's place, but Bayle didn't want to run the risk of anyone like a bus driver being able to place him in the area. He spent most of the trip resisting the desire to look over his shoulder every time a car horn or errant human voice announced itself and logically demonstrating to himself that a crime can only be said to be a crime if there is a crime scene, and that there can only be a crime scene when a person gets caught and charged with committing a crime. And since Bayle had no intention of getting caught it stood to reason that he really wasn't going to be doing anything criminal, just righting a wrong that, if the world ran on reason and not pettiness and mean-spiritedness, never would have required his righting it in the first place. So there.

Looking up to notice he'd just passed Davidson's street, Spruce, Bayle doubled back and detoured down its sidewalk. Nearly seven-thirty now and feeling fairly comfortable under the cover of an almost-darkness, he stood in front of the old man's unoccupied apartment.

Tonight was the first time since Davidson had been hospitalized that Bayle hadn't gone by to visit. Not that he did much when he was there anyway except steal guilty glances at just-showered Gloria fresh from practicing her routine at the rink (all-over workout-taut and whatever springtime scent it was she wore whenever returning from the arena kicking the death out of the hospital smell of rubbing alcohol and slow decay that upon signing in at the front desk always made Bayle temporarily loath to take the elevator up to Davidson's fifth-floor room). But once he got there and saw the grateful little half-smile Gloria always gave him when he came in the room and heard the grunt of recognition half-asleep Davidson always made when hearing Bayle's voice saying hello to Gloria, dread of disease and dying disappeared and nowhere else he'd rather be than in room #563, Hays County General Hospital, passing the hours between six and eight p.m. with his two friends.

And friends, Bayle thought, still standing there in front of Davidson's house, real friends, they'd do anything for each other. Anything. Because that's what friends do.

Bayle took one last look at the house and strided back down the sidewalk. He was only about ten minutes away from Duceeder's place and figured he could be there and done with what he had to do in fifteen, twenty-five minutes tops. Duceeder. That bastard.

36

"MR. BAYLE. I'm afraid you don't look at all well. I fear this horribly inclement weather is getting the best of you. Stay the course, young man. According to the weather forecast on WUUS a change for the better is on its way. A cool front down from Canada, apparently. And how about that? Relief for all of us, and all the way from where you call home."

Samson said his smiling-as-usual-as-he-said-it bit before turning his attention over to a question tug-on-his-sleeve posed by one of the two others on either side of him in press box row, the thick sideburns like furry porkchops and identical pot-bellies stuffed into tight-fitting white suits to go along with longhorn bolo-ties and enormous white cowboy hats leaving little doubt that the two men were from Texas, or at least willing to play the part in the made-for-T.V. movie. Duceeder also sat in the press box, but at the other end, his eyes never leaving the ice surface. It appeared as if he hadn't been invited to Samson's hoedown.

Bayle sat himself and his laptop down and looked where he was supposed to look at the rink below without actually seeing the quick two-on-one break right off the face-off converted into a Warrior goal by Robinson assisted on by Trembley at the 15:31 mark. Never heard the public address system announcement of the goal, either.

White as a sheet (or a ghost; or, alternatively, looking like he had just seen a ghost); sick as a dog; weak as a kitten; feeling like death warmed over: cliches, sometimes, exactly what the doctor ordered, the patient too sick with — fill in the blank with whatever ails — to come up with a witty way to say just how one hurts (and how). Dull language for a dull pain. In Bayle's case: fear, and all its still-echoing after-effects.

Bayle put his hands together with the celebrating others in the arena and struggled to quit looking at then quickly looking away from Duceeder smiling to himself at Robinson's goal. Struggled, but apparently not hard enough.

"Yeah?" the G.M. finally said, end of his tether at Bayle's peek-a-boo routine having finally been reached. He took a gnarled pen out of his mouth. "Yeah, what?"

"Good game so far?" Bayle said. Jesus Christ, what did I do? he thought.

Duceeder considered Bayle head to toe for a few unimpressed seconds and then stuck the pen back in his mouth, trained his eyes back on the ice.

"Mr. Bayle," Samson said, "I'd like you to meet Mr. Handy and Mr. Gunn. Gentlemen, Mr. Bayle. This is Mr. Handy and

Mr. Gunn's first hockey game, if you can believe it. Any tips from an experienced observer like yourself you'd care to pass on?"

Six eyes on him unblinking and awaiting, Bayle, wanting the force of the three men off him like sucking leeches on a twentieth-century sick man, feigned enthusiastic the first thing that came to mind: "Keep your eye on the puck!"

Each man hesitated; then, with the resumption of collective blinking, nodding in understanding agreement all three of them, turning their attention away from Bayle and back to the game. Bayle opened up his computer and plugged it in and tapped away at whatever keys his fingers happened to find, filling up his screen with absolute gibberish in order to buy some time to piece together just what the hell had happened.

Like most unqualified disasters, things couldn't have started out better.

More than once having heard Duceeder bitch and moan about the new patio door he'd just had installed, Bayle made it around the back of his house without, he thought, anyone seeing him, and went right for the glass door, giving it a sharp jerk and feeling the thing immediately give, if only an inch or two. Three more hard yanks and the door jumped from its track just like he'd heard Duceeder complain about. He looked around him — nothing: backyard blackness everywhere only — and slid the door easily open.

Which then promptly fell forward and crashed into the kitchen table, one of the wooden table chairs shattering right through the glass door. Instead of running the other way, though, Bayle was propelled by the glass explosion into the carpeted diningroom, the sliding of the patio door the last act he could with any exactness remember.

After this, only fragments of action and emotion to be ceaselessly replayed over and over, just like that infamous piece of film footage Patty during her conspiracy theory period had for so long lingered over of Kennedy taking one for the home team that one last time in Dallas. Frame by frame, slower and slower, maybe *this* time the meaning of the act won't escape with the end of the tape.

241

Fragments of action and emotion fifteen minutes in the actual doing but only an instant in the remembering:

The sound of the smashing glass still ringing in his ears even after the slivers and shards on the carpet were only a still pool of crazy water refracting jagged the entering beam of moonlight.

The screaming silence as soon as the ringing had faded.

The first uncertain steps toward ....?

Stopping, looking around, assessing the room.

Second, third, fourth uncertain steps toward ....?

I-Spying kitchen cupboards (no), counter drawers (no), teacup-and-saucer-filled corner cupboard (no), liquor cabinet (Alcohol ... Drugs ... Make sense? Yes). Placing the peppermint tin of cocaine out of eyeshot behind the Southern Comfort and bottle of gin.

On his knees in front of the cabinet and hearing the policemen's walkie-talkies as they came around the side of the house, sprinting into the other room with laptop in tow in search of the first cover he could find — the livingroom closet — mothballs gagging his throat and sweat stinging his eyes, yet too scared to wipe it away for fear of rustling the winterwear and overcoats.

The five-minute (five hours?) up and down the house search by the cops — always one downstairs when the other was up, never an opportunity to make a run for it even if he'd had the nerve to take the chance.

One cop calling the other one over to the diningroom.

"Whatta you got?" the deep voice said. Carpet steps toward the other voice.

Silence.

"Uh huh," the deep voice said, loud enough for Bayle with strain to hear from inside the closet.

"What do you figure?"

"At least a grand, maybe more."

"Too much for just him and the little lady for around the house, though, wouldn't you say?"

"Oh, for sure, for sure. This guy's selling. No doubt about it."

Silence.

"Liquor cabinet open just like this when you found it?"

"Yep. Open as the barn door. Thought I'd check it out for prints in case our B-and-E got a little thirsty before he left."

"Well, at least now we know what our visitor was looking for," said the deep voice.

"We must have spooked him off before he could find it."

"Uh huh."

Silence.

"So what do you want to do?"

"Find out where Mr. and Mrs. James Duceeder of 66 Maple are this evening, I reckon."

"I'll radio HQ."

"And tell them to send somebody over here with a dog. See what else this bastard has got buried around this place."

Back at the rink, Bayle's nose wrinkling, stomach slightly curdling, looking around for the sour source; tentatively sniffing, remembering, realizing, thinking: Shit. The skunk. I forgot all about the skunk.

But not any more.

After the cops had taken the coke and left, and before the next set of them arrived with the police dog, Bayle had beat it out of the house through the busted patio door with legs and arms pumping, if still with eyes alert for gawking neighbours and the like, terrified backyard wildlife, unfortunately, excepted. He didn't actually see the thing lift its leg and spray him — only saw it waddle off underneath the fence as soon as it saw him coming and felt the skunk's skunking burning away through the hairs in his nose — but right away Bayle knew that the skunk had got him. Christ, I stink, he thought. Man, I stink. I stink.

Fiercely rubbing at his eyes — all right; clean, unskunked — and wisely deciding he'd likely attract less attention if he calmly made his departure instead of flailing away down the sidewalk like a madmen being pursued by invisible demons, Bayle strolled away from Duceeder's house as cooly as he could, coolness of departure severely compromised, however, by the mist of stink he knew enveloped him. Bayle rubbed his eyes again and continued his retreat.

Eventually bringing him back to the Bunton Center where he now sat squirming on his stool desperately attempting to come up with a reasonable explanation as to why he smelled like, well, like a skunk, and wondering why no one, not even Duceeder, had said anything yet about his smelling so bad. Mid-Western manners, he decided.

The period ended and Duceeder got up and quickly left. One of the Texans said to the other, "C'mon, Tommy, let's get us smore of this here pig-farmer beer. It sure ain't Lone Star, but the fourth one don't taste half as bad as that first one does." The two men stomped off toward the arena lobby, leaving Bayle and Samson by themselves in the press box.

Bayle raced to cover up his skunky tracks.

"... and by then I didn't want to put Mrs. Franklin or any of her guests out by coming back to The Range during supper hour reeking like I did, so I went to a gas station near the bus stop where the skunk got me and tried to clean up as best I could. Then I walked around for awhile hoping that some fresh air might help."

"Really, as I've tried to assure you, Mr. Bayle, to my nose it's virtually imperceptible," Samson said. "Perhaps when Mr. Handy and Mr. Gunn return from getting their refreshments you could share some of your findings about minor-league hockey with them. They're only going to be in town until tomorrow, I'm afraid. Perhaps this might help rid you of your unfortunate preoccupation with skunks."

"Mr. Handy and Mr. Gunn: they're friends of yours?" Bayle said, latching on to the opportunity to be talking about anything other than his smelling like an acrid goat.

"Friends? Yes, I suppose you could say that," Samson said.

Leaning Bayle's way, "Here's a scoop for you, Mr. Bayle," he said. "The Warriors are moving to Texas next year, El Paso, in fact. Mr. Handy and Mr. Gunn are here as representatives of the generous business community down there that has convinced us to move our operations south."

244

It took Bayle a few seconds to process this. Eventually, "You don't seem too shook up about it," he said.

Samson smiled wide.

"But your bosses, the owners, Bunton Groceries, they don't want the team to move," Bayle said. "You yourself in the *Eagle*, you said as much, I saw it. I read it."

Samson smiled wider.

"And Harry and his articles about the arena," Bayle said, almost pleading now. "You all hated him. Duceeder even got the players to stop talking to him just to get back at him."

At this Samson slightly frowned, seemed even a little disappointed.

"Mr. Bayle, you're an intelligent man. Is it really so inconceivable that those boys simply believed what they read in the newspaper and heard on the radio every day and were merely frightened of losing their jobs?"

Bayle didn't answer; couldn't.

"And as far as any animosity I might have toward Mr. Davidson, well ...." Samson seemed to consider whether or not to finish his sentence. He leaned Bayle's way again.

"Hypothetically, imagine this if you will," he said. "A large corporation comes upon an offer to make one of its marginally profitable side interests much more so if only it could transfer said interest to a more prosperous market where corporate support is plentiful and the tax situation most favourable. Most favourable. Impeding the move, however, is the horrible publicity the corporation might suffer at relocating this much-loved interest out of state. The effect on its remaining interests — which are substantial, mind you — could be very, very injurious. If, however" — Samson stopped and looked at Bayle to see if he was still listening; he was — "if however an opportunity presented itself whereby some other party could be seen as responsible for the move of the corporation's interest — indeed, blamed and condemned for forcing the relocation — well, that would suit this corporation just fine, wouldn't it? Hypothetically speaking, of course."

Bayle felt like the last person in the movie theatre to

finally figure out whodunit, the music swelling and the credits already rolling down the screen. "You were glad Harry wrote those articles," he said. "You just wanted everyone to think you were all mad at him and that the owners didn't want to move."

Until he heard one of them speak, Bayle didn't notice the two cops standing at the press box at Samson's side.

"Excuse me. Mr. Samson? I'm officer Phil Tate and this is officer Peter Fitts. The usher said that a Mr. James Duceeder could be found down here."

Bayle thought: Deep voice. Familiar. Cop. Deep familiar cop voice. Shit ....

"Why, yes, he ordinarily can be, officers. Unfortunately, Mr. Duceeder seems to have stepped into the lobby, I believe, for a cup of — No, I stand corrected. Here he comes right now. And with young Bill in tow, too, it looks like."

Laughing, one hand resting easy on his son's shoulder, the two of them came joking down the arena steps, Duceeder Sr. not paying the two cops all that much notice. Settling down first Bill and then himself beside him at the press box, Duceeder looked merely surprised to find a policeman standing behind him on either side. He turned halfway around in his seat.

"James Duceeder?"

"You've got the right man, boys. What can I do you for?"

"James Duceeder of 66 Maple?"

The big grin of happy co-operation dropped off Duceeder's face. He looked from one policeman to the other. Bill looked at his father.

"Yes," Duceeder said, all polite seriousness now, "what is it, officers?" His face suddenly flashed panic. "Is it Carol?" he said, exploding up from his seat, knocking the stool to the cement floor with a loud wooden whack. Bill stood up beside his father. "Bill and I just saw her a few minutes ago in the lobby and —"

"Sit down, Mr. Duceeder," the deep-voiced cop said, putting a forceful hand on the G.M.'s shoulder. "Your wife is fine." The other, younger looking cop set back up the stool. Duceeder and his son reluctantly took their seats, each looking slightly more dazed with every second.

"We can do this two ways, Mr. Duceeder," the cop said. "One way is for you to quietly come along with us to police headquarters and answer a few questions we have. The other way is going to be a lot less pleasant for everyone involved, believe me." The cop looked from Duceeder, to his son, then back.

Duceeder shook himself loose from his numbed state and poked a finger in the cop's chest. "Hey, what the hell is this all about, anyway? I'm a taxpayer, buddy, and you're a civil servant who's supposed to be serving me. I want some Goddamn service in the form of some answers, and I want them fast, and I want them now."

The two cops looked at each other and shrugged. One of them unhooked the pair of silver handcuffs dangling from his belt and deftly clicked them on the incredulous Duceeder's limp, unresisting hands.

"James Duceeder, you are hereby placed under arrest under the authority of the Hays County Police Department for possession of an illegal substance with intent to traffic. You have the right to remain silent. Anything you say can and will be used against you in a court of law. You have the right to an attorney. If you cannot afford an attorney, one will be provided to you. Do you understand everything I just said?"

Duceeder nodded blankly, stared at the gleaming handcuffs binding his wrists, whatever fight there had been in him evaporated. He raised his gaze from the cuffs to his son. Frightened teenaged eyes looked back at him, dry lips slightly trembling, mouth open and gaping, unbelieving any of this was happening. The two policemen hoisted the prisoner to his feet.

Duceeder rose willingly, but would not be moved. "Bill needs to go home," he said. "I'm not going anywhere until I know he's gotten home safe."

The policemen looked at each other again. The younger

247

one took off his cap and scratched his head. "Your house is still being investigated," he said. "Nobody'll be able to get in there for a couple hours more at least."

Duceeder stood his ground; didn't resist, just wasn't going anywhere until he knew his son was going to be all right. He looked Samson's way. Samson cleared his throat.

"Of course," Samson said, "if it wasn't for my having to be responsible to Warrior ownership for entertaining Mr. Handy and Mr. Gunn tonight I would be more than happy to take charge of young Bill during this ... unfortunate episode, James. As things stand, however, my hands are tied. I'm sure you can understand." As if to illustrate his predicament, devoted company man Samson locked his fingers together on top of the press box tabletop, offering nothing else. For a long moment, no one else did either.

Eventually, piercing the silence, "Bill can stay with me until he can go back home," Bayle said. The press box swayed its attention Bayle's way. "I'm just going back to my room at The Range after the game anyway. The police can call us there when it's okay for him to go home. I'll make sure he gets back."

Duceeder's eyes seared Bayle's, bearing down hard trying to decide if he could entrust his only child with this fool. Bayle beared the stare. Briefly. Bayle lowered his eyes.

"I'll be okay, Dad," Bill said. "Go get mom and bring her home, okay? Figure out what this is all about, okay, Dad?"

Duceeder looked at his son. Smiled. He moved toward Bayle, the younger cop making a motion to stop him, the other one nodding that it was all right. Bayle's body tensed.

Inches from Bayle's face, "Thanks," Duceeder said. "I owe you one."

More than you know, Bayle thought. "No problem," he said.

Duceeder turned around and faced the police. "All right, let's go," he said. "It's time to get to the bottom of this nonsense." He winked at his son. His son smiled and winked back.

Duceeder was led away down the arena stairs by the two policemen. Fans turned around in their seats to stare at the handcuffed man being escorted from the rink.

37

IN SPITE of everything, Bayle still had a job to do — Harry's — and he did it, throwing together his game report for the *Eagle* from a cribbed combination of Bill's surprisingly vivid recounting of the first two periods and by sticking close to the timekeeper's official scoresheet. He even thought Duceeder's obviously shaken son started to relax a little when asked to remember as best he could things like how Trembley's first-period goal was scored and how many of the twenty-three shots fired at the Warrior net over the first couple of periods were tough saves. Bayle, too, seemed to wind down somewhat with attention turned over to the game and its piecing together.

Not wanting the boy to stew in worry all alone in the press box, Bayle took Bill along with him to the Warriors' dressing room as soon as the buzzer signalled the end of the game, another Warrior loss, this time a come-from-behind six-to-four Wichita victory. Here, perfunctory grunts from the main Warrior combatants, Bill standing close by as Bayle scribbled and nodded.

A knock, another, and then another at Coach Daley's closed office door elicited only, "Unless that's fucking Wayne Gretzky out there, go the fuck away!" Trembley, the game's leading scorer with two goals and an assist, noted that because of the uncharacteristically warm weather, "The ice, it was brutal out there, like skating in, what you call it, quicksand, oui?" And from Dippy, who renewed his season-long battle with the Wichita goon, Bladon, by going another two spirited rounds, the observation that, given the Warriors' disappointing two wins and five losses to start the season, "Something's got to give. One way or another, things have got to change around here." Scribbling and nodding, Bayle couldn't have agreed more.

Back upstairs at the press box, slap-dash article whipped off and faxed, Bayle looked around the empty, garbage-strewn arena.

"Okay," Bayle said. "Let's get out of here. I've got to lose these clothes."

"I don't smell any skunk," Bill said.

Polite kid, Bayle thought. Somone has taught him good manners.

"Let's go," Bayle said, the botched break-and-entry, the skunk, Duceeder's arrest, Samson's revelation — all of it stuck behind his eyes like the beginning of a bad sinus headache. "This smell. God. I'm starting to make myself sick."

Bayle vowed that if he did nothing else in his life, for the next couple of hours he was going to be the best host to Duceeder's son the world had ever seen. He felt like some kind of diabolic Big Brother to the son of the innocent man he'd just shot in the back. Smile, Bayle. Even if it hurts.

Potato chips and Hickory Sticks fortified with a can of root beer (for Bill) and a paper cup of black coffee (for Bayle) to do the washing down, two Snickers bars — shared favourite-candy-bar coincidence — to be saved for later, for dessert, Bayle and Bill with their salt and sugar loot horsed around, pushed and shoved each other past The Range's unoccupied front desk, Bayle the horsing-around instigator.

Bayle paid for the whole thing, for both of them. It had taken a solid ten minutes to get what they did, mainly because every time Bill went to punch in the numbers of the item he wanted, Bayle would attempt to foil his junk-food plans by trying to push a different number, Bill straining to keep him away with one hand while labouring to hit the right numbers with the other. They were going up to Bayle's room to listen to Bill's favourite rock station. Bayle bet Bill a dollar they'd play a Canadian band before they were done eating. Bill said two dollars. Bayle said okay you're on. The bulky manila envelope sticking out of mail slot belonging to Bayle's room behind the counter stopped him cold.

"Hold on," he said. He leaned across the desk and pulled out the packet. AIR MAIL. REGISTERED. IMPORTANT DOCUMENTS WITHIN. Return address: Johnson, Johnson, and Bailey, Barristers and Solicitors, 194 Bay Street, Toronto, Ontario.

"Looks important," Bill said.

"Bad news usually does," Bayle replied. Pistol-waving Ronald Reagan in the movie still on the wall over the desk would know how to deal with this, he thought. Easy for you: you're armed, on horseback, and have never met Jane Warriner when she's thoroughly pissed.

"Bayle."

A voice, somewhere from above; a voice, Bayle turned to see, attached to a body hurtling down the stairs two steps at a time upon seeing Bayle at the bottom of them.

"Hey, Ron," Bayle said. "Ron, I don't know if you know James Duceeder's son —"

"We need to talk," Ron said, ignoring Bill's raised-hand "Hi" and grabbing Bayle by the coat sleeve, pulling him back down the hallway into the darkened and deserted diningroom. The dull glow of the empty coffee urns on the banquet table on the other side of the room gave off The Breakfast Corral's only light.

"What the fuck is going on, Bayle?" Ron said, taking a quick pull from a litre-and-a-half plastic bottle of Coke Classic. And scratching his cheek. And rubbing his left eye. And scratching his right ear. And blinking. Blinking fast.

"Are you all right, Ron? Maybe you should slow down on the caffeine. You seem a little —"

"Fuck what *seems*, Bayle, what I want to know is what's my shit doing in some old guy's house over in — Did you just say that that kid's father is James Duceeder, the dude with the Warriors, the guy that just got busted? Look, I'm only going to ask you one more time, and I want some answers: What's going on?"

"How did you know Duceeder was arrested?"

"I know people who know people, all right? I don't need to buy the fucking *Eagle Beagle* to find out what's going on in this dump."

"But how do you know it was the drugs you sold me that they caught Duceeder with?"

"How? How Bayle? *Because not too many people keep their fucking stash in a fucking peppermint tin mail-order imported from fucking Vermont, that's how.*"

"Oh, no."

"Oh, yes, Bayle, oh, yes. And guess how many people who've cruised through this hotel over the last ten years and seen that same peppermint tin on that front desk out there can positively identify it as the exact same kind that's right now plastic-bagged and labelled at the crime lab downtown?"

"But that's not true. Your aunt's got nothing to do with any of this."

"No shit, Sherlock. But once it takes them about two seconds to figure that out, who do you think they're going to start leaning on around here? Look at me, Bayle. Who do you think?"

Greasy shoulder-length hair. Motley Crue concert shirt. Pock-marked face. Torn black jeans. Yep, Ron sure did look like a drug dealer.

"I don't know what to say," Bayle said. "I can't tell you how bad I feel that it worked out like this. It wasn't supposed to, though, I can tell you that much. I feel bad for you, Ron."

"You feel bad for *me*?" Ron said. He stepped through the darkness, nose almost touching Bayle's. "You might want to save some of that sympathy for yourself, Bayle. I'm a businessman, you understand? A businessman with expanding commercial interests that extend far beyond dealing shit in this hole of a town. I'm a fucking entrepreneur with his sights firmly set on riding that information highway right to a media conglomerate's motherfucking motherload! And you've potentially complicated all that, Bayle. Potentially complicated that big time." Ron took a last, desperate guzzle from the pop bottle before slam-dunking it into the aluminum garbage can near the door.

"But I haven't gotten myself almost to the point where I need to be by working this hard for this long, nickel-and-diming twenty-four hours a day, seven days a week, at every all-night coffee shop and freezing cold park in the middle of winter in this miserable little town just to get hung out to dry because some stupid Canuck fuck is playing some kind of sick joke on the old man of that kid out there."

Running his fingers through his long hair, calming himself as best as his caffeine-cranked system would allow, "Like I told you, Bayle, I'm a businessman," Ron said. "If my business happens to suffer a loss because of some other business, you can be sure that I'm going to retaliate just like any other smart businessman would." Then, this time with the tips of their noses actually meeting, "But I always make sure to employ other people to do my retaliation for me," he said. "That way, I know if a specialist does the job, it'll get done right."

Ron's running shoes softly padding away down the

carpeted hallway, Bayle was alone. Alone with a mind involuntarily set upon churning out one scene of organized injury to his person after another, each successive image more menacing than the last, crow-bar attack to his knees giving way to pistol-whipping to his head giving way to fatal drive-by shooting while sitting-duck waiting at the bus stop.

Bayle stepped into the light of the hallway and leaned against the wall, slowly sliding down into an uncomfortable squat. Bill approached cautiously from the reception area.

"What's that guy's problem?" he said, thumb-pointing down at the end of the hall at the rampaging Ron kicking and muttering a losing fight to the pop machine.

"Too much Coke," Bayle said.

Bill nodded.

"C'mon," Bayle said, standing up, throwing his arm around the boy's shoulders, "I'm going to get washed up and you're going to put on this supposed kick-ass radio station of yours. And get your two bucks ready, buddy. You can't keep a good Canadian song quiet for long."

After a long, soapy shower and after changing into some of his cleaner dirty clothes, and with a bite, maybe two if the bites were small left in Bill's and his Snickers bars, and just as Winnipeg's own The Guess Who saved Bayle two of his few remaining *Toronto Living* dollars, Bayle by the small window of his room grinned Bill a toothy chocolate-covered victory smile and gave an energetic thumbs-up to playfully rub it in. Then looked out the window and blanched at seeing Warren and his red Ford Ranger pull up in front of The Range.

Chewing his own bar, sitting on the edge of the bed, Bill wasn't ready to hand over his two dollars quite yet. "No way," he said. "Listen to the words. It's about an *American* Woman."

Bayle didn't listen to the words of the song or even hear Bill tell him to; heard only the argument in his head that said: It's okay, Warren is a friend — But did Warren know about the stash? — But how could Warren know? — But if Ron knew, Warren could know — But Warren's not Ron — That's right, that's right, Warren's not Ron — Warren is a friend — A friend wanting to know where in the hell his cocaine-addicted friend Bayle was at seven p.m. tonight instead of at his crucial first counselling session.

Argument into action, Bayle sprinted to the door and locked the dead-bolt and chain, killed the lights and radio, and ordered Bill to be quiet, not a word, not a single word.

Not knowing why, but talking in a whisper and squatting down in the dark beside Bayle on the floor anyway, "What's going on, Peter?" Bill said. "Is it about the music? Was the music too loud?"

"Sshh. No, it's not about the music."

"What is it, then? What's going on?"

"Sshh, quiet now, nothing. Nothing's going on. Just be quiet, all right? Please?"

Bill shook his head yes, mouthed an unspoken okay. Bayle smiled, patted the boy on the shoulder. Bill waited. Bayle waited. Bill waited for what Bayle was waiting for. Bayle waited for Warren's knock. Seconds into years. Squatting. Waiting. Bill waiting. Bayle waiting. Waiting. Bill noisily slurped his root beer.

"Little fuckhead, I told you to be —"

BOOM BOOM BOOM

"Peter," Warren said. "I knew you were in there. Open this door at once."

BOOM BOOM BOOM

"Obviously I underestimated the severity of your problem, Peter. I thought I could trust you to be at the church tonight of your own volition, but clearly I made a misdiagnosis. That's a mistake that won't happen again. But that's behind us now, isn't it? And now it's time for us to get ourselves on the road to recovery. How about we go somewhere for a cup of tea and start in on that path together?"

Nothing.

BOOM BOOM BOOM.

"I say, Peter, you come out of there this very instant or

I'm going to go downstairs and get the pass key from Ron. Either way, we're going to start getting that monkey off your back. Tonight."

Still nothing.

One last BOOM BOOM BOOM.

"Very well then."

Warren's footsteps down the hall to the elevator. Elevator ding, door opening, closing, Warren going downstairs to get the key.

Bayle rubbed the tips of his fingers over his forehead up and down hard; closed his eyes and hurried to think of what to do next; hurried to no apparent end. Wasn't aware of the silent tears running down Bill's face until he heard the boy unsuccessfully trying to noiselessly lick them away, hands occupied with chip bag and can of root beer.

"Bill," Bayle said, "it's okay. Really. Don't worry. It's okay."

"I want to go home now," Bill said, tears still trickling down his checks. "My mom and dad ... they'll be home by now, right? My mom and dad will be home now won't they, Peter? They'll be at home waiting for me by now won't they? You said you'd take me home, Peter. I want to go home now. You said you'd take me home."

The elevator dinged its arrival. Bayle looked at Bill, Bill looked back at Bayle, the boy wiping his running nose on the sleeve of his Warriors sweatshirt.

So long, American woman. Bayle took out his wallet.

"Here, take this," Bayle said, pulling out a five-dollar bill and sticking it in Bill's hand. "Ask the guy who's going to come through that door any minute now to drive you home. He's a nice guy, don't worry. Tell him this is for gas money. And tell him ... tell him I'm sorry."

"Sorry for what?" Bill said, sniffling, taking the money.

Bayle thought for a second. He could hear the elevator doors open. "I don't know," he said. "Just tell him I'm sorry."

He grabbed his leather bag and laptop and pushed open the small window as far as it would go.

"Where are you going, Peter?"

Bayle threw one leg over the window frame and tested his footing on the rooftop. He could hear Warren putting the key in the door.

"Home," Bayle said. "I'm going home too."

38

WHEN HE called from the payphone at the gas station it seemed like Gloria already knew something had gone wrong. Didn't seem upset, though; didn't even want to hear about it right now. Just asked him where he was, told him to stay there, not to move, and said she'd be there to pick him up in ten minutes.

Bayle stepped out of the phone booth and pulled up the collar on his suit jacket and stuck his hands deep in its pockets. So hot for so long, the cold wind that was snapping tight the Texaco and American flags flying high over the gas station took a minute to work its way from body to brain. But when it did, a deep instinctive whiff of damp night earth and the shiver of alive that only a northerner can know. When Gloria beeped her arrival from the other side of the pumps Bayle was leaning rumpled against the phone booth looking like he'd just blown his load.

"How about this weather, eh?" he said, throwing his gear in the back seat, the V.W.'s windows rolled right up and dry heat blowing out of the plastic air vents. "It's like it came out of nowhere."

"You high, Bayle?" Gloria said, giving him a good going-over.

"What do you mean, '"Are you high, Bayle?'"

"Well, you're acting like you are, for one thing."

Bayle frowned. "Does a person have to be high on drugs to be happy for two seconds?"

Gloria put the car in gear and pulled into traffic. "Might not have to be," she said, "but it sure does seem like it helps sometimes."

They were sitting at the kitchen table at Davidson's house. No music played from the boombox on the counter and Davidson wasn't sitting in the wooden chair that stood empty between them.

Judging that it looked like he needed it, Gloria had taken Davidson's bottle of Wild Turkey down from the cupboard and splashed out a generous shot or two for him. Untouched the entire time Bayle recounted the evening's events, the glass sat there in front of him, like a dare. He told her everything, everything including how in deference to Ron's aunt potentially painfully incriminating peppermint tin Bayle was taking the first flight out of town

262

tomorrow morning. Everything, in fact, but how there'd been no Duceeder-led insurrection after all. Bayle didn't have the heart.

"I tried," he concluded, closing his eyes, lowering his head, equal parts simple fatigue and regret over how things had ended up. He attempted to remember with his nose just how inexplicably good the blowing-cold breeze outside had made him feel not thirty minutes before, but all he could smell was the bourbon.

"I know you did," Gloria said. "I can tell how you feel about Harry just by the way I sometimes catch you looking at me in the hospital."

Slightly panicking, Bayle picked up his glass and briefly considered it. Considered putting it back down. Considered this only briefly. Swallowed, gulped, then took another drink. "What do you mean?" he said.

"No reason to get all embarrassed, Bayle. You're just not able to hide the concern you're feeling for a sick friend, is all. Nothing wrong with that."

Bayle attempted to show a sympathetic smile but settled instead on another drink of bourbon, emptying the glass in the process. Holding it aloft, "Do you mind if I ...?"

"You stay sitting and let me get it," Gloria said, standing up and tenderly kneading Bayle's shoulders on the way to the counter. "Your night's been long enough as it is."

"Mind you, I'm not saying I'm happy about the way things turned out," she said, "because I know my plan would've worked." She came back to the table and placed the glass down in front of Bayle, braless breasts like knives slicing through one of Davidson's white cotton workshirts as she leaned over to do the pouring.

"But at least that sonofabitch Duceeder is gonna get his. Even if it didn't go off just like the way we planned and things aren't ever gonna be the same again, something good's come out of all of this anyway. And it's all because of you, Bayle."

All because of me. Golly gee yes. You should be real proud of yourself, Bayle, what with putting an innocent man behind bars and likely making his son the pariah of Hays County Junior High.

Bayle raised his glass in fine faux-toast fashion and gratefully felt the first tingling effects of nascent drunkenness; shivered slightly, thinking: Did Gloria just tenderly knead my shoulder?

"Gloria, who's Dan Fenton?" Bayle said, the first thing that came to mind that didn't have a part of Gloria's naked body attached to it.

In a tone appreciably cooler, "Dan Fenton's nobody," Gloria answered.

"That's what you said the last time I asked you."

"Well, I guess it's still true then, isn't it?"

The booze starting to weigh in now, "C'mon, Gloria," Bayle said. "Duceeder said —"

"Duceeder! Why are you listening to trash talk from that sonofabitch?"

"He wasn't trash talking," Bayle said. "It's just that I was running an errand for Harry a while back, dropping off something for Duceeder's kid, and Duceeder mentioned a guy named Dan Fenton, and when I asked you about him before you said —"

"And so you think just because Duceeder knows who Dan Fenton is he also knows everything there is to know about everything?"

Bayle held up his non-drinking hand. "I don't think anything. That's why I asked you who Dan Fenton was in the first place."

Gloria gave him a long, sceptical look. Eventually she went to the cupboard for another glass. When she came back she topped off Bayle's and then filled the other one halfway.

"You wanna know who Dan Fenton is? All right then. I'll tell you who Dan Fenton is." She raised her glass within an inch of her mouth, involuntarily getting a whiff of the whiskey. Set it back down.

"Harry wasn't gonna go and die in some jungle in Vietnam just because Uncle Sam felt like kicking a little

Communist ass, all right?" she said. "That was the one thing he knew for sure. That's when he decided to make it on up to Canada, in the fall of '68."

"Harry was a draft dodger?" Bayle said.

Gloria stared at him.

"Sorry," Bayle said.

She picked up her glass, this time taking a drink and holding it in her mouth for a couple of seconds with closed eyes before finally swallowing. Almost wincing, she braced herself and took another drink.

"He knew his mother had a sister up in Alberta she didn't talk to much because of the man she was married to, a wife-beater supposed to be, so that's where he went. Didn't know a soul until he got there, but she was glad to see her sister's boy anyway because family's family, right?"

Bayle nodded.

"Okay, so one of the reasons his aunt's so glad to see Harry is because she's divorced by now and she's got a sixteen-year-old son by the name of James — Harry's cousin. No more than a week or two around town and Harry's already got himself a job writing at the local newspaper, a car, a nice little apartment downtown — all the things her son needs to see a man can do if he puts his mind to it and does more than drink beer and watch hockey on T.V. And everything's okay for a long time. Harry's not having to try and kill no Vietnamese and no Vietnamese trying to kill Harry, and his aunt's son and his best friend, a boy by the name of Dan, Dan Fenton, they both practically worshipping Harry. They stop skipping classes at the high school, both of them get themselves part-time jobs at the local arena, even start wearing side burns just like Harry." Gloria laughed. "You imagine that? Harry with sideburns? I've seen the pictures, I swear it's true." Bayle laughed too. They each sipped their drinks.

"But this Dan Fenton, he gets into some trouble with a girl from the high school. And not only does he put the girl in a family way, but if that's not bad enough, she's a girl from the reservation nearby, and that's something white boys from

265

good families just aren't supposed to do in Medicine Hat, Alberta, in 1968. Probably still not supposed to do. Doesn't matter none that the two of them say they're in love and wanting to keep the baby and wanting to get married and all the rest of it. Dan's parents just aren't gonna have their baby boy ruin his life because some squaw slut can't keep her panties on. So they think they're real smart and got things all figured out by convincing the girl to let them pay for an abortion in Calgary and getting her to agree to never see their son again. But what happens is the girl takes the five hundred dollars and runs off to Toronto to have the kid, and Dan, he joins the Canadian Armed Forces so that when the baby gets born he and the girl can get married and he'll be an officer and a gentleman and they'll all live happily ever after. And just before he enlists he gives Harry — Harry, mind you, not his friend James — all the money he's got saved up from working at the rink and asks him to hold on to it for him and to give it to his girl if anything should happen to him. Of course Harry tells him to put it in the bank or just give it to the girl now since she could probably use it, even if it is just four or five hundred bucks, but Dan ... Dan, he watches too many war movies and he wants Harry to keep it for him. Practically begs him to. Forces him to. Harry finally says okay, he'll do it, and thinks that's the end of that. Except that Dan gets shipped over to Vietnam within twelve weeks and is home wearing a toe-tag in fourteen."

Bayle looked down into his drink, Gloria too.

"After the funeral, Harry and his cousin try to get ahold of the girl as best they can, but the address they got isn't hers no more and nobody down in Toronto has heard of a pregnant Indian girl from Medicine Hat. Harry, he doesn't want this boy's money, so he tries to give it to Dan's parents. But they think he had something to do with Dan enlisting and dying over there so they say they don't want any Goddamn guilt money from a Goddamn draft dodger and slam the door in his face. Harry does the only sensible thing he can think to do: throws the money in the bank and forgets about it."

Gloria had finished her drink, Bayle only half. She lifted the bottle and poured nearly as much into his as she did into hers, bourbon quick to the brim of Bayle's glass and spilling over the edges. Gloria didn't notice. She wasn't looking at Bayle anymore, only at her own drink. Bayle watched the pool of liquid on the formica table slowly tide his way.

"Years go by and Harry moves away from Medicine Hat and gets a better job at a bigger paper in Edmonton. A nicer car, a nicer apartment, all of it. Lives his life. But when Carter, President Carter, when he makes it okay for everybody who was against the war and went north to go back, Harry decides it's time to come home."

"But why?" Bayle said. "I mean, it sounds like things were going pretty well for him up in Canada."

"People go home, Bayle. Don't need any reason. They just do."

Bayle nodded; took a sip and nodded again.

"But Harry, he feels sorry for his cousin still stuck back there in Medicine Hat, his cousin James who's done nothing with his life since Harry left except get his high school diploma and be a gopher for the junior hockey team. So Harry says he'll take him along with him when he goes south. Help him get settled, try to use his sportswriting connections to get him work in the hockey business." Gloria paused. "Harry takes Goddamn Duceeder along."

"Duceeder?" Bayle said. "You mean James as in James Duceeder? As in Harry and Duceeder are cousins?" Gloria didn't hear him.

"And then one day ...." She took a long swallow of bourbon — too long — and gagged slightly at trying to keep it down.

Steadying herself, taking a deep breath, "And then one day," she continued, "strung-out so bad I was almost hoping I'd get caught and somebody'd show me some mercy and put a cap between my eyes just to save me the trouble, I decide to car-jack Harry's truck on a Friday afternoon on the hottest day in August anybody around here has ever seen. And Harry — I think he's going for a piece when he reaches across to the glove box, right? So I put my blade right upside his kidney and tell him not to move unless he wants to feel seven inches of steel inside him — you know what Harry says to me when he pulls out his flask? 'You look like hell, woman. Have some of the bird.' I didn't know whether to stick him or laugh and have a drink."

"You didn't knife him, though."

"No, I didn't."

"You took a drink?"

"I took a drink."

"Did you laugh?"

"I wasn't quite ready for any laughing yet. But that flask of his passed back and forth between us until it was empty and we needed another bottle. And another bottle took us back to Harry's place, and that one put me to sleep on his couch where I woke up a few hours later with a splitting headache and a note on the pillow from Harry saying he'd be back in a few hours, that he was gone to the rink to cover the hockey game, and for me to use the bathroom to get cleaned up and to help myself to whatever I wanted in the fridge. I can't believe it. Broke and practically shivering for a fix by now, and here I am left all alone in the house. Except there isn't anything to steal! Black-and-white T.V. from God knows when, got no stereo, no computer, no cash stashed around the place as far as I could see. I finally just took the rest of the bottle of Wild Turkey and cursed the old bastard's name."

Forming a V with his hands on the tabletop, Bayle tried to stop the stream of spilt bourbon from his glass now threatening to run onto the floor. He turned back most of it, but some still managed to drip over the edge and onto his jeans.

"The next time I saw Harry I was lying on his front step at six o'clock the next morning with a serious case of withdrawal and holding on to an empty Wild Turkey bottle."

"What for?" Bayle said. "You knew he didn't have any money."

"I ask myself that."

"And?"

"And I suppose I'm still asking. And after Harry put me to bed and figures out he can't keep me drunk forever, he calls around and gets the name of a place in Kansas City that's supposed to have something like a ninety percent success rate with users. Except it costs twenty-one hundred dollars that Harry doesn't got. So Harry, he tries to get the money everywhere he can, but —"

"But wait, wait, hold on," Bayle said. "Go back. Why? Why would Harry care enough about a complete stranger — somebody who only the day before might have knifed him — to bother and try to scrap together that kind of money? Don't you ask yourself that one too?"

"Sometimes, yeah."

Both glasses empty, Gloria and Bayle each went to pick up the bottle at the same time, fingertips brushing at point of bottle-gripping contact. Bayle instantly pulled back his hand. Gloria calmly poured out two more big ones, dripping the last of the bourbon into Bayle's glass.

"Sometimes I do," she said. "But mostly I'm just thankful. Harry saved my life. If it wasn't for him eventually getting that twenty-one hundred dollars together, him remembering the five hundred and something of Dan Fenton's he put in the bank way back in 1968 and that after doing some digging it turning out to be nearly two thousand — that, and driving me to Kansas City in his pickup truck with the heat turned on full blast with the windows shut tight in the middle of August, me shivering like it's ten below zero and him doling me out codeine cough syrup every half hour to try and keep me from having a fit — I wouldn't be here talking to you right now. Maybe not that night on his step, maybe not the night after that, but sometime, some night not too long after, I'd be dead. You reach out for help like I did and then someone comes along and gives you your life back like Harry did, you tend not to think too much about the why of it all so much as just the fact that it happened. The fact that it happened and, no matter how bad things get after that, how glad you are you're here and not ... I don't know ... wherever it is you are when

269

you're not. But maybe you've got to be lucky enough to be saved like I've been to know what I'm talking about. Or maybe save somebody else." Gloria took a long drink from her glass. "Bayle?"

Nothing.

Placing her hand on Bayle's knee, leaning across the table to better see what was the matter, "Bayle? What's wrong?" Gloria said. "Bayle?"

Bayle looked up from the Rorschach bourbon-blot on his pant leg. Saw Gloria's fingers on his other knee, her leaning face, coming-close eyes, lips ....

Six seconds later and both of them with water in their eyes, Gloria softly crying at the kitchen sink with her back turned to Bayle, the sting of her hard, loud slap reddening the entire left-hand side of his face and tearing his eyes.

Gloria finally turned around from the counter. "Why did you want to go and do something like that?" she said. She wasn't crying anymore, but some of the tears she had were running down her cheeks. "Why?"

"I don't know. I guess I thought you wanted me to," Bayle said.

"You guess you thought I wanted you to?" The drying tears were still there, but the vulnerability he'd never seen before and that just a moment previous had gone with them was suddenly now gone. Long gone.

"And how the fuck do you figure that?" she said, crossing her arms. "You're saying that I led you on, Bayle? Is that what you're saying?

"I guess not, no."

"No guessing about it."

"No."

"No is right. I'm with Harry, Bayle."

Bayle hung his head. "Yes."

"You think just because Harry's sick and in the hospital and not here to see what's going on that I'm gonna betray him? Betray him and me and everything we've got between us?"

"No."

270

"No is right."

Head still down, Bayle picked up his glass of bourbon off the kitchen table. Set it back down. "But what has your having gotten clean have to do with Duceeder?"

Incredulous, "Christ, Bayle, what —? I think you better go home now. Right now."

"But I want to know."

"I think you should go home now, Bayle. Your story-time privledges have been revoked."

Bayle looked up. "I've go to know, Gloria," he said, almost begging. "I've got to know how it all fits together."

"How all what fits together?"

"I don't know. *Everything.*"

Gloria stared, hesitated; hesitated, but could see and hear Bayle's desperation. She sat back down at the table and looked at him long. Took a drink from her glass and looked at him again and shook her head as if she didn't quite believe what she was going to do. Took a deep breath and shook her head one last time. Finally spoke.

"So I got clean, all right? And Harry, somehow he finds out that the one thing my mother did for me before I split for good was sign me up for figure-skating lessons when I was 13 because one day when she was good and high and vegging out in front of the T.V. she convinced herself that Dorothy Hamil was the most beautiful white woman she ever did see and that I might have a shot at being a real lady if only I learned to skate like little Miss Dorothy. So Harry talks to Duceeder and convinces him that what the team needs is a mascot to get the fans more into the game. And before too long I become the Warrior. Gloria the Warrior."

Bayle smiled. Gloria almost too.

"Yeah, I know, there's the costume and all the rest of it, but believe me, it still beats working the late shift at Taco Bell five nights a week for five bucks an hour or dealing dope and every minute wondering whether you'll live to see tomorrow night. And I always did like skating, you know? Sometimes, when it seems like it's just me and the ice out there, speeding so fast and going round and round in big perfect circles, the air so fresh, so clean, not hearing a thing but the sounds of the ice giving way underneath my skates, it feels ... good. It just feels good. Even if that crackhead bitch was the one who got me started.

"So anyway everything's just hunky dory. Until one day a couple years back Harry comes home from covering the team three sheets to the wind at two in the afternoon and with a bee in his bonnet something awful. After enough jawing I get it out of him that the girl Dan Fenton had the baby with all those years ago, she's living out in B.C. now and she's gotten ahold of Duceeder that very morning after hearing about the money Dan set aside for her — don't ask me how, probably Dan's parents — and she's wanting it and wanting it right now because her and Dan's boy is twenty-something now and she's wanting to help send him to — get ready for this, now — chef school, the boy's big dream. But Harry doesn't have the money anymore."

"Couldn't he take out a loan or something?" Bayle said.

Gloria sat down her drink. "Take out a two-thousand-dollar loan so he could hand it over to some complete stranger so she can pay the way for her boy so he can play at being a baker?"

"I though you said he wanted to be a chef."

"Chef, baker, motherfucking hot dog vendor, have I been talking to myself all night here, Bayle? Harry used that money to save my life. Not to send me off to college or fix my car or get me a nose job. *To save my life.* Don't you think that's a little more important than some farmboy strapping on an apron?"

"Of course it's more important, it's just that ...."

"Just that what?" Gloria said.

"Well, just that it really wasn't Harry's money to give away. I mean, technically speaking."

Gloria looked at Bayle and slowly shook her head. Picked up her drink. Looked at him one more time. Drank.

"So what happened?" Bayle said.

Gloria looked up from her glass, the effect of the rare

evening of drinking showing in her face. She picked up the glass and drained it. Spoke as if performing the last tiresome task of the day.

"What happened next is real simple. Duceeder kept asking Harry for the money and Harry kept saying he didn't know what the hell Duceeder was talking about, that he doesn't even remember where he put that money. Until one day Duceeder somehow tracks down the bank and finds out that Harry withdrew all the money, with interest, the year before. Harry and Duceeder weren't exactly on the best of terms by this point anyway — Duceeder had started getting in tight with Able and Munson and all the rest of that crew by then. And the only reason Harry even goes by Duceeder's place anymore is to see his nephew Billy. But the thing with Dan's widow just makes things worse. Then those articles came out that Harry wrote on the Bunton Center and then the rumours about the team moving started and, well, that only made it final. Duceeder forgets all about all the good Harry did for him over the years and all of a sudden Harry's a no-good, trouble-making communist or something. And that's just about all there is to tell."

Bayle picked up his glass but there wasn't anything in it. Went for the bottle but it was empty too.

"Of course, none of that bothers Harry none — the less he has to talk to Duceeder the better — but Duceeder all of a sudden doesn't let him see Billy no more, and that does bother Harry some because Harry, he doesn't have much family left, you see, and even though that boy's not really his nephew, he treats him like he is. And from what Harry says, that boy, Billy, he's all right. In spite of who his father is. "

"I know," Bayle said. "He's a good kid."

"Harry tell you about him?"

Bayle shook his head. "Tonight, after they arrested Duceeder, I tried to make sure he got home okay."

Gloria's tired face brightened. "They took Duceeder away during the game? Right in front of his own son?"

"It wasn't pretty," Bayle said. "But all things considered, the kid actually handled the whole situation pretty well, I think."

"All right!" Gloria said, clapping her hands. "Let that boy see first hand what kind of man he's got for a father."

"He didn't do anything wrong, Gloria. I was the one who planted the drugs there, remember?"

"He may not be guilty of what he got arrested for, but he's sure enough guilty for what he did to Harry, how he deprived that poor man of his livelihood, the way he practically drove him into the hospital."

Bayle held his tongue so Gloria could keep on believing.

Gloria picked up the empty glasses and carried them to the sink. Turned on the faucet and squirted a yellow shot of dish soap in each. "Anyway, the way I figure it, thankfully it won't make much difference one way or the other to Harry now, anyway."

"Harry's all right, isn't he?" Bayle said.

"Harry's just the same as he was yesterday: no better, no worse. But I've got a feeling, I've got a real good feeling, that when I visit him tomorrow and tell him all about the team, him not covering them won't be such a blow anymore, won't eat him up inside like it's been doing, you know? I've got a good feeling that when that happens he'll be back on his feet again in no time."

Playing along, "Tell him what all about the team?" Bayle said.

Gloria turned around at the sink. "Didn't you hear?"

Bayle shook his head.

"The Warriors, they're moving. They announced it right after the game on WUUS. To Texas, they said. All of us, we're all done now, Bayle. It's over. For everybody."

PART THREE

39

THE NEXT day's *Eagle* flew with Bayle back home. The aborted hockey article was dumped in an airport trash can just before boarding.

News of the move was all over the newspaper, from its front page announcement, to the Local Scene ("*Local Business Braces Itself for Economic Affect of Warriors' Departure*"), to, of course, the sports section, where a hastily constructed capsulized account of the team's history filled up the entire top of the first page. The history lesson sat directly on top of Bayle's report of last night's game. The placement seemed fitting.

But right beside a short article reporting no new leads in the search for members of C.A.C.A.W. there was still room left over for one more page-one, Warrior-related story. The headline read *Warrior G.M. Arrested on Charge of Drug Trafficking*, the story going on to explain how Duceeder and his wife were each looking at twelve years of federal penitentiary time if convicted. The picture directly underneath of Duceeder entering the police station by himself, cuffed hands raised to his face unsuccessfully shielding his identity, said it all. Bayle crushed the paper into a messy ball and jammed it under his seat.

At Pearson International in Toronto nobody was there to greet him. Passengers were instructed to keep their seat belts on until the light at the end of the cabin said not to and the taxiing plane came to a complete stop, but everyone stood up anyway, scrambling around like panicked squirrels and clawing after their luggage in the overhead compartments and sizing up the competition next to them for the race toward the nearest exit. Bayle stayed strapped into his seat until the plane was empty. A flight attendant came by to ask him if he'd forgotten anything. Bayle said he hadn't like he wished he had and moved down the aisle toward the big hole in the side of the airplane where the captain and the other flight attendants stood around looking at their watches and tapping their feet while waiting to wish the guy in 46B who looked like he hadn't slept or shaved in three days a nice day and thank him for flying with them today.

The airport shuttle delivered him as far as the western-most subway stop; from there, rapid transit, right downtown.

H E R O E S

Coming up the stairs of the St. George station: the cold, grey, metallic-tasting everything of an enormous November downtown Toronto sky and an explosion of scurrying people sprung everywhere from somewhere making Bayle's head swim. Swim with people crossing the road, shaking hands and parting, shaking hands and back-slapping and walking off together, standing and talking calmly under elm and oak, bicycling along (patiently ringing their bells), jogging by (cheerfully mouthing words to songs only their headphoned ears could hear). Even — because St. George street borders the university — the odd odd academic type with pointed silver beard (stroked with every third step) and dangling red scarf sucking on a pipe (cherry-tobacco: sweet) with a thick hardcover stuck right there underneath his nose strolling his way through the throng of accommodating sidewalk strollers.

Bayle kept walking, swimming head making for eyes-everywhere gawking — the intoxication of a tourist in his own town — walking around and between as best he could dog-walkers, hand-holders, hockey-bag-and-stick-toters, chalk-on-pavement hopscotchers, after-dinner-tokers, hairy pan-handlers (always polite — answering, when told you have no spare change to give, "Thanks and have a good night anyway!"), and, finally, ending up at 177 Spadina Road, the three-storey brick house divided into six bachelor apartments that Bayle called home. Or, rather, had.

His key to the front door worked just fine, but the one to number three, on the second floor, Bayle's flat, proved a little more difficult. Actually, didn't fit anymore. Mr. Hart in number one on the first floor, occupant and superintendent, seemed more sad than angry at Bayle's prolonged indifference to his repeated but polite pleas for nearly three months worth of overdue rent, at the unfortunate but necessary decision to evict.

"And my stuff?" Bayle asked.

Another sad frown. "Until yesterday, I'd kept it all for you nice and neat right downstairs in the basement."

"And now?"

"Let me get the legal papers. A lawyer by the name of Johnson, if I recall, him and a moving man came by yesterday afternoon and took everything away, lock, stock, and barrel. I don't know what sort of trouble you're in, Peter, but I can't believe what they done to your things is right and square. Let me go inside and get the legal papers."

"Don't bother," Bayle said. "I've got my own set."

Handshake, best wishes, no hard feelings.

Laptop and bag in hand, Bayle waded back out into the night, delicate yellow covering of a slightly chilling setting sun transformed in the short time it took him to join the ranks of Toronto's increasing homeless population into a bitterly fucking cold Canadian night.

He walked to where Spadina Road met Bloor and set down his baggage on the pavement to try and warm his freezing fingers inside his pant pockets. Gloves for his hands, a place to put down his stuff, a warm bed for his head for the night: As suspected all along, the philosophers had been lying — *these* were the Big Questions.

Anti-intellectual thought thunk, who, then, but Smith, Bayle's thesis advisor, striding down Bloor Street with Italian-leather-gloved hands dug deep in the caverns of his enormous black overcoat with matching black felt beret tilted at just the right angle — the beret and tilt were legit; Smith and his wife cathedral and castle-hopped on the continent every summer and sabbatical they could. Without missing a beat:

"Okay, here's the deal, Bayle," Smith said. "I'll promise not to harangue you and demand an explanation for your presenting yourself *on the night before the most important day in a young scholar's life* because, obviously, no explanation could possibly suffice. Let us just hope that you've been holed up somewhere studying very hard for your defence. That would at least explain your looking like hell even more than you usually do. And tell me that you *did* give the medieval period a good going-over as I asked you to. Believe me, I sympathize entirely with your indifference toward all things Catholic, but you know as well as I do that Professor Allen is somehow going to manage to bring something up about the Middle Ages simply because the old goat doesn't know much about anything else. And how about if we just pretend that the revised copies of your thesis that you were going to have delivered to me two weeks ago got lost in the mail, all right? Thankfully, as I have tried to impart to you for more than a year now, there was nothing that needed revision anyway, so I took the liberty of having my own copy duplicated and distributed to the other members of your committee. Where are your gloves and hat, Bayle?"

"All the stuff in my apartment, it's ... I mean, all my ...."

"All your clothes are in lock-up somewhere because you've been evicted, correct? I thought it might be something like that when I stopped by your flat and the woman who answered your door claimed to never have heard of you. Not that you won't get them back, I'm sure, but except for your books and personal items, I can't say it's that much of a loss, really. You're going to have to buy a new suit for your interview with Hunter next week in Waterloo, anyway. Besides, you've only been evicted. There are worse crimes."

Yeah, Bayle thought. Like embezzlement, entrapment .... Then thought: Hunter?

"I never called Hunter," Bayle said. "I mean, I called him, but we never actually set up an appointment. I mean, I tried, but —"

"But you were understandably far too occupied chronicling the fascinating exploits of your hockey team to actually do anything more than leave a single message on his answering machine. I know. But luckily for us he had to be suddenly hospitalized a couple of weeks ago to correct an irregular heartbeat and, until recently, was entirely out of commission. When he started feeling better and began answering his phone again I told him you were simply too considerate to bother him with your merely professional concerns during his convalescence and it turns out he found your placing of his undisturbed return to health over improving your job prospects admirable in a young whippersnapper like yourself. Anyway, you *do* have an interview, he's even *more* interested in meeting you now, you *will* be wearing a new suit purchased with, I'm sure, substantial monies received from whoring around for your girlfriend's magazine, and you *will* get the job. Your letters of recommendation have been sent ahead and, as I said, I've read through your entire manuscript again. It's brilliant, Peter. You've captured the very soul of Empiricus. Even if the old boy would deny having one, of course."

"Jane's not my girlfriend anymore," Bayle said.

Smith took off his beret and ran a gloved hand over his balding, slightly sweating head. Bare hands still stuck in his pockets, Bayle began to slightly stutter-step in place, trying to keep warm.

"Where have you been staying then?" Smith asked. "I assume you've been back for some time now."

"I've ... been around," Bayle said.

It began to snow.

Smith put his beret back on, suitably adjusted it, and picked up Bayle's bag and laptop. He talked as he walked, Bayle keeping up alongside.

"I'll lend you my running outfit — it's freshly laundered, not to worry — and after a thorough hosing down in the shower and maybe if you're your usual charming self, Myra will put out an extra plate on the table and throw your clothes in the washer. About that sad excuse for a jacket there's not much that can be done between now and ten o'clock tomorrow morning so I'll have to lend you one of mine. We would appear to be about the same size. After dinner you can use my office to get some final studying done. There's a fold-out couch in there. I'll set the alarm for eight. The room is booked for ten but we should be ready to go fifteen minutes before then."

Inside the Spadina subway station Smith dropped a transit token in the cash box and walked through the silver turnstile, lifting Bayle's gear over top. Bayle on the other side picked through a palmful of American nickels, dimes, and pennies, not coming up with the necessary fare no matter how hard he tried.

Smith leaned over and dropped another token in the box. "Send me a nice tie when you get settled in Waterloo," he said, leaving Bayle to carrying his own luggage.

"Thanks," Bayle said.

"And please, please, at least skim through Part Two, Volume Two, of Copleston's *A History of Philosophy*. There are eleven chapters in there on Aquinas and I just know Allen will figure out a way to work him in somehow. It never ceases to amaze me how otherwise intelligent people can always find a way to put Christ's nose into all sorts of places He most certainly doesn't belong."

40

MYRA, SMITH'S wife, an architect
and accomplished amateur cellist, was kind,
intelligent, and charming. Their two children, Brad
and Zelda, ages 11 and 13, polite and bright. The
large house in Rosedale, while stylishly turn-of-the-
century and exhibiting the family's bookish, cultured
interests, never approached the pretentious. Bayle sat
at the kitchen table in clean grey sweatpants, a jazz
piano solo softly tinkling from unseen speakers, a
savoury wash of basil, garlic, and romano warmth
rising from his plate of steaming handmade linguini
gently massaging his face. Like the grade-schooler
who is astounded to spot his teacher at the grocery
store or shopping mall, part of Bayle felt certain that

the ball-busting academic he'd known at the university for the last several years simply couldn't be the same man sitting across the table from him patiently discussing the origins of the Israeli-Arab conflict with his daughter and joking with his son about the ineptitude of the Maple Leafs' present goaltending situation.

Smith poured his wife another glass of Casillero del Diablo. "Speaking of hockey, I bet you didn't know we've got a veritable expert staying with us tonight, Brad," he said to his son.

"Yes," Myra said, silently thanking her husband for his attention with a soft smile, "what exactly were you doing down in the U.S., Peter? I know where you were and that it had something to do with hockey, but Tom was a little sketchy on the details."

Bayle looked up from his plate of pasta, jarred from the simple joy of just being clean and warm and full of good food and a little buzzed on the red wine. He cleared his throat. "Basically I just spent a little time down there with a minor-league hockey team called the Warriors for a piece of journalism on the how and why of the spread of hockey in the lower States."

Smith's son set down his water glass, Bayle's stock suddenly rising from merely-aspiring-another-version-of-his-dad to a guy who got to hang out with a hockey team.

"And what kind of hows and whys did you come up with?" Myra said.

Bayle picked up the half-full bottle of wine and asked if anybody wanted a refill.

"No," Smith said, taking the bottle out of his hand and setting it back down on the table. "And neither do you. Not if you don't want the Middle Ages to actually seem that long ago tomorrow morning at ten."

Bayle slowly nodded his head in agreement but still eyed the bottle of Chilean red. Looked up to see the whole family, forks in neutral, waiting upon his answer. He could barely remember the question.

"I'm sorry, Myra," he said. "It's been a long day. What was that again?"

"The hows and whys, Bayle," Smith said. "The hows and whys of your trip."

"Right. The hows and whys of my trip. Well, after a lot of careful consideration, after a lot of research and investigation, I came to the conclusion that ... the whys most definitely outnumber the hows. Outnumber them big time. Outnumber them big time every time."

Myra smiled politely, drank her wine. Smith and his daughter returned to their pasta. Only Brad hung on a little longer before he eventually gave up, too. Without looking up from his meal, "The Middle Ages, Bayle," Smith said. "And don't forget about Aquinas."

Bayle thanked everyone for a wonderful meal and retired to the study.

Where Smith sure had a lot of books. Yes, sir (insert here long, slow whistle of appreciation at sheer enormity of number of editions), a whole lot of books.

And after scanning the spines on several of them and even taking a couple off the shelves to peruse the back — and after losing a best-four-out-of-seven of tic-tac-toe to himself scribbled on the front page of his thesis — Bayle spent the rest of the evening actually absorbed in one of the volumes until Smith knocked on the door of the study at eleven-thirty to say goodnight and deliver Bayle's washed-and-dried clothes. Bayle attempted to slide Smith's 1959 undergraduate yearbook from the University of Western Ontario down between the armrest and seat cushions of the couch

"Well, how's it going?" Smith said. He laid Bayle's clean clothes and a fresh towel for the morning over the end of the couch Bayle wasn't sitting on.

"Good," Bayle said. "Good."

Smith frowned. He walked around to the other end and pulled out the book. He held up the slim blue volume with one hand and, mute with amazement, could only point to it with the other.

"I didn't know you were studying to be a priest," Bayle said.

"No, and now that you do, you're just that much closer to acing your defence tomorrow, aren't you? I mean, really, Bayle ...." Smith dropped the yearbook on the floor and sat down at the wooden swivel chair at his desk with his back to Bayle, elbows on the desk top, chin in his hands. Bayle picked up the book and set it down on the couch beside him.

"You know," Smith said, still not facing him, "the only way I can get my mind around you sometimes is by thinking that you're either the coolest, most cocksure sonofabitch I've ever met who just might be Empiricus incarnate, or you really just don't care." He swivelled around in his chair and looked at Bayle. Bayle was looking at the yearbook.

"Why did you want to be a priest and why did you decide not to?"

"Did you hear what I just said, Bayle?"

"I heard you. Did you hear me? You go first."

Smith considered this for a moment. Rolled his eyes.

"I came from a little town in northeastern Ontario, right along on the Quebec border, where you were either Catholic or you were Indian. We weren't Indian so I was Catholic. Simple as that. My father, besides being an usher and serving on every church council he could and being the one who woke me up every morning at a quarter-to-six to go to mass, was the editor of the little newspaper we had there, so he made sure I got a decent enough education, that I didn't end up like the other guys who usually ended up working in the mines or joining the army. He sent me off to study philosophy and theology at Western when I was 17 so I could become a priest and get him just that much closer to God. That's my theory, anyway. But in second year I took one of my electives in analytic philosophy because the title of the course sounded impressive and worlds collided. Over the next couple of years I still took a bunch of theology courses and even got one of my majors in it so the old man would continue to foot my tuition and board, but after that one class I knew I wanted to do philosophy and that the study of theology was basically much ado about nothing."

Smith leaned back in his chair, gave a little that's-all-there-is-to-tell shrug and half-smile.

"That's it?" Bayle said.

"That's it."

"Losing your faith: it was just that simple?"

"Sorry to disappoint you," Smith said.

Bayle put the yearbook on his lap; flipped until he came to a picture of Smith in a group shot of the International Student Christian Fellowship, UWO chapter. He put his finger on the picture and shoved the book at Smith.

"The yearbook and that picture are both from first year," Smith said. "Before my Age of Enlightenment."

"But it's *you*, right?"

"Of course, it's me. What's your point?"

Bayle closed the yearbook. Leaned back against the couch and closed his eyes.

"So what's your story, Bayle?"

Bayle didn't answer.

"Well?" Smith said.

Eyes open, "Biggest day of a young scholar's life tomorrow, right?" Bayle said. "And I guess that Aquinas isn't going to read itself."

41

BOY-MAN IN a bubble.

Boy-man: Bayle.

Bubble: lip-blown (but by imbibing, not the usual way, by blowing); moderately impenetratable; and, if a constant source of eighty-proof bubble-juice continues to go down the gullet, enough of not others and other things outside the bubble to make moment to moment kind of all right. Or at least slightly more so than it might be if non-bubbled otherwise.

And, for the occasional diversion, five salt peanuts floating on their backs on an undisturbed draft beer lake with an ear tuned to the conversation at the bar a few empty tables away.

"C'mon, Stan, give me a beer. On the house. Bitch was on crack and stole my coat. Right here, right on your premises."

"Was that a new coat, Jimmy?"

"Did I say it was a new coat, Lloyd? Did I? No, I didn't. It was my old coat, the same coat I've been wearing ever since I don't know when. The same coat I've never had any reason to complain of. Does it gotta be a new coat for Stan here to compensate me for a crime committed at his very own establishment? All I'm asking for is one bottle of beer. Aside from the financial loss, that coat had great sentimental value to me, you know."

Before Jimmy has a chance to again relate how his father and his father before him proudly wore the raggedy-ass Sears and Roebuck castoff everybody around the bar knows he got for free at the Salvation Army at College and Spadina a month before, Stan Knott, owner and proprietor of Knott's Place, opens the glass-covered door of the refrigerator behind the bar and pulls out and cracks open a Labatt Ice.

Setting the bottle down on the bar but not letting go when the old man eagerly latches onto it, "One beer, Jimmy," Knott says. "And not one more sob-story about drug addicts stealing your flea-bitten coat, no tales about long gone relatives, and for Christ's sake drink it by yourself, over by the juke box."

With eyes only for his beer, Jimmy rapid-yeses like a chicken at its feed and motors over to a table in the far corner as fast as his spindly legs can carry him.

The only one left standing at the bar, Lloyd — another daytime drinker with a varicose soul but with a dependable source of disability cheques that make beer-begging anecdotes unnecessary — asks, "How can you tell if somebody's on crack, Stan?"

Knott opened up the place at noon and it's only a quarter-to-three now, but he peels the cellophane off the day's second pack of Rothman's Unfiltered, ignoring the bold black warning on the package that kindly cautions that smoking could be hazardous to the health of his baby. Lit up, he snaps shut the lid of his silver lighter and inhales deep like a suffocating man taking in pure oxygen. At an even six-foot and three hundred and twenty-five pounds, he doesn't need to employ a bouncer.

"Anybody that sucks my cock without my having to pay them," Knott says. "That's how you can tell if somebody's on crack."

Lloyd snorts into his pint of draft beer and adjusts his torn galosh on the foot rail underneath the bar. "The Price is Right" soundlessly plays on the fuzzy T.V. hanging over the pool table. Bob Barker can't give away the self-cleaning ovens and sparkling sets of golf clubs fast enough.

Knott glances up at the television, flicks his ash into an empty draft glass, looks out the window. Through a driving, freezing November rain he watches the Queen Street steetcar stop out front taking some on, letting some off. Another streetcar will be back in another ten minutes to do the exact same thing. Knott will be standing just about where he's standing right now to watch the whole glorious affair happen. And happen again. And again.

Back to the bubble. (One of the chief reasons for diversions being temporary relief from desiring any more diversions.)

But the bubble needs blowing. And blowing means more bubble-juice. Must feed the bubble, Bayle.

"Same as before, Professor?" Knott says, taking the empty beer pitcher and shotglass Bayle has carried to the bar.

Bayle nods into his shirt and pulls out a ball of bills and fistful of loonies, twonies, and other, less-valuable coins, spilling the entire clattering sum onto the bartop. Knott counts out how much Bayle owes him for another pitcher and shot of C.C. and pushes the rest back across the bar.

Refilling Bayle's jug from a tap beside the cash register, "You might want to think about putting your change inside your wallet, Professor," Knott says.

Knott's been calling Bayle "Professor" ever since the first time the normally quiet/occasionally berserk but always generously tipping Bayle came into his place utterly wasted and alone one night near closing time a year or so ago and matter-of-factly announced, when asked by one of the old boys at the bar what he did for a living, "I don't do anything. I'm going to be a university professor instructing others in the wisdom of scepticism. That's the wisdom of not doing anything."

Stuffing the bills into his wallet and dumping the coins into his pocket, Bayle nods again, his head like an anvil teetering on a neck made out of rubber. He motions Knott his way with a slow-moving index finger. Knott moves closer but Bayle keeps curling his drooping finger so he'll come even nearer. As far as his enormous stomach allows him to Knott leans across the bar, Bayle whispering what to him is a whisper but, to Knott, who never takes his first drink before six p.m., is the tell-tale sign of the drunk who is approaching that crested point of intoxication where a whisper to the soused is a scream to everyone else. "Please don't call me that anymore, Stan," Bayle says. "Professor, I mean. Please don't call me that."

Still leaning, Knott nods understandingly, the first rule of running a successful tavern being that the drunken customer is always right. He eases himself back upright into his customary standing position behind the bar and looks up at the muted "Price is Right" people continuing to hop up and down. The Queen streetcar rumbles to a stop outside the window and Knott lights up another cigarette. Bayle carries his pitcher of beer and shot glass of whiskey back to his table by the jukebox.

A quarter slid down the juke box slot rolls deep into the wired guts of the machine, any combination of a single letter followed by two numbers getting you a song. A randomly selected letter followed by two just as arbitrarily chosen numbers and, suddenly, pounding out of the juke box speakers, music. E-34 buys you something from *The Best of BTO*, apparently, "Takin' Care of Business," specifically. And at this, his entirely uncalculated song selection, Bayle grins *bona fide* for the first time all day. Taking care of business, oh, yeah. And working overtime, you bet.

Fat biographical tomes like to tell how personage X performed life-altering act Y because of well-deliberated decision Z, from thought to action with all the perfect logic of a full bladder of beer meaning a quick trip to the bathroom. But Bayle the night before had simply been cold and hungry and had nowhere else to go so he'd followed Smith home, going along with the charade of preparing for his thesis defence the next day because it just seemed easier that way. And when suit-and-tied and cologne-smelling Smith rapped on the door of the study at eight the next morning, saying, "Let's go, Bayle, pancakes and coffee in twenty minutes sharp, I want to be out of here by nine," Bayle was awake to the world again and right back where he'd started.

He showered and shaved and was saying he didn't mind if he did to seconds of Smith's blueberry pancakes and another cup of coffee by 8:40. Smith's wife had been at her architectural firm since seven and Brad was at hockey practice, Zelda volunteering some of her before-school time at a downtown soup kitchen as part of her social studies class. By the time he was soaking up the last of the syrup on his plate, vague thoughts of escape began to float to mind. But soon he was wearing one of Smith's tweed suit jackets with a plain brown tie to match and sitting in the passenger seat of his BMW as they backed out of the long driveway and motored toward the university a few miles under the speed limit in deference to a steady, grey morning rain.

And then they were there.

The door to their assigned room on the third floor of the School of Graduate Studies was unlocked and Smith sat Bayle down at the heavy oak table and slapped a freshly bound copy of Bayle's dissertation on the table in front of him.

Bayle tentatively flipped through the pages of his manuscript while Smith busied himself with his own notes. If Bayle wasn't impressed by the words within — he wasn't; the long-ago-completed manuscript holding about as much interest as last Tuesday's weather forecast — he was a little touched, at least, by the professional care Smith had put into having the correct departmental forms signed and inserted in all the right places and making sure the page numbers were the correct amount of space from the top of each page.

Smith's pride at never having "lost" a Ph.D candidate in twenty-one years as a thesis supervisor was common knowledge around the department, no one whose dissertation he oversaw ever failing to graduate, find a teaching post, and eventually make a contribution in his or her field. So Bayle knew it was as much for Smith himself as it was for him that the older man remained so determined to see Bayle through to his academic end. But Bayle turned each crisp, graduate-school-approved page with something not unlike gratitude anyway. Concern, after all, was concern. And to a starving man a waxen banana in a bowl full of plastic fruit can look a lot like breakfast.

"I'm going to get everybody coffee," Smith said. "And donuts, if I can find any. If Allen shows up before I get back, just smile and nod to whatever he says. He's practically deaf and never wears his hearing aid *or* his dentures, so don't worry if you don't understand a word he says or don't answer back if you can't make out what he's saying. He's used to it. Just remember: smile and nod."

Bayle smiled and nodded. With cupped hands, loudly: "Whatever you say!" he said.

"Look over your manuscript again, wise guy," Smith said. "The Inquisition will be here soon."

But Bayle couldn't possibly go over his manuscript again because he'd never looked it over a first time the night before, neither that nor the Aquinas. He'd turned out the lights almost as soon as Smith had finished with the story of his lost teenage faith, leaving them on only long enough to take a leak in the little washroom connected to the study Smith had had constructed for privacy-while-working sake.

Standing over the toilet bowl and doing his thing, Bayle had looked up to see a silver cross hanging by itself on the wall over the toilet. He finished, shook, and put his dick back in his underwear without once taking his eyes off the crucifix. It couldn't belong to Myra, Smith's wife, because, Bayle knew, she was Jewish. And besides, it was Smith's own personal washroom. Bayle fell asleep wondering why an avowed atheist would keep a cross up on his wall.

"Congratulations, Dr. Bayle."

And then it was all over.

Because if you pull a hockey puck out of your coat pocket and suddenly fling it in the direction of a retired, out-of-uniform, out-of-shape goalie, chances are he'll catch it. Or at least block it with his body. Or at least go down trying.

So: congratulatory handshakes, back-slapping, and the oddest sensation of being sentenced to life membership in an exclusive club Bayle had a difficult time ever imagining wanting to belong to. Essentially, buffaloed into joining the sacred brotherhood, a gun to the head and the trigger gets pulled unless the funny tasselled hat gets put on with pride and the secret handshake is performed with real gusto.

Back in the BMW Smith wanted to go somewhere for a drink and to grab a late lunch to celebrate. As proudly pleased about how things had gone as Bayle had turned quiet, every one of Smith's spirited suggestions that they do something to commemorate the occasion elicited from Bayle only a tide of mumbling about how he was completely exhausted from the four-hour defence, how he should get the confiscated things from his apartment back from out of hock as soon as possible, and how he would appreciate it if Smith could just drop him off anywhere near Queen and Bathurst, where his impounded stuff was being stored. Eventually, Smith reluctantly gave in and pulled the car over in front of a boarded-up building near the intersection where Bayle wanted to be.

"Right here's great," Bayle said, pulling up on the door handle before the car even stopped moving.

Smith put the car in park. He turned in his seat, seatbelt still on. "Where are you going to put all your things when you get them back?" he said.

"A friend said he'd hold on to them for me until I get settled." Lie.

"I imagine there's a lot of stuff," Smith said. "How are you going to get all of it to this friend of your's house?"

"Another friend has got a truck." Lie. "He lives near here and I've just got to give him a ring and he'll help me bring it right over. To my other friend's house." Lie.

"You're fortunate to have such good friends," Smith said.

"You know what they say about friends."

Smith waited.

"Well, what *do* they say about friends?" Smith said.

"I haven't got a clue," Bayle answered. "I thought you might know."

Bayle opened the car door and watched the dirty rainwater gushing away down the gutter, a stream of his own thank-you's and I'll-call-you-soon's greasing his getaway. But before he could disappear into the afternoon Queen Street throng, Smith put his hand on Bayle's shoulder, freezing him in his seat.

"You did well, Peter," Smith said. "I'm proud of you."

Bayle nodded a few mute times at Smith's praise; in spite of the cold rain eagerly unbuckled and shifted his body on the car seat to get his feet on the street. Knott's Place was only a five-minute walk away. Two minutes, if he ran.

Smith squeezed his shoulder harder. "It's going to get easier, Peter. Think about today for instance. You had no choice. You were forced to do your job and you did it admirably. You'll see. You get older, things become expected of you, things need to get done, and you do them. Things become clearer. You'll see what I mean. Once you get settled in at St. Jerome's you'll know what you're supposed to do and, knowing you, you'll do it splendidly. Without ever having to think about it twice."

Only the faintest threads of Bayle's pant fabric remained on the edge of the passenger seat. Feet side by side in the icy, torrenting gutter, Fast approaching thirty, Bayle thought, and still waiting to be dismissed.

Smith still had his hand on Bayle's shoulder waiting for a response. Waited, but it didn't come. He pulled his hand away and Bayle at once got up out of the car.

Before Bayle had a chance to mutter any more so-long bromides and shut the door, Smith asked, "How much did they say it was going to cost you to get your stuff back?"

"What stuff?" Bayle said.

"The stuff from your apartment, Bayle. How much to get it back? I presume that's how this sort of thing works."

"Oh, that stuff. I, uh, I didn't ask."

"You didn't ask." Smith shook his head and pulled out his wallet, took out two fifty-dollar bills and handed them to Bayle. "This was supposed to be our celebration money, but I guess your beginning to get your affairs in order is probably the prudent thing to do at this time." Bayle hesitated.

"Oh, take it, Bayle. You're going to catch the flu standing there like an idiot in the rain. I know things are tight right now so just take the money. Besides, if you want to, you can always pay me back. Don't let on that you know when you meet with him next week, but Hunter told me that the St. Jerome's job pays forty-nine per to start. You shouldn't have to worry about any boarding house evictions then."

Bayle took the bills and stuck them in his pocket. "Thanks," he said.

Smith nodded; started up the car engine, flipped on the wipers. Flashing Bayle a smile, "You're welcome," he said. "*Doctor*."

Bayle rapped twice on the roof of the car and walked

away. He watched Smith's BMW join, then get lost in, a cautious procession of east-bound automobiles all with wipers dutifully working to provide their careful owners an unobstructed view of what was out there in front of them and even what just might be.

Bayle pulled off Smith's tie and stuffed it in one of the pockets of the borrowed tweed jacket. Felt the hundred dollars in his pant pocket. Knew where he was going.

Jimmy raises his empty beer bottle from two tables over in homage to Bayle's choice of juke box song. Politely inquires if another jumpy tune like that last one is coming up and if, seeing as Bayle is, like himself, sitting all alone, might he, Jimmy, join Bayle for a glass from his pitcher of beer.

Another song, another round. *Ad infinitum.*

42

UTTERLY SOUSED, it's simple, really: lacking a reason to get up off the barstool, invent one.

Something like: Who got my stuff? My stuff my stuff. I want my stuff back. My stuff belongs to me. That ball-breaking, two-timing, lawyer-hiring germalist of an ex-girlfriend, she'll know where my stuff is. Because my stuff my stuff. Wait a minute, already said that. Okay, then. Just one more pint and off to get my stuff. Because my stuff my stuff. Wait a minute, already said that.

"Cancel that pint, Stan," Bayle said. "People to go and places to meet."

"You mean you don't want your beer?" Knott said, pint glass already poured out and sitting there beading on the bar top waiting.

"Already said that," Bayle said.

Pockets weighted with what was left of Smith's money, a quick cab ride deposited Bayle in front of 1118 The Esplanade, an eighteen-floor ode to yuppie fashion and cultivated consumer convenience. The building itself couldn't be said to be of any particular architectural period or style, but it *was* very clean and very tidy in appearance — even the potted plants in the lobby were spotless — with a wine store, dry cleaner, and frozen yogurt shop all within easy walking distance. Throw in free cable and a good Thai restaurant nearby that delivers until four a.m., and what is the meaning of life but that movie by Monty Python where that fat guy eats so much supper he explodes all over the place. Hilarious, that. Just fucking hilarious.

Bayle lurched around for a bit on the sidewalk in front of the building straining his neck and trying not to fall down while attempting to locate through the driving cold rain Jane's fifteenth floor apartment. Beginning to feel slightly dizzy, he moved closer to the wall, managing to get only slightly less out of the rain. But the effort had paid off. He'd found her apartment and the lights were on. She was home.

He waited for someone to come along and open the code-accessed front door while trying not to look like he was waiting for someone to come along and open the code-accessed front door. It was after nine now — he'd spent the better part of six hours at Knott's Place — and between the booze, lingering dizziness, and the icy November rain that hadn't let up the entire time he'd been inside the bar, Bayle didn't know how long he could wait it out. The steady downpour drumming against the green canopy hanging over the entrance to the building wasn't helping matters either, the pounding rain lulling his eyelids, gently thawing his resolve. Equal parts alcohol- and adrenaline-fuelled visions of making a dramatic entrance and just-as-dramatic claim for his belongings were soon replaced by altogether soothing thoughts of simply falling asleep under three layers of blankets in Smith's overheated study. Bayle leaned against the wall of the apartment building. Closed his eyes. Leaned ....

Until a beautiful blond woman in her early twenties — tall and then taller still in four-hundred-dollar heels, face all cheekbones and perfect, elevated nose, exactly the sort of beautiful that getting caught in the rain can only succeed in making even more dripping beautiful — weighted down with an armful of delicately string-tied packages and lovely cream-coloured shopping bags swiped her plastic identification card through the slot and made it through the door and into the white marble lobby.

Bayle slipped inside.

He pushed the UP button on the elevator and waited; ran his hands through his soaked hair a couple of times and coughed. The elevator finally arrived and he was inside, pressing 15 and thinking that maybe now was a good time to figure out just what he wanted to say when he got to where he was going. But the elevator door too-soon dinged and Bayle coughed and sneezed himself into the lovely, hardwood floor hallway, finding himself staring at #1503, Jane's apartment door.

Which, lucky him, opened up without Bayle having to even bother knocking. Opened up just as Bayle was trying to decide how to best deal with a long, dangling green string of freshly sneezed snot. And with Jane and what could only be boy-toy August at her side looking on — boy-toy August himself blond, buffed, and looking just like the better men's

303

magazines told him to — Bayle decided it best to go right to
the root of the problem, a sharp pinch of the nostrils and
quick flip of his wrist flinging said trail of onerous mucus
directly onto *Untitled, Number 37*, the apartment-building-
supplied contribution of tastefully framed culture to the strip
of wall beside Jane's door.

In a calm, even slightly bored voice, "I'll call security,"
August said, peeling off his brown leather gloves, Bayle having
apparently just caught the couple on their way out the door.
August turned around and headed for the phone inside the
apartment. Seeing that Jane hadn't immediately closed the
door and bolted the hatches, "For goodness sake, Jane," he
said, "shut the door. You don't want to encourage these sorts
of people. Who knows, he could be dangerous."

"Only to himself," Jane said, crossing her arms, looking at
Bayle. "It's all right. I know this one."

August hesitated for a confused second; set down the
receiver to the phone but didn't remove his hand. "You don't
want me to call security?"

"Not yet, anyway."

August walked back to the door and crossed his own arms.

"I think I can handle this," Jane said.

"Are you sure?" August said, giving the soaking and now
violently coughing Bayle a considered once-over.

"I'm sure."

August only momentarily lingered before nodding and
disappearing back inside the apartment, saying over his
shoulder as he did so, having apparently already forgotten
about the potential menace in the hallway, "Don't let's be late
for dinner tonight, all right? We told everyone we'd be there
for ten sharp."

Bayle still hacking away, face flooding red, "The only
reason I can possibly think of why you're here," Jane said, "is
that you've managed to come to your senses and have with
you, *in full*, the twenty-five hundred dollars that *you stole*
from *Toronto Living*. And even then, technically speaking" —
she pulled up the arm of her heavy overcoat and checked her

watch — "you're approximately thirty-six hours late. The magazine's lawyers made it clear, I thought, that all moneys were to be repaid at their offices by cash or certified cheque no later than nine *a.m.* yesterday morning. It is now" — she consulted her watch again — 9:06 *p.m.*"

Bayle finished his coughing spasm and took a couple of deep breaths, hands on his hips like an exhausted runner at the end of his race. Swallowed with difficulty and wondered who had dropped the razor blades down his throat when he wasn't paying attention. Felt like his knees were about to buckle and the top of his head was ready to blow off. Said, more like he was asking permission to go to the bathroom than demanding his inalienable rights, "I'd like my stuff back. I'd like to know where my stuff is."

Jane looked at the sniffling Bayle in his soaked-through suit jacket and squishy black Oxfords. "I'm sorry about that part, Peter. I didn't want it to come to that. But after you repeatedly refused to respond to any of my numerous faxes and phone calls asking for some kind of explanation, well, that's when the lawyers needed to be brought in and, well, they ...." She looked up. "Come inside and towel off. I think there might even be one of your old sweaters still here. I'd offer you something to drink to warm you up but by the looks of it you've had enough already. Obviously some things haven't changed. August can put on some coffee. There's a late dinner party we have to be at directly, but we've got a few extra minutes."

Obviously-eavesdropping August seriously begged to differ, however, greeting Jane with watch-on-arm extended for an up-close inspection just in case she wasn't quite aware of the late and getting-later hour. Jane immediately shot him one of her patented fuck-with-me-at-considerable-personal-cost death glares that Bayle well remembered putting an end to the direction of many a late-night discussion she wasn't prepared to go, saying only, "Coffee, August."

August yanked his jacket down over his watch and huffed off into the kitchen. The sound of coffee mugs and spoons being slammed onto the kitchen countertop could be heard clearly in the livingroom.

"Wow," Bayle said.

"What?" Jane said. She was on her knees, searching around on the floor of the hall closet.

"Nothing," he said. "It's just hard to believe that that used to be me in there."

Jane pulled out what she was looking for, a small cardboard box, and from it a very large and very expensive wool sweater. She stood up and turned around to see Bayle staring at the doorway to the kitchen. "Meaning?" she said, hard lines tightening around her mouth and eyes, the beginning of the dreaded death glare.

"Nothing," Bayle said, "forget it." Knowing he was out here and August was in there was enough. Gave him, even, an unexpected return to focus. "Look, to tell you the truth, I don't feel so hot, and I've got a feeling it's not just the start of the world's worst hangover, either. Tell your houseboy thanks for the refreshments, but if you could just let me know where and how I can get my stuff back I'll let you two be on your way. Because my stuff my stuff."

"Because your stuff your stuff."

"Exactly," Bayle said.

"I think you've being hanging around that hockey team too long," Jane said. "Here." She tossed him the sweater. "At least you always did have good taste in sweaters."

"You bought me this," he said.

"Oh."

She pushed the cardboard box back into the closet with the toe of one of her heels and shut the door. Discovered and proceeded to carefully pluck off an offending piece of lint that had made its way onto her overcoat.

"So?" Bayle said.

Lint free, looking up, "So, what, Peter?"

"So where's my stuff?"

"I'm sure I haven't the foggiest. That's something you'll have to discuss with the lawyers. And one word to the wise: I'd be at their offices bright and early tomorrow morning. And you might want to be a little more presentable than you are right now. By then you'll be almost two days late with the return of the money."

"Who said I had the money?"

"What do you mean?"

"I mean, I've got maybe twenty dollars in the world to my name."

Very un-Janelike, it looked as if Bayle's ex-girlfriend and ex-employer was going to either drop a kidney or blow a gasket, whichever was more physiologically possible.

"Why do you think I avoided your faxes and phone calls in the first place?" Bayle said. "Because I had it?"

"August!" Jane called out.

In came August from the kitchen doing his best to hurry up and heed his master's voice and, at the same time, balance a silver serving tray loaded down with coffee pot, cups, spoons, milk pitcher in the form of a white porcelain cow, sugar dish — in short, everything necessary for a nice hot beverage shared between friends on a cold and rainy night. "Christ, I'm coming," he said. "It's not like I could make the pot brew any faster, you know."

"Put that tray down," Jane said. "We're going."

"But I just ...." August looked down at the tray. He *had* done a lovely job; what with the porcelain cow as the centrepiece of the tray and a handful of gingerbread cookies laid out all around the edge of the platter.

"Put down that fucking tray and go and get your coat. We're leaving. And don't forget Simon's present to me in the bedroom."

Remembering the dinner party seemed to make giving up the tray a little bit easier. August set it down on the coffee table, if with slight regret, and disappeared down the hall.

Jane turned around, looking stunned that Bayle was still standing there.

"What? What do you want?" she said.

"Nothing I can get here, I guess," Bayle said. He

thought about putting on the sweater (he was cold and it was his), but somehow it seemed to make more sense to just leave it behind.

He tossed the sweater onto the couch. "Give this to your butler, will you? One size fits all." Bayle headed for the door.

Jane called out after him. "Do you see what happens when you try to help someone? I go out on a limb and give you an all-expense paid chance to get some distance on your life, to re-establish your priorities, to save your very own career, and what do I get in return but all the ridicule and headache that comes from having an ex-lover of mine steal from my employers."

Bayle turned around. "'A chance to re-establish my priorities'? Jane, you purposefully flew me out of the country so you could start screwing someone else. If that's what you really think, if that's what you really call trying to help somebody out, then you're even worse off than I thought you were."

"I knew the first day that I met you there were a lot of things you weren't going to do and be in life, Peter, but I never figured you for a common criminal. I thought you had a bit more going for you than that."

Bayle opened up the door. "Yeah, well, the more I think about it, there are a lot of things I never figured myself for, either. And you know something? Maybe you did do me a favour, maybe you and that magazine of yours did buy me a chance to get away from it all. Because from where I'm standing right now, common criminal doesn't even come close to being the worst of them."

And when August returned to the livingroom all bundled up and ready to go with a Union Jack folded neatly over his arm, a distinguishing white bleach spot right there in its upper right-hand corner, Bayle suddenly felt ten times as drunk as he'd been all day and more sober than he ever thought possible. Pointing at the flag, "Where did ....?"

Doing up the buttons on her coat, "Actually, this might be of some interest to you, Peter," Jane said. "A very good friend of my father's, Simon Johnson, got that for me, one of

the lawyers who is going to prosecute you to the full extent of
the law. I rather offhandedly mentioned to him when visiting
my parents ages and ages ago that I'd been invited to a mock-
United Nations dinner party where everyone was supposed to
bring with them a national flag, and what do you think he
presented me with just this last week? A Union Jack. That's
the kind of man you're going to be dealing with, Peter. A
mind like a steel trap. A brilliant man of the law. A mind that
never forgets anything."

Bayle took back Patty's flag with little struggle from
August and grabbed a bottle of Absolut Vodka off the top of
the liquor cabinet as he stalked out the door and down the
hall. Just over the noise of his flopping wet shoes, heard:

"Oh, let him go. The last thing I need is another reason to
have to deal with Peter Bayle."

"But what about the British flag? Now we don't have
anything for the party. Jane, we need a flag."

"That tacky convenience store over by the video shop
has got every flag under the sun in their t-shirt section. We'll
just pick up another one on the way. And who said it had to
be British? Let's be a little different, shall we? I'll bet
everybody and his brother will be bringing a British flag with
them tonight."

43

HE HIT every bar that would take his money. At those that wouldn't, he hit whatever he could still manage to see, a list that included a doorman at Grossman's Tavern who was just doing his job and a beefy waiter at The Rex Hotel who demanded that Bayle either quit waving his Goddamn British flag around in the faces of the other patrons or take his business elsewhere. It was just the sort of invitation Bayle had been waiting for.

The waiter popped him once hard and square in the nose and led Bayle, nauseous with pain and half-blinded with booze and blood, out into the still-pouring night. He sat on the curb, rain rivering down his face, one hand holding his bloody nose, the other Patty's flag. The Saturday night Queen Street foot traffic walked right around him.

Eventually, Etobicoke, his mother's house, around dawn. His mother put him to bed in his old room and did her best for four days to keep the fever down. But Bayle's temperature just kept going up. When he started hallucinating, calling out Patty's name and a bunch of others his mother didn't recognize — Davidson's, Gloria's, Warren's, Duceeder's and his son's — she called for an ambulance.

For nearly two months Bayle wore a clear plastic wristband that identified him as patient number 387366, Ward Three, Etobicoke General Hospital. At first it was just pneumonia, albeit a severe enough case — tubes to feed him and a succession of nurses to clean him — to cause the doctors to be concerned for awhile and to keep his mother bedside every day during both afternoon and evening visiting hours. Then a lung that filled up with fluid when he started to get better from the pneumonia, and, after that, a reaction to the medication for the problem with the lung. He finally went home with his mother early in the new year, thirteen pounds lighter but walking on his own and without the wristband.

Mostly he just slept and ate and lay around on the couch watching television. The Maple Leafs were their usual lousy selves again after teasing their fans with respectability for a couple of brief years in the early nineties, but the Wednesday night game on Global and "Hockey Night in Canada" on Saturday were the highlights of Bayle's week. For the first time since his father had died Bayle knew exactly where he'd be whenever the Leafs were on T.V. Bayle had become a fan again.

And the empty expression stuck to his face since he'd gotten out of the hospital seemed to say that he watched the hockey with no more interest than he did MuchMusic and the black-and-white late-night double feature on CBC. But his mother could see the slow signs of change in her son as the days began to get longer outside and the Leafs briefly flirted with the last Western Conference playoff spot.

At first, just the occasional comment from his now customary horizontal position on the couch to his mother sitting in her old armchair working away on one of her "Find and Circle the Hidden Word" game books when an especially pretty Leaf goal was scored or, more often, a feverish Toronto comeback late in the game fell short. In time, leaning up on his elbows to get a better view when a replay of a disputed goal or contentious penalty was shown. Eventually — and before a late-February, six-game losing streak all but mathematically eliminated the Leafs from the playoff picture — sitting up on the edge of the couch only a few feet from the set the entire game long, anxiously tapping his feet whenever Toronto would get boxed in their own end while killing a penalty, pumping his fist and shouting "Yes" and smiling his mother's way when the Leafs managed to put one in the net.

Once, in the middle of an incredibly exciting four-goal third period outburst that put the Leafs ahead to stay against arch enemy Detroit, Bayle got up to dance around the T.V. and generally whoop it up only to look up and see tears running down his mother's face. Bayle froze in mid-celebration.

"Oh, don't worry, Peter, I'm all right," his mother said, balled fist almost immediately taking care of the uncommon tears, a tender smile taking their place. "I just couldn't help but see your father in you just now. That's what he used to do all the time, you know. Look at me so happy and proud when Toronto would score. Sometimes his yelling when they'd finally get one would test my nerves, I won't lie to you about that, I don't mind telling you that now. But he *would* look so happy. Just like a happy little boy. Just the way you looked just now."

That Bayle, in the absence of his impounded own, had been wearing his father's clothes ever since he'd gotten out of the hospital — blue and brown cotton work shirts and pants, all carted in from the garage by his mother and laid out on his bed waiting for him the day he arrived home — only made him more uncomfortable with his mother's rare show of emotion. He didn't have to worry.

"Don't forget about those butter tarts I put in the freezer this afternoon," his mother said, dried eyes already back on her puzzle book. "Just pop a couple of them in the microwave for thirty seconds or so and put a scoop of ice cream on top afterwards if you want. I don't care what Dr. McKay says, I say you're still a little underweight."

Bayle relaxed, looked at his mother. "You must miss Dad a lot, don't you, Mum?"

His mother just kept looking intently at her book.

"Hey, Mum, I said, 'You must —'"

"Ah ha!" she said. "Found you, you little sneaky Sam!" His mother had discovered the hidden word she'd been searching for. Pleased with herself, she grinned and circled.

Bayle smiled. "Maybe I will have a couple of those butter tarts," he said.

"Have as many as you want, dear, that's what I made them for," his mother said. "They don't do any good just sitting there in the freezer."

Bayle looked back at the television just in time to see the Maple Leafs congratulating each other at game's end on their come-from-behind victory.

"These Leafs aren't going to go down without a fight, Harry," Bob Cole said to colour man Harry Neale.

"It sure doesn't look like it, Bob," Harry said. "As long as there's an ounce of hope left in these young fellas, you can bet they're going to give it everything they've got."

44

AND THE black-and-white movies and the music videos started to get old real quick and Bayle began puttering around the house, growing even more bored in the process, getting under his mother's feet all the while. When the secretary from the philosophy department called to ask him to please clean out the small office he'd been assigned as a teaching assistant he felt relieved at having another reason besides his mother pleading with him to get out of the house for the first time in almost two months.

The subway ride downtown; the walk from the station to the philosophy building in the nippy afternoon air; the oh-so-serious and oh-so-beautiful-for-it undergraduate girls going in and coming out of the library in their heavy sweaters and faded jeans with not one smile for all the men instantly falling in love with them (and them all the more beautiful for it): it felt good to get out. Admittedly a little awkward at first — the man at the subway station having to pound on the glass to remind Bayle to put his ticket in the cashbox — but good. Good for no good reason. Bayle wondered if this was how people who claimed to be happy all the time did it.

Five seconds inside his tiny office and he knew he wouldn't need a moving van. He'd never kept any of his books here, and nothing even remotely personal like photographs or a print or a poster disturbed the bare white walls. What there was was lots and lots of paper covering his desk and virtually everything else in the room. He considered the paper blizzard only briefly; left and came right back with the blue recycling box from the secretary's office and swept every surface clean and emptied every desk drawer with real passion. When the box could take no more he hauled it down the hall and dumped it in the big plastic recycling bin the janitors used and came back for more. Done, no trace of him left anywhere in the room, he didn't even take a last look, just flicked off the light and locked the door behind him.

Returning the recycling box and key to the secretary's office, he almost slammed right into Smith coming out with his mail.

"Bayle," Smith said, looking up from his handful of letters.

"Smith."

They stood there in the doorway not knowing what to say until an anxious existentialist needed to get by. They stepped out into the hall.

"I was just ...." Bayle held up the bin and the key to his office.

"Right. So the new crop can move in. Actually, I just the other day met a new Ph.D candidate for the fall down here all the way from Colorado, Jeffery something or other. He's thinking of having a go with the Hellenistic period, your old stomping grounds. I think it's quite possible he might do some very interesting work."

"That's great," Bayle said.

"Yes," Smith said.

"Yeah."

"Yes."

"Well, I better get this stuff back before they think I've run off with it," Bayle said.

"Right. All right, then, Bayle." Smith and Bayle shook hands. Smith walked down the hall to his own office and Bayle returned the bin and key to the secretary.

A couple of minutes later, as Bayle waited for the elevator, Smith came back down the hallway with his unopened mail still in his hand.

"I just have to know this one thing, Bayle," he said. "I've thought about this and thought about this and I simply have to know." The elevator arrived and slowly opened.

"Okay," Bayle said.

"If you weren't going to meet Hunter — if you knew you weren't going to meet him — why didn't you at least call to let him know? Or even call later and give him an excuse why you didn't show. It's simply not feasible to me that you didn't realize how difficult if not downright impossible it was going to be for you to get a decent job in this country after literally standing up a man of his reputation."

Bayle stepped into the elevator and faced Smith. "I'll answer your question," he said, "if you answer mine."

Smith seemed slightly taken aback. "All right," he said. "What?"

"Why does an atheist keep a cross hanging up in his bathroom?"

Smith stood silent for a few seconds. "Is this some kind of joke?" he said. "What are you looking for, Bayle, a punchline? My question was sincere."

"So was mine," Bayle said.

Bayle pushed GROUND, waved to Smith a final goodbye, and the elevator doors closed tight.

Home, his mother had left his mail out for him on the kitchen table, two letters and a large manila envelope, quite a haul considering he hadn't told anyone where he was. The kitchen was oven-warm. Bayle guessed meatloaf.

Two of the items he couldn't even be bothered to open. The latest envelope from the offices of Johnson, Johnson, and Bailey went right into the garbage pail under the sink. The letter from the government he didn't even want to guess. The last, however, appeared to be an actual letter from an actual person, Bayle's name and the address of the U of T philosophy department printed in careful, childlike script, the word CANADA in blocks and underlined twice. He checked the postage and saw that it was postmarked Kansas City, KS, NEXT DAY DELIVERY, and had been forwarded to his mother's house by the school.

Dear Bayle,

Harry is dead. He died this morning. After you left he never got better like I thought he would. The doctors said Harry died of I forget the exact name but a hemmorage the main idea. All the other things that were wrong with him that they never figured out just got worse and helped make way for the hemmorage they said. The doctor says he couldn't have felt much and we all kind of saw it coming. My mother used to say the only thing a person can wish for in this life is to die in their sleep so I guess there is that.

After they announced the team was moving and all the people that were going to lose their jobs it's like a cementary around here. Oh well not my problem anymore because I'm leaving for Macon, Georgia, as soon as the last game is over this Saturday night and I'm all done as the Warrior. A cousin whose got a restaruant down there says I can help out until I get something somewhere else. Who knows? You won't believe this but they've got a hockey team down there now called the Macon Whoopi. Maybe I'll be their mascot next year. Ha ha.

I guess you wouldn't know but right after Duceeder got bail the case against him for the cocaine got thrown out because of something to do with the police and illegal entry or something else his lawyer cooked up and he got let off. Which means you and that peppermint tin you were so worried about is off the hook now. But Davidson did get fired by the team and him and his family moved away from town and that's better than nothing I guess. Samson in the Eagle said something about the Warriors being a family business and them having to keep up the team's image.

I wanted you to know about Harry and to let you know we are going to bury him four days from now on Saturday. Harry has some cousins and an aunt up in Alberta and I'm hoping by waiting they can get here. I guess I could have called your school to try and talk to you but I know you probably can't come all the way down here. But I thought I should send this letter because I know Harry would have wanted you to know. Harry liked you Bayle. He said you were all right. And Harry doesn't say that about too many people I bet you know that.

Take care of yourself and don't worry if you can't make it. But I thought you should know.
Yours truly,
Gloria

Bayle put the letter back in its envelope and then in the pocket of his workshirt. He called to his mother in the livingroom that he was going out for a walk.

"Make it a short walk," she said. "That meatloaf is only about thirty minutes away from being ready."

Like most Etobicoke homes, Bayle's parents' house wasn't so much a part of a neighbourhood where one could, as Bayle later learned to love to do in Toronto, walk for wonderfully distracted hours with an always-changing cityscape scrolling by, as it was simply one of several houses that formed a street which in turn formed part of a block. The schools where the children went; the variety stores where the adults bought their cigarettes and lottery tickets; the sports bars that had the satellite dishes: all meant getting on a bus or driving your car. Unless one wanted to walk the forty-minute walk along the busy road that all the traffic had to travel on in order to get to the stores and subway station in downtown Etobicoke, it wasn't possible to do anything *but* take a short walk up and down one's own street past all the identical houses or, maybe for a little variety, the virtually indistinguishable street two or three over. But there was the hydro-electrical field.

Ten minutes from Bayle's parents' house there was a large, overgrown field, almost a quarter acre of knee-high grass and weeds, out of which grew eleven hydro-electrical towers. Eleven mighty steel oaks with thick twisting cables connecting them all at their tops according to some unfathomable system of hydro-electrical science. No one, not even Bayle's Ontario Hydro-employed father, knew exactly how the towers did what they did, but everyone knew that the hydro towers were somehow responsible for keeping their part of Etobicoke pulsing alive. And everyone knew that you were supposed to stay away from them.

But for all the strong warnings Bayle and Patty and all the other children on the block were given as soon as they were old enough to understand the danger of playing near the towers, there wasn't anything like a ten-foot-high brick wall or a barbed wire fence to keep them out. Only a modest, five-foot high version with a rusty padlocked gate. It wasn't as good as having somewhere nice to walk to or anything to do like a nearby park or playground, but the high grass that hid them and the simple fact that they weren't supposed to be there made the hydro field a veritable place of rite of passage for every child who grew up in its shadow. Bayle and Patty were no different.

Bayle was initiated into the secret, just-turned-teen joys of poring over somebody's father's copy of *Playboy* and smoking your first cigarette in the camouflage of the tall grass by a gang of local boys led up by a fat bossy older kid everyone called "Skipper." And conscientious big brother that he was, Bayle did the same for his sister, although loner Patty's tastes ran more toward solitary afternoon Dunhills while working her way through a fat summer stack of paperback novels.

As far as Bayle and all the other kids knew, no one ever came even close to getting injured in the field. Many long summer afternoons, in fact, were spent lounging in the grass smoking and idly wondering how someone actually could get hurt. There were no hanging wires to touch. And the towers themselves weren't going to fall down on you. Everyone always agreed that the only way anyone could possibly harm themselves was by climbing up one of the flat-sided smooth steel towers — not impossible, but a fairly impressive athletic feat all the same — and literally putting their hand against one of the exposed, curling electrical coils and waiting there suspended for a charge to come. And like anybody's going to do that. As if.

Inevitably, with the beckoning of high school, the summer shelter of the hydro field got left behind in a cherry Kool-Aid mist, right there along with Pixi-Sticks and hockey cards and Saturday night sleep-overs. Hanging out in somebody's car, sharing a case of beer at a house party, going downtown to Toronto — that's what a real Etobicoke teenager did. But never being one to do what was she was supposed to do, Patty never entirely quit the field. And even if her solo meditations there were occasionally compromised by a new generation of shrieking first-time smokers and porno-readers, Bayle always knew where to find his sister if she wasn't in her room listening to music or reading up on a recent enthusiasm.

The day after Bayle went out to his parents' house at his mother's insistence and Patty refused to see him, his mother called him up again, this time in a panic because she hadn't seen Patty all day, didn't know where she was, couldn't find her anywhere. She'd found Patty's bedroom door wide open late that afternoon for the first time in over a week, but without a note or anything saying where she'd gone.

His mother had checked out all the places she might have been in Etobicoke — the local library branch, the little greasy spoon she sometimes liked to linger over a plate of fries at and read, the repertory movie theatre — but no, nothing. Had Patty called him? his mother wanted to know. Was there someplace in Toronto she might be that his mother should look? Should she call the police? And all this, his mother said, after Dr. McKay, their family doctor, had been good enough to agree and squeeze her into his busy schedule tomorrow morning to see if he could try and figure out what might be wrong with her.

"Don't go anywhere else or call anybody until I get there," Bayle said.

Downtown, from the St. George subway stop, west, to the Royal York station. From there, usually no more than a five-minute wait for a bus that took you to the stop closest to Bayle's parents' house. Or, the bus stop before, near the hydro field.

The grey steel towers looked like some giant child's tinker toy set in the soft yellow glow of the after-dinner setting sun. Bayle pulled the buzzer and stood up without knowing he was going to get off until he did.

He hopped the fence of the field for the first time in years and worried he might rip his pants or worse. But the motion going over came right back to him. The field was only cut once each summer and was almost chest high now, mosquitos and little buzzing black things passing in front of Bayle's nose and eyes, circling around his head. He kept his eyes directly in front of him, on the grass and weeds falling underneath his steps. He kept his head down.

All he had to do was shut her eyes and gently close her mouth and it was Patty. He picked up the copy of Pascal's

Pensees lying beside her and opened it up to its only paper-clipped page and read the highlighted and starred line.

What must I do? I see nothing but obscurity on every side.

Bayle hurled the book as far as he could. Heard it disappear in the tall grass with a soft settling swoosh.

Later, after the chaos of his mother and the ambulance and the police and the gawking neighbours, in the middle of the night in his housecoat and slippers and armed with a flashlight and a bottle of Canadian Club, Bayle was determined to find the flung Pascal. He looked for hours, over and over swiping the beam of the flashlight through the grass and weeds of the field until he got so tired and drunk he had to sit down and take a rest. When he woke up near dawn in the dew-soaked field, every inch of his flesh exposed to the night and the mosquitos had turned into a red pulpy mess.

When Bayle's mother heard him come in the front door back from his walk she called out from the kitchen for him to wash up because it was almost time for dinner. Bayle answered back that he'd be there in a minute and not to set the table, he'd do it, but there was something else he had to do first.

Not much from the night of over three months before when he'd ended up on his mother's front step remained clear, but her shock at seeing him dragging Patty's Union Jack behind him through the door being almost as great as her distress over his disorderly and obviously ailing state Bayle remembered almost perfectly. Also, before peeling off his wet clothes and while his mother prepared a scalding hot tub and pot of tea, where he'd put the flag.

Bayle went upstairs to his old room and got down on his knees beside the bed. Eyes closed, he felt around on the carpeted floor until he had it. He pulled out the flag and opened his eyes, snapping it tight in front of him a few hard times to get rid of the dust and lint. He laid the flag down on the bed and carefully folded it. When he came back downstairs and his mother at the stove saw him and it coming through the kitchen, she started to say something but didn't. Patty wasn't something Bayle and his mother talked about. Not because they'd forgotten about her. Not because they didn't care. Not because of anything except it just wasn't something Bayle and his mother did.

Bayle kissed his mother's forehead. "Don't set the table, Mum, I'll do it, I'll only be gone a minute," he said and went out the back door.

He flipped on the light switch in the garage and the long florescent tubes slowly crackled to life. It seemed like the garage never changed, time and more cardboard boxes only making it more like itself.

A twenty year-old couch Bayle could still remember him and Patty as kids being so excited about trying out the day the big Sears delivery truck backed into their driveway. Four new snow tires his father had gotten a great deal on at Canadian Tire the spring before he got sick and didn't have a chance to use. The family's long-gone cat Freddy's kitty litter box and claw-ravaged scratching post. And cardboard boxes. Boxes and boxes and still more boxes. Bayle knew the one he wanted.

He set his mother's old sewing machine on the cement floor and opened up the mildewy box underneath. Patty's "British Thing" box. The six volume set of Kipling, bard of a long-gone empire upon whom the sun was every day closer and closer to setting. Her English bone china tea service with the missing saucer and the pot with the spout that never poured straight. A deflated soccer ball. Bayle gently placed the folded flag on top. He replaced the cardboard lid and put the sewing machine back and closed the garage door.

His mother was sitting at her place at the table with her hands folded in her lap staring off into space, steaming plates and pots already out, the table set for two.

"Mum, I told you I'd do that," Bayle said. "It's about time you stopped waiting on me hand and foot around here."

"I didn't know how long you'd be out there," she said. Bayle sat down across from her.

"I wasn't gone that long was I, Mum?" he said.

324

"No, but ...."

"No but nothing. I had something to do and now it's done and now I'm back."

His mother looked at him and almost smiled. When Bayle picked up his knife and fork and banged them down on the table and opened up his mouth as wide as it would go, pointing with the fork at the empty cavity, her almost smile turned into a did. She picked up one of the serving ladles and plopped an enormous scoop of mashed potatoes onto Bayle's plate.

"Good," she said, "I'm glad you're back. Now we can eat."

She ladled out more potatoes and then green peas and then began cutting off a huge slice of meatloaf.

"And I want you to eat everything I put on your plate," she said. "It's about time you started putting some flesh on those bones of yours. You're getting stronger all the time, but you've still got some room to go."

45

"IF I knew you were coming, we would've waited. But I never heard from you, Bayle. To tell you the truth, I never really expected you to make it."

Gloria and Bayle sat at Davidson's kitchen table. Bayle had on his funeral clothes — the suit jacket and tie that Smith had leant him for his thesis defence and a pair of his father's better blue work pants — but the service and burial had been over for more than an hour by the time Bayle managed to catch a bus in from the airport. Gloria and Wilson from the *Eagle* were the only late Saturday morning mourners, the Reverend Warren, Bayle learned, officiating in what was his last bit of official business in town before heading off to his new job heading up another church in Athens, Ohio, a small university town. It wasn't the eastern seaboard like Warren had hoped, but it wasn't here either, Bayle thought. World without end, Chuck. And try to take it easy on the hard stuff, buddy.

Gloria made them each a tall glass of iced tea from an old jar of humidity-hardened instant tea crystals she found at the back of Davidson's cupboard. She stirred and stirred each glass to try and get the chunks of crystals to completely dissolve, adding plenty of ice cubes when the clinking of spoon to glass had stopped.

Spring — just a rumour just five hours before in thawing but still chilly Toronto — was, here, already full-blown, the warm, sap-scented air making the bees and everything else alive tinglingly restless, the good new goo of springtime teeming pushing through the winter-weary veins of leaf, bee, and human body alike. Bayle's suit jacket and tie hung over the back of his chair, the sleeves of his white dress shirt rolled up to the elbow.

"It took a couple days for your letter to be forwarded to me from the university," he said. "I guess I should have called you when I got my flight, but it was late and I was sure you had enough on your mind already and I thought that if I left early enough this morning and was here by noon ...."

Gloria sipped her iced tea and crossed her black-stockinged legs, the sound of sheer to sheer the sound of pure sex to recent late-night black-and-white movie buff Bayle — every 1940's B-movie seduction scene, it seemed, ending up with one of those long black stockings hanging over the lampshade. Bayle had never seen Gloria in anything but her Warrior outfit or jeans or the same grey sweatsuit, so the stockings, modest heels, and black dress were, even if entirely bereavement acceptable, a little overwhelming. Bayle crossed his own legs, hoping to hide his approval at Gloria's choice of mourning clothes.

"That you took time out from everything else and came all the way down here is as much as Harry could ask for," Gloria said. "You dropping everything like you did shows your respect for him just fine. Being there when they put that box in the ground wouldn't have done any more."

"Thanks," Bayle said. "Because I wanted to be here for you. For Harry, I mean. You know what I mean."

"I'm glad you came, Bayle," Gloria said, giving his hand a quick squeeze as she got up from the table to get more ice cubes for their drinks.

Bayle looked around the kitchen as a way of not looking at the outline of Gloria's firm ass through her dress as she walked away from him. "What's going to happen to all of this?" he said, gesturing around the room. "To all of Harry's things."

Gloria plopped two more ice cubes in her and Bayle's drink. Pulled an envelope out of her purse sitting on the other chair and placed it on the table.

"What's this?" he said.

"Harry's will."

Bayle hesitated then touched the edge of the envelope. "I never really thought of Harry as the will-leaving sort."

"That makes two of us," Gloria said. "Imagine how I felt when it turns out he left everything to me." Bayle looked up from the envelope. "Oh, it doesn't come to much money-wise," she said. "After paying for the funeral and some of the hospital costs his insurance at the *Eagle* didn't cover there's maybe a few hundred dollars left. But that's not what I care about. What this really means," she said, tapping the envelope with her finger, "is that instead of some cousin or whoever coming in here and selling everything off at some yard sale or something, I get to take with me anything I want that will help me remember Harry by."

Bayle thought of Gloria in her new home in Georgia making herself a cup of lemon tea in Harry's old white teapot; smiled.

"It's funny, you know?" she said. "The last time I saw my mom was when I was 13, but still, she was my mom for those years, right? But I'll be damned if I can remember what she looks like. I mean, I do, it's there, but it's not, you know what I'm saying? I didn't exactly ask for any family photos when I got smart enough to bust out of there, and it's not like I'm every day needing to remember her and all the hell she put me through, but still, you'd think I could remember if I wanted to. But that isn't going to happen with Harry. When I make my move from here I'm gonna take enough of him with me so as I can remember him as long as I got all my marbles."

They both sat there looking at the white envelope on the table until Gloria finally stuck it back in her purse. "But what about you, Bayle? You teaching at that college of yours yet, or is that in the fall? I forget what you said before."

"No," he said. "That job ... no, that job didn't work out."

"What have you been up to then? Teaching at some other place?"

So Bayle told her about getting sick and being in the hospital and recovering at his mother's house and how actually only when his mother retrieved and opened up the letter from the government that he'd tossed in the trash the night before did it turn out that his income tax refund from the year before would supply him with the money he needed to make the flight and be here, and then only barely.

"You're telling me you spent everything you've got just to get down here for Harry?" she said.

"It really wasn't that big a sacrifice. Really. It was found money. And like I said, I wanted to come."

Gloria smiled and crossed her legs again. Causing Bayle to avert his eyes and once again cross his.

"I don't know what your plans are," Gloria said. "But like

I already wrote you, I'm leaving for my sister's place as soon as I can manage. But Harry's apartment, it's got five more months of rent paid on it that I can't get back, I already checked. You're welcome to stay here if you want. Rent free. Maybe you could ask Wilson for your old job back at the *Eagle*. He seemed pretty mad at you for just leaving like you did, but maybe not that mad."

"Thanks, but I've got to get back. My ticket's non-refundable, return date tomorrow. I thought I'd stay for the game tonight, but I'm going home tomorrow."

"Of course you want to get right back, what am I thinking?" Gloria said. "Like you want to be working for some newspaper like the *Eagle*. You probably want to get back as soon as you can so you can start looking for another teaching job now that you're feeling better again, right?"

"I'm going back tomorrow because I told my mother I would. I'm all she's got now." Bayle lifted his glass and finished his iced tea. "Besides," he said, "as good as she's been to me, I've really got to get some kind of work — any kind of work — and find a place of my own back in the city before we end up driving each other crazy. Grown men weren't meant to live with their mothers and I wasn't born to live in the suburbs. And they tell me the Monday morning newspapers have got the best help-wanted ads."

"Do they advertise the kind of job you're looking for in a regular newspaper?"

"I guess I'll know that," Bayle said, "when I start looking."

Gloria nodded and rose and rinsed their glasses in the sink. Shut off the tap and turned around, stepped out of her shoes, yawned.

"It's been a long morning," she said. "And I've got to have my pre-game nap."

"I thought only players slept before games," Bayle said.

"Anybody that works as hard as I do out there at what they do deserves to have a pre-game nap. Player or not."

"Gotcha," Bayle said. He picked up his jacket and tie off the chair and started for the livingroom.

HEROES

"Aren't you tired too?" Gloria said. "I mean, what time did you say you flew out of Toronto this morning? Quarter to seven?"

"Maybe that's a good idea," Bayle said. "Maybe I'll just crash out here on the couch for awhile. Just make sure you get me up when you do, okay? I wouldn't want to miss the last game in Warrior history."

"Then maybe you should come and lay down with me," she said. "I always set the alarm for six. We can ride to the rink together and you can be there early enough to get the best seat in the arena."

Bayle looked down at the floor. "But before, when I tried to ... I mean, you said before you'd never betray Harry."

Gloria slowly padded over to where Bayle was. Kissed him, first, soft on the cheek. Then long and hard on the mouth. Took his hand.

"Harry's gone now, Bayle. That's why your not being here when they threw that dirt down on that box this morning doesn't mean nothing next to to you showing up and not forgetting about him. You remember Harry and I remember Harry. And that's good. That's the important thing. But Harry's gone now. And you'll be gone from here forever tomorrow and me not long after. But right now, we're still here. And there isn't anything anybody can do about that."

46

AN EARLY arrival at the arena and a great seat to watch the game, just like Gloria promised, right at centre ice, seven rows up. Bayle scratched his nose and smelt his fingers and thought of a tuna fish sandwich and just how nice it felt to once again feel gloriously loose as a goose in body and soul from the back of your tired calves to the top of your nicely cloudy brain after spraying sweat and sucking face all lovely afternoon long. If only he hadn't bought today's *Eagle* before Gloria left him at the concession stand downstairs to get ready for her act. Bayle munched from his box of popcorn and read the newspaper the same way you run your tongue over a sore tooth you know you obviously shouldn't but can't stop from doing anyway.

To commemorate the Warriors' last game the paper was full of plenty of pie charts and graphs to show how the loss of the team was going to be the biggest hit the town had taken since the G.M. and International Harvester plants moved to Mexico in the early '80s. Another article on the same page reported how a series of long-promised federal grants intended for rust-belt towns to re-train the significant number of unemployed former employees of the long-gone auto and steel industries had been scrapped in the Republican senate. The article went on to note how Washington insiders were all abuzz over the highly successful anti-grant lobbying efforts of newly nationally syndicated radio talk show host I.M. Wright. Since just before Christmas Wright's show had been picked up by thirty-seven new affiliates and the list was growing every day.

Although relegated to page four, C.A.C.A.W., Bayle discovered, was still going strong. Silent since his own departure from town in November, the militia group had just recently sent a new dispatch to the *Eagle* offices saying that a new "political action" intended to observe both the "local misgovernment's persecution of the Bunton family that has forced them to move the Warriors to Texas" as well as the anniversary of the "constitutionally unjust murders by the federal misgovernment of the Branch Davidians at Waco" was "imminent."

Bayle crunched his empty popcorn box under his foot and kicked it and the folded *Eagle* under the seat ahead of him. The stands had begun to fill up while he'd been reading, and as much as the words in the newspaper, the faces of the crowd told the town's story.

The men, as usual, slurped at their giant paper cups of beer and stared down at their game programs. The women wore their Warriors sweatshirts and blew on their styrofoam cups of steaming coffee. And the children had their Warriors pennants to wave and hot dogs and ice cream bars to munch on. But replacing the expectant buzz that always filled the Bunton Center just before the players took to the ice was a heavy silence. A couple of banners made out of white bed sheets and red paint sagged from the upper sections declaring *We'll Miss You Warriors* and *Warriors Forever!* but when the home team came out for their last ever pre-game skate the noise from the crowd was only at its usual pitch for one or two loud minutes. The warm-up for both teams in full swing, Bayle could actually hear the players down on the ice calling out for a pass, the hard, wooden slap of the puck coming off the stick.

Once the game got under way it quickly became apparent that both the Warriors and their opponents from Wichita, the Tornados — the only other South Central Hockey League team not to make the playoffs and, as a result, really with nothing to play for — shared the crowd's lack of interest. Neither team seemed overly concerned with actually winning the game, each squad content to play most of the period in the neutral zone and to simply dump the puck into the opposition's end without much desire to skate in after it. The loud rock music that blared between every stoppage in play seemed just annoying, no one singing along or stamping their feet or clapping their hands during the parts they were supposed to.

Only when the Warriors' Dippy and the Wichita enforcer, Bladon, briefly renewed their season-long antagonism by rubbing their gloves in each other's face before each finally managed a single shot to the other's head after a quick whistle in front of the Tornado net did the crowd just as briefly come to life. The players raced in tight and surrounded the two heavyweights to lend support — each skater grabbing hold of a potential sparring partner from the other team by the jersey in case Dippy and Bladon's gloves got dropped — and everyone in the stands let out a loud roar and rose to their feet.

But the linesmen managed to get between the two enforcers and order was quickly restored. The game resumed at its previously sluggish pace for another few dull moments before the horn sounded to end the first period. Bayle filed into the arena lobby along with everybody else.

Waiting in line at the concession stand Bayle never saw Able, the Warriors' play-by-play voice, until he had Bayle by the hand and was shaking it with his customary vigour and telling him how darn nice it was to see him again and how much he'd enjoyed Bayle's pieces in the *Eagle* when Davidson had gotten sick and how surprised he was to see him back in town because he'd heard he'd left for good. When Bayle told him he'd returned to attend Davidson's funeral Able seemed stunned.

"Today? The funeral was today?" Able rubbed his bald head and stared down at the garbage-littered arena floor.

"I called Gloria as soon as I found out Harry'd passed on but she wouldn't talk to me," he said. "I mean, the woman just wouldn't speak to me. All she'd say was that me and Duceeder and everybody else who had anything to do with the team were just as responsible for putting Harry in the ground as that hemorrhage was. I just wanted to know where to go to pay my respects, but there was nothing about a service in the newspaper and she just kept hanging up on me. I mean, sure, maybe Harry didn't see eye to eye with the rest of us over how things should get done around here, and maybe we teased him a little too much sometimes, but to say that we were responsible for ...." Able looked up at Bayle.

"My mother died around the same age as Harry did, you know? And I just wanted to come by and pay my respects. But Gloria wouldn't talk to me. She just wouldn't talk to me."

By now Bayle was at the front of the line and the acne-scarred teenager in the Warrior golf shirt and visor behind the counter snarled at Bayle demanding to know what he wanted because there were, like, other people besides him who wanted to get served today too. Then Able looked at his watch and said he guessed he'd better get back to the broadcast booth before Munson had a fit.

Bayle gave the kid his order, turned to Able, and told him that the very fact he wanted to go to the funeral so bad was indication enough of his intentions, and not to worry what Gloria or anybody else thought. Surprising himself,

Bayle even patted Able on the back a couple of solid times as he said it.

Able said thanks, shook Bayle's hand heartily, and turned around as he was leaving to say thanks again before disappearing into the cigarette-smoke fog of the arena lobby. Bayle got his Diet Pepsi and popcorn and walked back to his seat not sure if he should feel as good as he did about making Able feel better or as bad as he did for being disloyal to Gloria by talking to him. Eventually decided it was really all right to feel both.

Most of the second period was a repeat of the first, a zero to zero tie looking not all that unlikely. Bayle even saw more than one person leave their seat and not come back. Bored himself, he strained to see who was at press box row, spotting only Wilson, obviously covering the game for the *Eagle*, and Samson, puffing away on a fat cigar and smiling his usual big smile. The counter looked empty without Duceeder and Davidson sitting at their customary opposite ends.

But then with about seven minutes left in the period things began to pick up. An interference call against Robinson and a minor roughing penalty to Dippy for shoving Bladon from behind gave Wichita a two-minute, two-man advantage that the Warriors killed off like it was really no advantage at all, energized, it seemed, at the obstacle suddenly placed in their way. The crowd began to wake up as well, cheering louder and louder each time the Warriors would successfully ice the puck into the Tornado zone. When the power play was over and Robinson and Dippy skated out of the penalty box the fans stood up to give the Warrior penalty-killing unit a quick but noisy standing ovation.

Then it was Wichita's turn. All the pressure they hadn't managed to exert during their power play they somehow mustered now, for several long minutes keeping the pressure almost entirely in the Warrior zone, driving shot after shot at the Warrior net. Some were rocket slapshots from the point that missed high and wide but blasted along the glass right back to a waiting Tornado defenceman for another go. Some were drives from the top of the face-off circle that Warrior defencemen were able to throw themselves in front of and keep from getting through to the net. And some were point-blank shots from right out front, the final piece of a bing-bang-boom passing play from Tornado to Tornado to Tornado. But none of these nor any others got behind the goal line and chants of LET'S-GO-WARRIORS-LET'S-GO! echoed off the Bunton Center walls.

Just when the Warriors started to return the favour, though, peppering the Tornado goalie with several difficult blasts of their own, the horn sounded and the second period was over. The crowd, most of it on its feet and all of it, Bayle included, loudly applauding the attacking Warriors, seemed caught slightly off guard by the noise of the horn and the sudden stop in action, like someone discovering while gleefully belting out their favourite song they're not at home alone after all. The large doors at the north end of the rink slid open and the zamboni rolled onto the ice. The crowd quietly sat back down in their seats.

But not for long.

Before Bayle or anyone else had time to decide whether to stay where they were or visit the washroom or get something to eat or drink from the lobby, Gloria shot out onto the ice like a streak of silver light, aluminum sheathed as usual and with the plastic cannon strung over her shoulder, whipping around the rink like a mad speed-skater racing desperate and alone against some kind of terrible clock.

A few wildly reckless circles of the rink while feverishly pointing and jabbing her cannon at every section of the crowd were followed up by a whole series of sinew-stretching jumps, twists, and backward skating flips that didn't appear to follow any method other than what her never-ceasing-to-move legs instructed, but which thrilled the audience all the same. Somewhere between a figure-skater and a runaway train on blades, Gloria had the crowd in an applauding frenzy.

Winding up her final laps as the Warrior, she pulled the last of the tennis balls out of her ammunition belt and hurled them into the furthest reaches of the rink as she raced around the ice surface faster than she'd ever gone before.

All the tennis balls pitched into the stands, the zamboni having long since done its job and left the ice, the players for both teams standing at their respective benches waiting to come on for the start of the third period, Gloria, although it seemed impossible, somehow managed to crank it up yet another notch, convincing her exhausted legs to carry her around the rink even faster still. At a speed that transformed her into a blur of silver, Gloria began peeling off her uniform and tossing it into the stands.

Still tearing around the rink, first went the plastic cannon, lobbed into the second row behind the Warriors' bench. Then came her ammunition belt. And then, last lap almost over and tearing toward the opening of boards at the north end of the arena waiting to collect her, off came the glaring robot headpiece, tossed high over the glass into the waiting, outstretched hands of a young man in the seventh row behind one of the nets, the silver head hanging suspended in the air for a split second for all to admire like a beheaded trophy flung fresh from some intergalactic chopping block.

Too late now to throw on the brakes to stop, Gloria left her feet where the playing surface met concrete and flew off the ice and through the air like a crouching ski-jumper, right through the opened boards and down the black-rubber-carpeted hallway out of the fans' sight. The doors slammed tight behind her and the crowd erupted. Spilling out of their benches, the players for both teams banged their sticks on the ice in tribute to the performance.

From the opening drop of the puck the Warriors and Tornados did not play but combated like it was the seventh and deciding game of the championship round and not the last, meaningless contest of an unsuccessful regular season. Every charge up ice by the Warriors brought the home town fans to the literal edge of their seats, a steadily building

murmur of excitement as the puck was head-manned down
the ice culminating more often than not in an excellent
opportunity to score and a disappointed but still thrilled
Ohhhhhh as the puck either just missed the net or was
stopped by the Tornado netminder — just as when the now
thoroughly detestable visitors rushed toward the Warrior net,
the crowd's loud *Ohhhhhh* an *Ohhhhhh* of relief this time at
a thankfully wayward shot or save. And the body-checking
on both sides now turned ferocious, every time a
defenceman retrieved the puck from his own end or a
forward made a pass in open ice he paid for it with a
crushing hit that sent him hurtling into the end boards or
the almost-as-punishing empty air.

When the Tornados finally broke the scoreless draw a
little over fifteen minutes into the period on a seeing-eye low
slapshot from the point, the crowd quieted down, but only for
a few numb seconds. Before the Tornado goal could even be
announced they were right back into the game, each fresh
Warrior attack on the Wichita net heralded and capped by a
storm of cheering that seemed more the rooting roar of one
enormous booster than of an arena of thousands clapping and
yelling on their own.

The Warriors heard their fans and fed off the noise,
skating faster and hitting harder, pounding the Tornado net
with slapshots from way out, wrist shots and backhanders from
close range, dekes and one-timers from close in tight. But the
Tornado goalie was good, and when he wasn't good, he was
lucky. And when the Warriors lifted their goalie for an extra
attacker to try and help get the equalizer, Wichita shot the
puck into the empty net with thirty-three seconds left in the
game and that was that. The crowd sat back in their seats and
were quiet for the first time since Gloria blazed onto the ice
at the beginning of the second intermission.

What happened next, Bayle saw from the first.

Scanning the Warrior bench after the clinching empty
net goal, Bayle spotted a red-faced Coach Daley screaming
into Dippy's ear and Dippy, staring straight out at the ice,

emphatically nodding his head again and again. And then, just before the face-off at centre ice, Daley smacked him hard on the shoulder pads with both hands and Dippy hopped over the boards to replace Trembley in the face-off circle. The puck was dropped but Dippy likely never saw it, racing right for Bladon manning the right defenceman's spot before the puck even hit the ice.

Sometimes a hockey fight is like a baseball fight where two people who really don't want to fight push each other around a little bit and wait for someone to get between them and break it up. Sometimes it's like a football fight where, even if the two do have a score to settle, all they really manage to end up doing is hurting their hands smashing them on each other's helmet. But sometimes a hockey fight is everything a boxing match rarely is, two men standing toe to toe for what each believes to be the very best of reasons, pounding away at each other until their faces hurt so much they don't feel anything, not even pain, and their arms grow so tired and heavy from hitting that at the end it takes all their effort just to lift them from their sides for one last punch.

Dippy and Bladon stood no more than a foot and a half apart, barely moving on their skates, repeatedly hitting each other in the face, head, and neck. If their fists were flesh jackhammers, their heads were like those Easter Island stone statues — unmovable, expressionless, stoic. The other players paired off in customary form, clutching at each other by the jersey, but no one could be bothered to do much of anything but watch the team's two enforcers fight their final bloody battle of season-ending honour. Bayle winced at every shot Dippy took to the head and howled with delight with every punch he landed; felt sad but happy wishing his father could be there to see what he could see. Thought: The old man would have *loved* this.

And because the entire crowd was standing on their feet screaming for Dippy and against Bladon, the first, smaller explosion went virtually unnoticed. But when the second pipe bomb went off behind the net at the south end of the rink,

341

blowing plexiglass and whole hunks of wood from the boards all over the ice, the riot began in earnest.

Bayle became one with the panicked, shoving mass trying to squeeze its way through the exits and into the lobby and out of the arena. Like all the others Bayle ran up and down the stairs trying to find an opening not jammed full of people. So much more out of what had suddenly become the ordinary then to see Samson sitting by himself at the press box with his elbows resting on the counter enjoying his cigar while watching the anarchy of the crowd, as if the whole thing were somehow some sort of private spectacle being put on for his own amused benefit.

"Samson?" Bayle said. Maybe he's in shock, he thought.

"Ah, Mr. Bayle. I'd heard you were back our way. I never did receive a copy of that article you were working on so diligently down here. Did all our hospitality go for naught?"

"Samson ...." Bayle gestured around him with both hands, mouth hanging open.

"Yes, it's terrible, isn't it? Although it doesn't appear C.A.C.A.W. will be claiming any fatalities this time, thankfully."

Bayle looked around him at the screaming confusion. Samson and himself were the only ones in the arena not scrambling for their lives.

"Why the hell are you just sitting there!" Bayle yelled.

Samson took a long pull on his cigar, exhaled a trail of blue smoke. "From what I understand, it's really the same principle as what to do when in the midst of any catastrophe, actually. Those who seek shelter are usually the ones who get hurt, you see."

"Besides," he said, "considering the difficulty we were likely going to have unloading the Bunton Center once we moved to Texas, this little ... incident tonight might, after all, be just the best bit of luck that could have happened. Only from an accounting point of view, of course. Still, I'd have to say that our insurance should take care of us nicely. Very nicely."

Firemen, policemen, and Bunton Center security personnel were pouring through the exits the other way now. For the first time Bayle had a chance to panic at the thought of Gloria and whether she was all right.

Bayle watched Samson drop his cigar stub to the ground and carefully crush it dead underfoot; looked at the ice surface down below still littered with Dippy and Bladon's abandoned sticks and gloves left over from their interrupted fight; wondered once again how Gloria was and felt his stomach slightly curdle; drew back his fist and punched Samson so hard right flush in the face that Bayle thought he saw a tooth or two mixed up with the blood and saliva that flew from Samson's mouth as he crumpled to the ground. He stepped around the motionless body.

A black-bag-toting medical attendant at the exit excitedly asked Bayle if he was all right.

Bayle heard the man's question but kept walking toward the cleared exit; didn't bother turning around to answer, just kept on moving.

GAME OVER, tie game, 3-3, Toronto needed the win but they'll take the point. Oh, well.

So I missed the game. That's what "Sportsline" at 11:30 and highlights are for, right?

And no problem. They're on T.V. again next week against the Red Wings and I'm not going anywhere. And, hey, the Maple Leafs versus the Red Wings, the old man's favourite Saturday night war, what more could you want? A comfortable chair, clear reception, and maybe a cup of hot chocolate between the second and third periods. Laugh if you want, little sister, but there are worse Blessed Trinities to live by.

But you wouldn't laugh. You'd say, Just as long as there *is* a Father, a Son, and a Holy Ghost. And there is, sometimes. Sometimes there is, sometimes there isn't. And when there isn't, you just have to wait around and shine your shoes and stare at all the pretty girls on the subway ride to work and read the sports page and wait around some more and hope that there will be again. And there will be. Maybe not as soon as you'd like, maybe not as often as you want, but there will be.

And when there is, be thankful, be grateful, give thanks. And when there isn't, be like a smart goal scorer stuck in a ten-game scoring slump: keep skating hard, keep going to the net, keep your stick on the ice. Because you never know what's going to happen out there. And sooner or later the puck's going to go in the net and the red light is going to come on and the crowd is going to rise to their feet and all of a sudden your arms and stick will be raised in the air over your head in celebration just when thirty seconds before you wondered — you really, really wondered — if you'd ever feel this good again. And you do. You will.

But hockey's not, as the t-shirt on that skinny kid I used to watch screaming himself hoarse behind the visitor's bench at the Warriors' games says, life, right? Hockey is just a game; a game, not life. But you try and tell that to the old man, okay? Yeah, right. You try and tell him.

It's late. I could order another drink but I won't. Bar nuts aren't supper, though, even if they are the expensive smoked kind, so if they're still open I'm still going to get that pizza from Papa Ciao's on the way home. And if they're not, there's always Pizza Pizza where I know can get a couple of slices. The pizza isn't even half as good, but at least they'll be open and at least I won't have to go home and cook. Thank heaven for small miracles.

I wish you could feel how hungry I am. I wonder what you'd think of the new Spadina streetcar. I'd like to show you where I work now. I wish you could feel how good it's going to feel going to sleep tonight. I wish we had talked like this a long time ago. I wish I knew then what I think I know now. I wish I wasn't just talking to myself. I'm not just talking to myself. I'm not just talking to myself.

Let's talk again, little sister. Let's talk.